Lust, Love, & Lies

A Novel by
Eric Fleming

Street Knowledge Publishing LLC
Website: www.streetknowledgepublishing.com
Myspace: www.myspace.com/streetknowledgepublishing

LUST, LOVE & LIES®
All Rights reserved © 2008 Street Knowledge Publishing

LUST, LOVE & LIES

Published by: Street Knowledge Publishing
Written by: Eric Fleming
Edited by: Dolly Lopez
Cover design by: Marion Designs/ www.mariondesigns.com
Photos by: Marion Designs

For information contact:
Street Knowledge Publishing
P.O. Box Box 345
Wilmington, DE 19801
Email: jj@streetknowledgepublishing.com
Website: www.streetknowledgepublishing.com
Myspace: www.myspace.com/streetknowledgepublishing

ISBN 10: 0-9799556-7-X
ISBN 13: 978-0-9799556-7-9

Dedication

This book is dedicated to all my fallen soldiers: Sylvester Elliott Sr., Sylvester Elliott Jr., Mary Elliott, Robert Smith, Gracie Fleming, and Victoria Colemen Rose

Rest In Peace

Acknowledgments

On bended knee I give thanks to God for His merciful grace. I thank Him for His unselfishness in sending His son Jesus Christ. If you haven't taken the time to develop a relationship with God, I beg you to do so. It's very simple to do, just go to church and my brothers and sisters in Christ will happily guide you the rest of the way into the bosom of Christ our Lord and Savior.

To the greatest mother in the world, Leuwenia McAfee. You have been a rock for me no matter the circumstance or situation. As you get better with age, I promise to be there for you whenever you need me to be. You raised my child during my incarceration and you've done an excellent job. You are priceless Mom.

To my seed, Quin Mercel Fleming, I want the world to know that your father is very proud of the person that you are. I know that it hasn't been an easy ride. You've weathered the storm and you stayed strong. Keep your head held high, never bite your tongue, and go forth into the world and seize a piece of it.

Victoria Coleman Rose, I wish that you were still of this earth so that I could share with you the joy of our creation. Rest in Peace Vicky.

Renee, Bianca, and Desiree, you are three ladies that will forever hold a special place in my heart. Renee, you've helped me stay sane in a world filled with loneliness, pain, and despair. No matter what, I will always owe a debt to you; and you will always be in my system. You have done an excellent job as a single mother and I am very proud of you. No matter what, we will always be more than friends.

Sheila Fleming, I have to give a special shout out to you too, sweetie. You've not only been there for me, Chrissy, Aaron, Starlett and Kenisha, you've been there for our children. You've kept our father Ken Fleming from falling when he refused to man up and stand on his own two feet. You are a rock sweetie and I love you, not for what you do, but for who you are. You will always be special to me.

WHAT IT DO.......Allen, Johnny, Ilean, Charles, Cathy, Levester, Joe Boy, Sharon Ross, Stephanie Boyd, Byron Williams, and Robin Jones my two Ninjas for life... My partner in crime Derrick Jefferson, A dub done son!! Donna Johnson, Lisa Staley, Yolanda Turner, I definitely have to see you ladies once I hit the bricks!! Get at me Rodney Heslip, Darrin Ard, Robert Aguilar, Sharlyn, Lelah, R.B., Jennette, Millecent, Devina, Shawn Edwards, Lil' Allen, Dex, Ryan, Michael Robicheaux, Damion Mobley, Tracee, and the rest of Kenisha's Prairie View Posse, I look forward to meeting you ladies. A special What It Do to Kenisha's book club, and all the book clubs down South, My Lil Bro Robert, Angela and Nicole, Funkytown Rabbit and Fred, Weinsy, Quinton Black, Steve, Mud, Weisel, Tree, what up playa, Derrick Rainwater if it wasn't for you I'd have a life sentence, I got your back, once I touch bricks that's on my word!!! Aunt Menyon, Ruby, Lucille, Rest in Peace Aunt Gracie, Sister, Rosy, Helen, Mary, Cora, Essel, and my dog Aunt Betty-Stay strong girl!! Janet, Sandra, Bruce, Kennard, Karla, Stacy, Author, Felicia, Veronica, Jackie, Bigg Wigg, Big D'bo, Terrence Jones, Bozo, Mike Jones and Ced. All of C Block, and last but not least my beloved grandmother Carol Elliott, I'll be home real soon sweetie!!

Peace to my hustlin' ass Liaison Linda Williams. You not only dug a brothas talent you knew what to do with it.

Word up, to all the talent under Street Knowledge Publications. Let's do the damn thang and blow the competition out the water. Be sure to cop my homeboy's novel 'Don't Mix The Bitter With The Sweet' by Gregory Garrett.

I welcome any feed back on my work. You can contact me via snail mail at:

> Eric Fleming #26436-077
> Federal Correctional Institution
> P.O. Box 9000
> Seagoville, TX 75159-9000

Prologue

The young man was so engrossed with writing a letter to his girlfriend that he paid little notice to the mailman as he approached from the end of the block. He was parked four houses down from a custom home that belonged to a guy his employers were interested in. Originally, all that he was supposed to do was make a phone call once the guy showed-up. He was bored out of his wits and half asleep when a big Mercedes Benz pulled into the guy's driveway around two in the morning. When he attempted to alert his employers of the man's arrival, he was unable to get through because his cheap cellular phone kept breaking up. When he did get through he was ordered to sit tight and wait for a call back. Glancing at his watch he noted that it was a minute or two past ten. Shit!

He'd popped a half box of No-Doze and filled four coke bottles with urine. If he'd known that he would have to sit inside his car for this long, he'd never taken the job! Luckily he'd brought along a pen and pad to catch up on his correspondence. His girlfriend was away taking summer classes at UCLA She'd been pissed the last time he'd called because he hadn't written a reply to her last two letters. He was trying to think of the right words to explain just how busy he was lately, when he noticed the mailman walk past the big Mercedes and head back up the block, the same way that he'd come.

It never occurred to the young man that the mail carrier failed to stop at any of the other homes that sat along the block.

●●●●●●

The man groggily rolled over and opened his eyes. Someone was pressing on his doorbell incessantly, like they'd lost their damn mind! He didn't get to bed until a little after three in the morning.

He squinted his eyes in an effort to read his alarm clock. 10:07 a.m.

"Shit!" he said, as he struggled out of bed before snatching up his bathrobe.

The man stumbled out of the bedroom. Someone was fixin' to get cursed out! He had just returned from a tiring and stress filled three-week vacation with his girlfriend. They were delayed in Florida because airport security was a bitch ever since 9-11. Their connection flight into Dallas Ft. Worth didn't land until 12:30 this morning. Once they got off the plane and found their luggage, finding his Mercedes hadn't been an easy feat to accomplish in the huge parking lot.

When they finally found the car, he had a flat tire. To further complicate matters, after changing the tire, he got into an argument with his girlfriend because he insisted upon dropping her off at her own place. He liked the woman a lot, but he was hoping that by taking her to her apartment, it would bring her ass back down to reality. She was actually starting to believe they were married for God's sake! For the entire trip it was Mr. and Mrs. This and Mr. and Mrs. That! He wouldn't be surprised if it was her crazy ass standing on his doorbell.

As he walked slowly down the stairs holding on tight to the banister rail, he could see the silhouette of the mailman through his glass door. "Can't he see the damn mailbox along the curb in front of the house?" he asked himself as he unlocked the door and violently snatched it open.

"Why in the hell are you ringing my doorbell like you've lost your damn mind?" he yelled, as he watched the mail carrier reach into the leather mailbag over his shoulder.

"I apologize for that, but I have a delivery that can only be delivered in person sir," the mailman replied.

"What, a package?" he asked curiously as the mailman slowly began to remove his hand from the mailbag.

"No. A bullet!" he replied, as he withdrew a pistol and shot the man in the center of his forehead.

Chapter One

Brandon

Brandon was thinking about his past, present, and future as he toiled under the hood of his father's old truck. His dad had purchased a new Ford F-150 last year. His mother had persuaded his father to keep the old truck to ensure that their only child had transportation when he finally returned home from college.

Growing up, his parents had been work-aholics. They loved him, but they rarely had time to spend with him. Once he won a football scholarship to pay his way to The University of Southern California for five years, he informed his parents that he wouldn't return until he graduated from college. Obviously, he must have finally gotten their attention because they traveled to California twice a year during his college tenure.

After Brandon graduated with a degree in Business Management, he was determined to succeed by any means necessary. Deciding to capitalize off the cellular phone and custom car stereo craze by opening his own shop in California, Brandon, armed with a sound business plan, proceeded to solicit several banks to finance this venture. But it wasn't to be. He was denied for every loan that he applied for. His parents didn't seem too disappointed with the news of his failure. They didn't particularly like the idea of him making California his permanent home anyway. As a matter of fact, his dad was sure that the banks back home in Texas would look out for their own. So his parents cut off all financial support except the exact amount needed for a plane ticket back home to Texas. It was all to no avail, but he tried to explain to his father that all financial institutions operated by the same system.

With a little time he could have found a job to tide him over. But he developed a severe dislike for being in the employ of someone else. Every summer, wealthy alumni would provide the schools' football players with jobs. But just because they were good athletes they would be paid double the hourly wage of a person who had done the same job for twenty years in some cases. Little things like that and several others left him with a sour taste in his mouth. That's why he was determined to become an entrepreneur.

Before he buckled down and hit the books in his senior year of high school, he ran wild in the streets with his best friend, DJ. They both grew up in a lower middle class neighborhood called South Oak Cliff, on the southern side of Dallas. They would steal cars so that they could ride around and commit robberies. They would mug unsuspecting illegal aliens as they staggered up the street drunk from a night of partying at the club. Sometimes these incidents would go off without a hitch and sometimes they turned violent. But they did whatever they had to do to put some extra money in their pockets.

DJ eventually moved on to dealing drugs and hanging out late on school nights. Brandon tried it himself with DJ's encouragement, only to find that he didn't like the way users neglected their children just to get high. Most often those same kids were his neighborhood friends and classmates.

When his coach had gotten wind of his activities, he received a long lecture. Then his coach reached into his desk drawer and retrieved a stack of unopened letters from different universities addressed to him. His coach told him that he had talent and an opportunity to go to college, if he stayed focused on his grades and football.

He took his coach's advice and left the street hustling to DJ. But since he returned three days ago to his old room in his parents' three bedroom wood frame house, he noticed that a lot of guys in the neighborhood were doing real good for themselves. Brandon was constantly running into guys who had made a lot of money in the drug trade. But what shocked him the most was how far his best friend had risen. Supposedly, DJ had become the biggest hustler of them all. If this was true, Brandon knew that he could borrow the capital that he needed. But knowing DJ, he would insist on being his partner. Brandon couldn't allow that to happen, because if DJ were ever caught dealing drugs, all assets would be seized if it could be proven that they were obtained through illegal proceeds. No, he wouldn't ask DJ for the money. But a plan was forming in his mind, and to carry it out he would need the help of his friend.

Brandon was jolted out of his daydream by the telephone in the house. He hurriedly wiped his hands and entered the house from the garage. He ran through the kitchen and into his bedroom, and caught the phone on the fourth ring.

"Hello!"

"Hello yourself, stranger! Why are you breathing so hard? You have a woman over there already?"

"Who's calling?" he asked sarcastically.

Brandon knew it was his high school sweetheart, Stephanie. She had married another man a year after he went away to college. He eventually got over the feelings of betrayal. But he vowed to never fully trust another woman ever again.

"Don't play with me Brandon Elliott! This is your woman."

"My woman! Must I remind you that your marriage ended all that?"

"No! Your going off to California forced me to look elsewhere for companionship. But that doesn't change the fact that I still care about you, Brandon."

"What about your husband, Stephanie?"

"What about him? He's out of town all the damn time working anyway. You know how I am. I get lonely," she purred.

Yeah, he knew how horny she was. They had started out experimenting with each other's bodies at the age of 16. By the time they were 18 years old they could've passed for porn stars.

"So what do you expect me to do about this loneliness you're feeling?"

"Well, I do want to see you, Brandon. I missed you so much while you were gone. If you come over tonight, I'll show you just how much," she said, seductively.

"How did you know that I was back home anyway?" he asked, trying to change the subject.

"Dee Dee called me last night to tell me how fine your ass is. You know that's my girl."

Brandon walked over to the window and opened his blinds. He could hear the rumble of someone's car stereo coming down the street.

"Dee Dee is your spy and you know it!"

Brandon could never get over on Stephanie in high school because Dee Dee would always rat him out. He hated the day he even introduced Stephanie to his nosy neighbor.

"What time are you coming by tonight?"

"I guess that I can make it around 7:00."

"You guess?"

"I'm hooking up with DJ today. Then I have to go by my mom's job at four."

A forest green Lincoln Navigator with 22-inch chrome rims was pulling into his parents' driveway.

"Well, call me if you can't make it. Do you have caller I.D.?"

"Yeah." He looked at the white box on his dresser.

"Do you see my address and phone number on it?"

"Yeah. I'll see you tonight."

Brandon set down the phone. His mind wasn't on her anymore. By the time he got out the front door, DJ had climbed out the SUV. Brandon immediately knew that the rumors he'd heard were true. DJ wore an expensive Boston Celtics throwback jersey and sweatpants with matching Nike Air Force Ones.

"What's up, stranger?" DJ asked, as he gave Brandon a big hug. "Man, let me look at you." He held Brandon at arms' length to check him out. "Man you're huge! They kept you on those weights I see."

"Did you get to check out some of my games on TV?" Brandon asked.

"Hell yeah! Won a lot of money too. You know I have a few gambling houses, right?"

Brandon focused in on his friend's platinum chain with a diamond encrusted cross.

"I didn't know about that, dog. But I can see that your decision not to follow me to college has paid off."

DJ looked Brandon up and down. "I'm going to show you how well it's paid off. I'm taking you shopping. Then we'll cruise by my crib so you can check out how I'm living."

"Alright, let me lock up the house and we can roll out."

He ran back into the house to grab his wallet and house keys. *Man, it was good to be home*, Brandon thought.

Chapter Two

Tabitha

Men! Tabitha was sick and tired of falling for the wrong men. Since she moved to Dallas she had given her time and heart to two dogs that she now despised.

First there was Mike. He was a good looking dark skinned man that she met in Barnes & Noble bookstore. They were both purchasing books by authors Gregory Garrett and DeVanté D. Andre, her favorite authors. So quite naturally she had to compliment the man on his good taste. Mike took the compliment as an invitation to flirt. One thing led to six months. Suddenly she was getting hang-ups on her telephone, so she called the phone company and request that a caller I.D. box be installed. Come to find out, the heifer that was hanging up in her face was Mike's babies' mama. After a lengthy discussion with the tramp, she believed beyond a reasonable doubt that Mike was creeping with the hoe. And to top it all off, the bitch was a white girl!

Hell no! A sista from the South don't play that. She had nothing against interracial relationships. But if her man was going to creep, it had better be with another Nubian Queen. So having no patience or understanding, she dropped his ass like a hot potato.

Two months after her birthday in January, she met the latest knucklehead to disappoint her, Larry. They met at church. She had become a member of International Body of Christ, because she felt comfortable with the young congregation.

Larry was a Deacon there. He was a brown skinned brother with a tongue smoother than silk. They too hit it off right away, and they also had a lot in common. But his smooth ass tongue helped him tell one lie too many. Unknown to her, several women complained to the pastor about Larry's nocturnal visits to their homes. It was all good until they realized he was playing them. Hell, to tell the truth, Larry had her feeling good too on cold and lonely nights, the dog! The pastor made him confess his promiscuity in front of the entire congregation last Sunday. Thankfully Larry didn't tarnish anyone's reputation by mentioning names. She was embarrassed enough as it was.

Every time that she was betrayed by a man she tried to find fault within herself. But when a man tripped and fell into the arms of another woman, it was his own damn fault! Never the less, she couldn't help but wonder if she was doing something wrong.

She was 23 years old, with a college degree from LSU in her home state of Louisiana. She had a damn good job as an accountant for Parkland Hospital here in Dallas. She had almond shaped eyes with a pretty face and honey colored skin. Tabitha took pride in her hygiene and wardrobe. She didn't have any children. And she was willing to do whatever it took to please her man in the bedroom.

She was currently sitting in her cubicle at work daydreaming and absentmindedly thumbing through an apartment guide.

Tabitha currently lived in Eastern Dallas. Her neighborhood was a melting pot full of different cultures. But it was fast becoming a majority of Latinos. That didn't particularly bother her. She wanted a change of address because Mike and Larry both had come knocking at her door after she cursed their asses out. She knew that she would eventually find the right man. And when she did, she didn't need her past mistakes to come back knocking at her door while she was getting her groove on.

Tabitha found a nice apartment complex in North Dallas. That section of Dallas was upper middle class to wealthy. That's just where she needed to be. Reaching for the phone, she decided to make an appointment to view a one bedroom today after work.

"Amber Tree Apartments, how can I help you?"

"May I please speak with the manager?" she asked.

"This is Leuwenia. I'm the Manger of Amber Tree. How can I help you today?" The friendly feminine voice asked.

"I'm looking for a one bedroom apartment and I was hoping that you might have one available. I want to get out of my present location as soon as possible." Tabitha was using her finger to twirl her long wavy hair.

"I have a nice apartment ready for immediate move-in," Leuwenia said. "Let me ask you a few questions, sweetie. Do you have any children?"

"No, ma'am."

"Okay, what about pets? We charge extra for pets now," she warned.

"No pets either."

"Good, that's good. Where do you work, sweetie?"

"I'm an accountant at Parkland Hospital," she said.

"Okay, the apartment calls for a $500 deposit and $520 a month. If you can make it by my office today before 6:00 I can show it to you and have you in it as soon as tonight or tomorrow."

"That sounds great!" she said. "I'll see you this evening."

"I'm sorry sweetheart, but I didn't get your name."

"Tabitha Smith," she replied.

"Alright Tabitha, I'll see you this evening."

Yes! Today was Friday. But more importantly it was payday. If she could get moved-in by Saturday she could take her best friend and co-worker up on her offer of a girls' night out. She hadn't gone out in a while with Shon. She had tried to beg off, but Shon knew she needed to have some fun to help take her mind off of her bruised heart. She sighed. Maybe Shon was right. Tabitha reached for her phone again to tell her friend that they were definitely on for Saturday night.

Chapter Three

Brandon & DJ

DJ had spent over $6,000 in the Galleria Mall on Brandon's new wardrobe. They had Versace, Polo, FUBU, Sean John, Tommy Hilfiger, and Armani gear piled in the back seat of the SUV.

Brandon couldn't believe how DJ was spending money. They were on their way to DJ's house when Brandon reached over from the passenger seat and turned down the radio.

"Man, you were spending money like it grew on trees back there. What type of money are you pulling in, a hundred thousand a year or two?"

DJ had a smug expression on his face. "Dog, that's chump change to me now!" he said while griping the steering wheel tight. "But understand that my income is derived primarily from hustlin', and a wise man never mentions how much chedda' he's clockin'. I also own a couple of gas stations and a car wash. But I could never launder all my money through shit like that." He looked at Brandon. "You were always book smart, Tank. If you can come up with a way to launder some major cash, I'll break you off something proper," DJ said, calling his friend by his street name.

Brandon did some quick calculations in his mind before he replied. "I have some ideas that I'll run by you one day. But I probably won't be ready until a year or two."

"Why so long?"

"Because I have some plans of my own that I need to put down. And I can use your help with putting those plans in motion."

DJ chanced another glance in Brandon's direction as he entered the off ramp. "What kind of help?" he asked warily.

"We'll talk when we get to your house." Brandon turned the music back up and bobbed his head to the Ja Rule CD.

DJ pulled into a circular driveway in front of a two story new styled brick home. All the houses in the neighborhood were beautiful with professionally manicured lawns. Brandon noticed a brand new forest green 2002 Corvette sitting on 20-inch chrome rims, and a black 2002 Mercedes Benz ML500 in the paved driveway.

After they climbed out the Navigator, DJ threw Brandon a set of keys.

"I told you that I had a graduation present for you," DJ said.
Brandon was speechless for a second. He kept comparing the Corvette emblem on the key chain to the actual car.

"Man, when did you have time to get this?" Brandon was checking out the rims on his new whip.

DJ followed him, happy that he could afford to bless his homeboy with a dream car.

"My momma called and told me you were home as soon as you arrived. You know Dee Dee is the neighborhood grapevine."

Brandon hit the button on the key chain and de-activated the alarm. "I'm going around the block."

"Alright, just come inside when you get back. And throw your gear in your own car!" DJ said over his shoulder.

●●●●●●

"Where the hell did you go?" DJ asked, while trying to hold the smoke in from his blunt.

Brandon ignored the question. One block had turned into ten. He couldn't wait to get that bad boy on the open highway.

"Good lookin' out. I really appreciate all you've done for me, dog."

DJ waived him off and rose from the leather sofa. He was mellowed out from the weed. "That ain't shit Tank. You've been there for me man." He grabbed a Heineken off the coffee table and took a long swig. "Look in the fridge and grab you a beer or somethin'. It's hot as hell out there. Meet me upstairs," he said, as Brandon went into the kitchen,

DJ was happy that his best friend was home. Growing up, they had done everything together. Hell, they even lost their virginity together to the same girl. He had christened Brandon with the nickname "Tank" after Brandon had ran him over in football practice one day.

After his friend had gone off to college, there were times that DJ wished he had followed. But after he hooked up with his Colombian connection in Houston, the money started piling up faster than he could count it. Eventually, he said fuck college! He was always told that you went to college to get a degree, so that you could find a good job. But most college graduates' first year earnings were less than some people paid in tuition in any given year at some colleges. No, he made the right decision. DJ's only regret was that he didn't have enough knowledge about business to be in a position to spend his money freely. He was tired of putting his possessions in other peoples' names and paying exorbitant prices to have third parties circumvent his income to evade IRS detection. Tank's new Corvette wasn't only a present, it was an investment that he was willing to make to insure that his best friend knew where they stood. They were closer than common friends; they were family. And DJ loved him like a brother.

As Brandon walked up the stairs sipping his orange juice, he was looking around taking in all the soft oriental statues and paintings mixed with African art. It was a nice smooth blend that left you feeling at peace.

When he got upstairs he counted three bedrooms and a huge game room, all fully furnished. The master bedroom had a masculine look with a hint of femininity. The king size waterbed was covered in black silk. The carpet was champagne, and up against the window sat a matching love seat. The dresser and nightstand were black lacquer with champagne lamps.

"Tank!" DJ yelled from the closet.

"Man, this place is tight! I'm going to get me a crib just like it," he said, while admiring DJ's wardrobe in the huge walk-in closet.

DJ was inside sitting on top of a huge black safe.

"Check this out, Tank. I have my hand in a lot of shit homey, and I could really use your help." DJ took a sip of his beer and continued. "I need someone that I trust by my side. Whatever you need, you got. Just say the word."

Brandon didn't know if DJ was asking him to distribute dope or what. But he knew that the dope business wasn't going to be his business.

"Look DJ. You know that I'm not going to slang. I have my own plans that I have to put down. And if you want me to help you clean the money in your safe, I'm going to need your help to get where I need to be."

DJ looked at him suspiciously. "What plans and what type of help?"

Brandon sighed and blew out a breath. He knew that DJ wasn't going to like this. But he also knew that his friend would never turn him down.

"Since I've been home I noticed that a few cats have come up with a lot of money. It's time someone relieved them of it."

DJ dropped his Heineken to jump off the safe. "Are you fuckin' crazy? That shit that we did in high school wasn't shit! We were rollin' drunks, Tank. You're talkin' about hitting high level dope boys who are expecting it!" DJ bent down and raised his pants leg and withdrew a chrome revolver from an ankle holster. "You see this?" He was holding the revolver in the palm of his hand. "Every guy out there that's in the game packs one of these! Not because they want to hurt someone, but because someone will eventually try and hurt them! In the game you have to be wary of two groups of people; Jackers and the Police!"

Brandon noticed that DJ's yellow skin had turned beet red. Some how he had to make him understand. He grabbed DJ by the shoulders.

"Listen, dog," he said calmly. "I've set goals for myself, DJ. And by any means necessary, those goals will be accomplished. I know that it's unorthodox for a guy with a college education, but I can handle this, DJ. I've given it a lot of thought. These cats are busters and marks. And with your help, hopefully I'll only need to knock off just one."

DJ turned back to the safe. "Tank, look at this safe, dog. It's full of cheese. Hell, I have two more just like it. Take what you need man, please."

Brandon shook his head and took a step back. "No, DJ. That's your safe and your money, man. I didn't stay home selling dope. You could have played college ball just as easily as I did. But you chose this route and you made the game pay. I respect that, man. But let me choose my own route to success, homey. Don't start tripping with me because of the path that I've chosen to take. I know what I'm proposing to do and I know the consequences. You just have to trust me."

DJ picked up his empty beer bottle. "You always were difficult and shit. But you're right, a hustle is a hustle. And since I'm in the game, I have to respect all aspects of it." He looked Brandon in the eye. "And if you're going to be in it, you'll have to do the same." He jumped back on the safe, "What do you need from me?"

"I need you to point me in the right direction. I need a guy that's got some serious cash."

DJ thought about that for a few seconds. "Alright, I have someone in mind. But I might have a better idea. When we learn that someone is going around jackin', we get together over a dice game. Every dope boy there has to put at least a grand on the table to go toward the bounty that'll be paid on a contract to kill the jacker. I would much rather see you do that."

"Do what?"

"Become a hit man," DJ said.

"How much does it pay?"

"No less that $15,000. But I have seen them reach as high as $100,000 before."

"That's good money. Unfortunately I don't feel like waiting for a jacker to come to town. And I don't have to worry about your comrades placing a bounty on my head, because you're the only person that'll ever know my identity. And here's the kicker homeboy. I want your competition. Because the more money that you make by taking over his territory, the more I'll eventually make for washing it.

DJ eyes brightened at the prospect of taking over an area that he should have had anyway. His greed won out over his better judgment. But he was confident that Brandon could pull off anything.

"Alright, dog!" He looked at his Rolex. "It's 3:10. Didn't you say something about visiting your mom at work?"

"Yeah, I forgot about that." He looked down at his jeans and Polo shirt. "Let me change right quick. If I'm gonna drive a Vette, I have to at least look like I can afford it," he said, before running down to his car.

Brandon changed into a pair of brown Sean John slacks with a matching button-down shirt. He accessorized it with his new alligator shoes, belt and watch. When he finished dressing, he found DJ shooting pool in the game room.

"How do I look?"

DJ looked up while trying to line up his shot. "You look perfect for the Vette." He dug into his pocket and tossed Brandon a big roll of bills. "Gas money."

"Good lookin', dog!"

"Come back by 6:00 or 7:00 and we'll roll to a spot I know. If this is done right, you just might come up."

"You know me. I don't half-ass or play games."

When Brandon was on the highway on his way to visit his mother, he couldn't help but wonder what the rest of the day would bring.

Chapter Four

Brandon & Tabitha

"So how did you like the apartment, Miss Smith?" They were walking back to the office.

"Leuwenia, will you please call me Tabitha. I want us to be on first name basis." She had asked the older woman twice already to address her by her first name. But the lady remained a complete professional throughout the showing.

"Only if you'll except the apartment." The pretty brown skinned woman was willing to compromise.

"I love the apartment, especially the loft style. Where do I sign?" The apartment had a half-bath, kitchen and living area downstairs, and a full bath and bedroom upstairs that allowed you to view the entire living room downstairs.

They entered the office and the slender older woman handed her a clipboard and pen. "Sign your life over for six months, sweetie."

Leuwenia watched the pretty woman fill out the application. She had wanted to get all her apartments filled by the end of June. And with this new tenant she would make it with three days to spare. The owners paid her a bonus every quarter if she had full occupancy. Leuwenia planned to use her bonus to put a down payment on a new car for her son.

"Finished?" Leuwenia reached across the desk to retrieve the clipboard that contained the apartment application.

"Yes, ma'am."

While Leuwenia looked over the application Tabitha admired the nicely decorated office. She could tell a woman decorated it. The style was very feminine. The curtains were a plum color mixed with pink swirls. There were three chairs in the office. One was behind the desk where Leuwenia sat and the other two were directly in front of the desk where she sat. They were a cream color that matched the carpet. She also had a big graduation picture of a handsome man on her desk, along with a portrait of her and her husband.

Tabitha could hear the bass of a car stereo outside. It was way too loud for this neighborhood. She could see that the manager was annoyed by the disturbance. Leuwenia sat the clipboard down on her desk. "Excuse me, Tabitha!" she rose from her seat. "I want to see who's making all that dang noise."

Before she could get around her desk the music stopped, and in bounced the sexiest man that Tabitha had seen in a long time. She quickly recognized him from the portrait on Leuwenia's desk. But nothing could prepare her for the aura of confidence exuding from him as he strolled up to kiss and hug the older lady.

He was about 6-feet tall and 215 lbs. with a well developed physique that included a nice tight ass. His skin was light brown and he looked damn good working a high bald fade with waves and a neatly trimmed goatee.

After he pulled away from his mother she angrily said, "Brandon Elliott, was that you out there making all that noise?"

He kissed her on the cheek again and the woman actually melted. *Hell*, Tabitha thought. *She would have melted too. Damn he was fine!*

"I'm sorry, Momma. I'm just so happy to be home that I forgot I was in your work place." Brandon smiled at his mother.

This was the only woman he would ever trust to not break his heart. "How was your day so far?"

"Fine. But don't try to change the subject. Whose car are you driving? Cause I know that your dad's old truck doesn't have a radio."

He laughed and Tabitha noticed his pretty white teeth. She squirmed in her seat. She was getting wet just from looking at him.

"DJ gave me a Corvette for a graduation present." He glanced at Tabitha.

"I figured as much. That boy is always giving away cars!" Then she looked at Tabitha and remembered her new tenant. "Oh Tabitha, I'm sorry sweetheart. Where are my manners? This is my son, Brandon. Brandon this is my new tenant, Tabitha Smith. She's moving in this weekend. Isn't she pretty?" She gave Brandon a little nudge.

Brandon turned away from his mother and walked around the desk to give Tabitha his full attention.

"Actually, Momma, pretty doesn't do her justice," he offered her his hand. "She's beautiful!"

As Tabitha rose to make his acquaintance, he quickly checked her out from head to toe. When she looked into his eyes she knew that this was a man that she would like to spend some time with. His grip was firm and strong. She also noticed that his large hands engulfed hers.

"It's nice to meet you, Miss. Smith."

With her 5'5 height, she had to look up to make her buttery and southernly smooth reply.

24

"The pleasure is all mine, Brandon. But I insist that you call me Tabitha." She continued to shake his hand and gaze into his brown eyes.

"I'll call you anything that you want me to, Tabitha. Anytime and any place," he said.

Lord, have mercy! She damn near embarrassed herself. A chill had gone down her spine and threatened to buckle her knees. But she quickly composed herself and smiled as he released her hand. When Tabitha looked at Leuwenia, she was beaming with pride. Tabitha couldn't blame her. She had watched her handsome son turn a woman into jelly with a smile and a handshake.

This man was dangerous for a lonely woman like her. She had to get the hell out of there.

"Leuwenia?" She took a step back trying to break his penetrating gaze. "You said that I could move in this weekend. Don't you want a little more time to process my application?"

"Well, sweetie, you do work for Parkland Hospital. And I recognize a Chanel suit when I see one." Everyone including Tabitha looked down at her pink suit. "I'm just concerned about you getting your rent in on time and respecting your neighbors. So you can move in as soon as you like." She reached into her desk drawer and handed Tabitha a set of door keys. "Just slide a check or money order through the mail slot when you move in. I'll need the deposit that we discussed and the first month's rent for July sometime around the first and fifteenth."

"Thank you, Leuwenia, I'll do that," she said, chancing a glance at Brandon as she turned to leave.

"It was nice to meet you, Brandon."

"You too, Tabitha. Hopefully we'll see each other again," he said, as she hurried out the office door.

As good looking as Brandon was, she couldn't allow her loneliness to be the sole reason that she chose a man. She knew that women were beating down the door trying to get some of his fine ass. And the last thing that she needed in her life was another man that couldn't control his dick. She walked into the parking lot and deactivated the alarm to her red Toyota Camry. She was going home to start packing her things. Hopefully, she could get Shon to help her move in. She wanted to be finished by noon tomorrow, so that she would be fresh when they went out.

Chapter Five

Brandon & DJ

Brandon had a cup of coffee with his mother and met a few of her tenants. After he left, he headed over to Houston School Road and checked out a few up to date novels on forensic evidence, along with some documentaries on true crime from the public library.

At 6:30 exactly, he pulled up to DJ's mini mansion. DJ came out the house as soon as he came to a stop.

"What's up, dog?" DJ asked, as he hoped into the passenger seat.

"Nothing much, just enjoying my new whip," he said, smiling. "Where to?" Brandon asked, as he pulled away from the curb.

"Let's roll over to Camp Wisdom Road." DJ looked at Brandon, "Do you remember that car wash where everyone use to hang-out? You know the one, it's right across the street from McDonalds."

"Yeah, yeah! Is that still the spot?" Brandon down shifted the Corvette and entered the on-ramp of the highway.

"It's the spot alright, but not for teenagers," DJ warned.

When they were in high school, everyone went to the car wash on Friday nights. Brandon and DJ went to listen to loud music, look at pretty girls, and dream of someday owning one of the fly rides that captured all the girls' attention.

Camp Wisdom Road was only a couple of miles from DJ's house. As Brandon cruised up the street, DJ told him to pull into the McDonalds across the street from the car wash. It was a beautiful Friday evening, and there were over twenty clean ass rides sitting on the three acre parcel that made up Camp Wisdom Car Wash. There were eight stalls in the middle of the lot that provided hot manual wash and wax jobs to its patrons, and eight more stalls in the back with eight high powered vacuum cleaners where customers could clean out their cars' interior and dry them off if they chose. At present, every stall in the car wash was being used.

Brandon and DJ sat back bumping a Scarface CD from the stereo and observed the action across the street for a while. Brandon noticed about six prostitutes going from one luxury car to the next. A few others were openly giving blow-jobs in the front seat. "Shit!"

DJ looked at his friend with a worried expression on his face. "What's wrong?"

Brandon was looking at his watch. "Damn, it's after seven! I was supposed to hook up with Stephanie at 7:00!"

DJ laughed. "Fine-ass Stephanie? Didn't she get married or some shit like that?"

"Yeah, but he's out of town."

"Are you trying to get her back?"

"Hell naw! She made a decision to marry that cat and that was a lifetime decision. But if she wants me to hit it, then I'll tear that ass up. What's in the past needs to stay in the past." Brandon looked at DJ. "Who's your woman these days anyway?"

"Until I can find me a professional that's God-fearing and fine as hell, I'm going to forever remain an eligible bachelor."

Brandon laughed, "They're out there, my friend. You've just been looking in the wrong places."

DJ returned his attention to the car wash.

"Every Saturday morning, there's this dude that calls himself Popcorn who comes up here to wash his car. Sometimes he's alone and sometimes he brings along one of his boys. I know this because I charge those hoes down there to work on my property."

"This is the car wash that you own?" Brandon sat up in his seat in surprise. This particular car wash was a gold mine because of its popularity. The prostitution was just an added bonus. "So you're a pimp too?"

"Hell naw! I don't get down like that. They just needed a safe place to work. Plus they keep me informed about what's going down in the street. You'd be surprised at what they hear, anyway."

DJ changed the subject. "Popcorn will either drive his red Lexus Coupe or the Red Lexus SUV. We don't have no beef, you understand. This is business. He's the primary distributor to cats that live in the Red Bird area. With him out of the way, I can take over his clientele."

After DJ revealed his plan, Brandon thought of the area that he wanted to control. It was a nice middle-class community, full of brick homes and shopping centers, dominated by the Southwest Center Mall, which was on this very road. He liked this area. Brandon planned to put one of his stores over here someday.

"What does he look like?"

"He's a dark-skinned guy around 6'3 or 6'4. He probably weighs around 230 lbs. You can't miss him or that red-ass Lexus. He's a gang member."

"Let me guess, Blood, right?" Brandon had learned all about gang bangers in the five years that he'd spent in California. The tentacles of the Bloods and Crips had spread across the country.

"You guessed right, and he'll be packin' some heat too," DJ warned, as he opened the car door. "Let me walk over here and collect some money from these hoes. I'll be right back."

Brandon went inside the McDonalds and ordered them a couple of Big Mac's. When he came out of the restaurant DJ was standing next to the car counting his pimp money.

"Big pimping, baby!"

DJ got defensive. "I'm not a pimp! My mother would kill me if she thought that I was pimpin'. She don't play that shit!"

They got back in the car and DJ handed his newly acquired cash to Brandon. "Here's some more pocket money." Brandon counted $400 in fifty's. "Man, you gave me about three grand earlier today. But I ain't given' it back," he said, as he put the bills in his pocket.

Then he turned his attention back to DJ's business. It was getting dark, but there were plenty of lights all around the car wash. He familiarized himself with the boundaries of the business. There was a service station to the left of the car wash. The back yards of homes ran down the right side. Also on the right side, a fence had been erected from the street to the back of the car wash as a barrier for the homeowners. The back of the lot had a six-foot concrete wall along the entire width of the car wash. Brandon figured that he could scale it if a fast getaway was needed. He hoped that it wouldn't come to that, but you never knew.

"DJ, I'm going to need a few things before I do this."

"Just name it and I'll get it."

"I need two clean and untraceable guns. A 9mm Glock and a .22 single shot with a screw-on silencer and shells for both weapons. I also need a dark colored late model Crown Victoria with black-wall tires, on factory rims." He looked a DJ. "I need it to look very plain. I also want a CB with an antenna installed on the car. Make sure that the car is untraceable to you, or anyone you know."

DJ nodded his head. "Is that all?"

"Yeah, that's it."

"I'll have everything ready by Monday night," DJ said.

"Good, because I'm going to do this next Saturday." Brandon started the car.

"So what's up for tonight and tomorrow?"

"Well, I'm going back home to see if Stephanie is still trying to hook-up. If she's not, then I have some reading to do. But I'm free tomorrow."

"Good. Throw on that Versace and I'll scoop you up around 10:00 tomorrow night. And please be ready cause I don't want a lecture from Mrs. Elliott. You know how your momma is."

After Brandon dropped DJ off, he went home to call Stephanie, but he ended up talking to her answering machine.

"Hello, this is Stephanie. I'm not able to come to the phone right now. But please leave your name and number and I'll call you back...beep!"

"This is Tank. Give me a holla." He didn't like leaving a message on a married woman's answering machine, so he kept it short. When he hung up the phone the first thing he noticed was the stack of books and tapes that he had checked out of the library. Oh well!

●●●●●●

Brandon and DJ were kicking it in the VIP section of Club Lakeside. They were watching all the fine ass women pass by as they enjoyed their drinks. Brandon was having a Remy Martin while DJ sipped on Hennessy.

The club contained three different levels. The upper level served as an observation deck where people could just hang out. The second level was the Hip-Hop floor. It contained two bar areas, a couple VIP areas, a DJ's booth, and a huge dance floor. The third level was in the basement where you could enjoy a live jazz band if you were into jazz. It too contained double bar areas and a dance floor.

After entering the club and walking through the thick crowd of dancing bodies, they both had been stopped and asked to dance twice. They politely declined each time and proceeded on to the VIP area. But after having three drinks, Brandon wanted to mingle.

"DJ, I'm going to walk around a little bit." Brandon set down his empty glass and rose from the table. "I'll probably check out the jazz band for a minute.

"Take your time dog, I'm cool!"

Chapter Six

Tabitha

"I'm going to the ladies' room, Tabitha. You want to come with me?" Shon asked.

"You go ahead girl. I'll watch our drinks and keep your seat." Shon slid off the comfortable bar seat and brushed out the wrinkles in her slinky Donna Karan black dress, which hung down provocatively low over her ample breasts.

"I'll be right back."

Tabitha was enjoying herself tonight. The atmosphere of the jazz club was made for couples. The lights were turned down low, as candles burned at each table casting a romantic glow. The jazz band was playing a smooth slow number. Almost all of the twenty or so tables were empty as couples swayed to the soft music. She had been asked to dance several times. But jazz was romantic music to her and she just didn't feel like faking the funk with a stranger.

While she was daydreaming, someone slid into her friend's seat. Damn! She turned to explain that the seat was taken.

●●●●●●

DJ was bored. The club scene just wasn't fun anymore. Maybe it was time to settle down and start a family. But before he could do that, he had to meet a special woman that was worth his valuable time. DJ looked at his watch, 1:07, and he was already ready to leave. He sat down his drink and got up to find Tank.

When he reached the bottom of the steps, he looked towards the live jazz band and the dance floor. He noticed Tank out there slow dancing with a woman in a red dress. She was a beautiful woman too, lucky dog! He was trying to check out the back of her dress. Damn! DJ was so engulfed with Tank and his dance partner that he walked right into a woman leaving the bathroom and damn near knocked her down.

"Oh shit, excuse me!" DJ held the woman's arm to keep her from falling. The first thing he noticed as he helped her steady herself was her beautiful dark breasts. When he tore his eyes away from her chest and looked into her brown eyes, he was mesmerized by her beautiful face. "Damn! I'm really clumsy sometimes."

She ran her left hand through her black shoulder length hair. "No harm, no foul," she said.

"Let me make it up to you." DJ ran his tongue around his lips. "Are you here alone or do you have a date?"

She smiled, "No, I don't have a date. But I'm not alone." She turned her attention to the dance floor where her girlfriend was getting her mack on. "I came with my girlfriend, but I see that she's occupied."

DJ smiled and offered her his arm. "Well, let's go to the bar and I'll buy you a drink. By the way, my name is DeJuan Jones, but my friend's call me DJ. And you are?"

"Shondalyn Edwards, but my friends call me Shon."

"Well Shon," DJ was leading her towards two empty barstools. "It's nice to meet you. Let's get that drink and get to know each other a little better."

As Brandon walked towards the empty bar seat, he couldn't help but notice the woman sitting alone next to it. She had honey colored hair piled up and pinned on top of her head. The hairstyle magnified the flawless honey colored skin on her back. She was wearing a red dress that was open all the way down to her ass. Before he slid onto the barstool, he forced himself to focus on the bartender. He had to play it cool. He didn't want to seem eager to meet her. Using his peripheral vision, he timed it so that they looked at each other at the exact same time. Brandon smiled and offered her his hand.

"Hello, Tabitha."

"Hello yourself, Brandon Elliott." She shook his hand. "How is your mother?" She was so shocked that she couldn't think of anything else to say.

"She's fine. But I don't want to talk about my mother right now." Brandon signaled for the bartender. "Give the lady a refill of white wine please, and I'll have a Remy Martin." After they got their drinks, he paid and tipped the man, then turned his attention to Tabitha.

"As I was saying, I would rather talk to you about us."

Tabitha looked surprised. "Us?"

"Yes, us. When I met you yesterday the first thing that came to my mind, was that you were the sexiest woman I had ever seen." He took a sip of his drink. "But it's kind of embarrassing to tell a woman that in front of your mother, if you know what I mean."

They both laughed and it broke the tension between them.

"You're a very sexy man yourself." She was starting to flirt back. "I know that someone as fine as you are has got to have a woman."

Brandon knew that she was fishing. "No, I don't have a woman." He looked deep into her pretty eyes. "But, I would like to have someone that I can call my very own." Brandon sat his drink down and hopped down from the bar seat. He took Tabitha by the hand. "Let's dance."

He had taken charge. How could she refuse?

Damn! This man looked good, felt good, smelled good, and danced good.

"Brandon, a girl could get use to this," she whispered into his ear. He was holding her tight and swaying to the smooth sound of the saxophone.

"I want to see you again, Tabitha. Let me take you to dinner Monday night."

"I go to church on Sunday morning and again on Monday nights. But I'm free for Tuesday." God, she hoped she didn't sound desperate to see him again.

He smiled but she didn't see it because her eyes were closed and her head was tucked nicely in between his neck and shoulder. "Tuesday it is then. I'll pick you up at 8:00."

"Okay, Brandon," she sighed.

When the music ended they pulled apart reluctantly and held hands as they walked back to the bar.

Tabitha noticed that Shon was giving goo-goo eyes to some yellow brother that was probably the biggest playa in the club. She never trusted yellow men!

Chapter Seven

DJ

DJ was really diggin' this woman. She was an accountant with a degree from Paul Quin University in Dallas. She spoke well, went to church, and she was fine!

"So Shon, what are you and your friend doing after you leave the club?"

"We haven't planned on doing anything," she threw up her hands and her tits jiggled. "Go home and get into bed I guess."

"That sounds boring and lonely if what you say is true about being single." DJ had to test her to determine if she was a tramp or not. "But I have an idea."

She gave him her attention. "What's your idea?"

"Let's go back to my house and I'll cook you breakfast. As a matter of fact, I'll cook you dinner too," he smiled.

"I don't think so DJ. It's a little too late to be going back to a man's house that you just met. It is for me anyway. I don't get down like that," she said seriously.

DJ wasn't disappointed at all. She was setting the rules of engagement. That was fine with him. It just let him know that she was a lady. He would respect her for refusing and she knew it.

"I like that about you, Shon. Give me your number and I'll call you tomorrow. I'd like to get to know you better."

She borrowed a pen from the bartender and wrote her number down on a napkin. As he tucked the napkin into his pocket, he noticed Tank and his beautiful dance partner approaching.

"Shon, I would like for you to meet my best friend, Tank. "Tank, this is Shon," DJ said.

He shook her hand, "It's nice to meet you, Shon," Brandon turned towards the lady in the red dress.

"Shon, DJ, I would like for you to meet Tabitha." Both ladies giggled as DJ shook Tabitha's hand.

"This is my best friend, silly," Shon explained.

"Oh, okay. What a coincidence. I guess that we both have great taste, Tank. We picked the prettiest ladies in the entire club," DJ said.

"Well actually, I met Tabitha yesterday in my mom's office," Brandon said.

"And she never called you Tank," Tabitha added.
"I gave him that name a long time ago. I'm probably the only one that still calls him that."

Shon looked at her watch. "Tabitha, its 2:10, girl. Are you ready to go? Cause we have to get up for church soon."

Tabitha could feel Brandon's hand on her back slightly tense at Shon's question. Well, she would make him chase before the capture.

"Yeah girl, I'm ready. My feet are tired anyway. Brandon wore me out." She looked up at Brandon. "No pun intended, baby."

Brandon smiled. "Give me your number so we can hook-up next week."

"Walk us to the car and I'll give it to you out there," she replied.

When they got to the top of the stairs and entered the Hip-Hop section, the Deejay was playing Tupac's Ride or Die. Then unconsciously, Brandon looked directly into Stephanie's sexy eyes. In a tight blouse that enhanced her breasts and a tight pair of white Capri pants, she looked good, and she knew it. Stephanie didn't say a word. She just walked up to Brandon, took him into her arms, and slid her tongue into his mouth. She slid her hands down his body and aggressively put her hands on his ass to pull him close.

Brandon was stunned and angry for being weak for this woman. He pushed her away! "Stephanie, you see that I'm with somebody! He turned to apologize to Tabitha, but she just walked away.

Stephanie said, "Oops, not anymore." She tried to hug him again.

Brandon pushed her hands away and went after Tabitha.

Men! Tabitha knew he was too damn fine to be single. There's just too many lonely ass women in this city. Tabitha stormed out of the club and into the parking lot in search of her car. She heard a commotion behind her and turned to see Brandon pushing through the crowd around the entrance to the club. *Damn!*

Brandon was trying to catch Tabitha before she reached her car, but people were congregating outside the club like they were at a church social. By the time he caught up to her she was sliding into her car and locking the doors.

"Tabitha, wait!" he knocked on her window, "Let me explain, come on now, let me talk to you, baby!"

She cracked her window. "I'm not your baby! Your baby is still in the club. And if you want further proof, I'll lend you my mirror and you can see that you're wearing the bitch's lipstick! You didn't have to lie to me, Brandon Elliott."

"I didn't lie, Tabitha. Stephanie is an old friend from high school. She was just happy to see me, that's all!"

"Whatever. You're not my man so I don't care who you kiss or let squeeze on your ass!" She rolled up her window.

"Well if you don't care, roll down your window and give me your number."

"For what? You don't need my phone number. Go call that bitch in the club, because I don't need this shit!"

When Shon and DJ strolled up holding hands, Tabitha rolled down her window and yelled at her friend, "Hurry-up Shon! I have to go to church in a few hours."

DJ looked at Tabitha as she yelled at Shon. *Damn!* Tank fucked up. But Stephanie was fine as hell; he wouldn't fall off too much if he lost Tabitha. Oh well, He was glad that his women knew how to act in public, because he would have cursed Stephanie's ass out for embarrassing him like that. Especially when he had a woman on his arm.

Brandon looked like he had lost the love of his life. It just wasn't playa to be sulking over a woman in the parking lot of a club.

"Listen Shon. I'm going to call you real soon, alright? I'm really diggin' your style. You know what I mean?"

She blushed and nodded her head shyly as he took her into his arms to let her taste some of him. Babygirl pulled on his tongue like a professional. When he slid his tongue back into place, he deftly reached down and palmed her ass. With the other hand he opened the car door and gently guided her into the passenger seat while softly palming that ass. *Pretty soon, that ass would be his ass*, he thought.

"You ladies drive carefully. And it was nice to meet you, Tabitha."

Tabitha didn't reply. She just gunned the engine and shot out of there like a rocket.

Chapter Eight

Brandon

Monday night, Brandon caught a cab to DJ's car wash to pick up the Crown Victoria and the guns he requested. He took the car to a storage facility about two blocks from his parents' house. Once it was safely stored, he placed a Hard Castle lock through the door hinge of the shed and snapped it closed. Brandon had chosen the Hard Castle because it was resistant to bolt cutters. If the homies wanted to break into his shed, they would have to bring along a cutting torch.

Brandon spent the next few days in the library viewing documentaries on videocassette. Tabitha would enter his mind from time to time. But he couldn't afford to allow his mind to constantly dwell on what might have been. He had to stay focused on accomplishing his mission.

Stephanie kept leaving messages begging him to return her calls. But she ruined his chance of possibly finding happiness with someone he really liked, and Brandon couldn't forgive her for that.

Thursday, Brandon caught the DART city bus downtown. He remembered seeing a uniform shop down there that specialized in law enforcement accessories. Once he found the shop, he entered and purchased four sets of handcuffs, a utility belt and holster that would accommodate the 9mm Glock, and a package of gold lettered iron-on patches. He hurriedly left the store and delivered his purchases to the storage shed. Brandon smiled as he walked home. So the game begins.

Friday, he went to a K-Mart store and purchased an iron, a pair of size 12-1/2 black boots, a blue baseball cap, a blue T-shirt, a huge blue duffel bag, and a pair of blue baggy Dickey pants with extra pockets on each side of the knee. On his way to the storage facility, Brandon stopped at a drug store and bought a roll of gray industrial tape, a box of surgical gloves, a straight razor with blades, a pair of aviator orange lens glasses and a pair of leather gloves. He proceeded on to the storage shed and placed all of the purchases from the last two days in his new duffel bag, including the guns and shells that he got from DJ. Once he re-locked the shed, he drove home and fiddled around the house in anticipation for nightfall.

At midnight, Brandon slipped on a black T-shirt and a pair of black Levi's with black sneakers and walked to the storage facility. After Brandon retrieved the car, he drove to a dope infested motel off of Old Highway 75. Checking into a room and paying with cash, he requested a wake-up call for 6:00 am from the Middle Eastern motel clerk.

With the duffel bag over his left shoulder, Brandon entered the nondescript room. It was just like any other cheap motel room he had ever seen, void of any personality. The dresser and television were to the right of the door, a queen-sized bed was to the left with nightstands on each side of the bed. He could see the plastic cups in the back of the room on top of a counter, which also served as a washbasin.

Brandon dumped the contents of the duffel bag onto the bed before going to the bathroom to grab a quick shower. Still naked from his shower, Brandon slipped on a set of surgical gloves and proceeded to wipe down the shells with a dry rag. After he loaded the guns, he set them to the side and turned his attention to the iron-on patches. Completing that task, he slid a fresh blade into the straight razor and laid it down next to his pistols. Brandon decided to wipe down a set of handcuffs. He didn't plan on leaving them behind, but he had to prepare for the unexpected in situations such as this.

Once he finished, he stepped back to survey his work. The blue outfit was lying out on the left side of the bed. The guns and shells were lying on a dry wash cloth on the dresser. The room was a piece of shit, but it served his purposes for the night. Brandon removed the latex gloves and lay down on the bed in the dark room to meditate on what he had to do tomorrow.

●●●●●●

It was turning into a beautiful Saturday morning, Popcorn thought. He had two kilos of cocaine in his trunk that he was going to sell for $22,000 a piece, if the punk ever showed up! Popcorn sold to any and everybody. Shit! Money didn't care who spent it, so why should he? His homeboys had got mad at him when they found out he sold to their arch rivals, the Crips. But he didn't care what color they wore, just as long as their money was green.

Popcorn heard a car pull into the car wash. *Bout time*, he thought to himself. He was down on his knees polishing his chrome 150 spoke rear Dayton rims, so he didn't see the brother in the unmarked police car until he pulled in front of his Lexus Coupe, successfully blocking him in. Shit!

●●●●●●

At 9:10 am, Brandon had the 9mm Glock cocked and ready in his lap. He left the McDonalds and crossed the street when he saw the big man drop down near the left rear wheel well. Popcorn had parked in the rear of the car wash in one of the stalls used for vacuuming automobiles. As he blocked the gangbanger in, he made sure that his tinted windows were rolled down so that Popcorn could have a full view of who he was. Brandon wore the uniform that struck fear in the heart of every dope dealer in the U.S.A; unofficially, they were called the "Jump Out Boys" because they would jump out of a car or a nondescript van and kick in drug houses. Law abiding citizens like Brandon had learned about them by watching the show *C.O.P.S.*

He had ironed on patches to his hat and T-shirt that identified him as a member of the Dallas Police Drug Task Force. Brandon took a good look at Popcorn as he stood up. Yeah, he thought, he fits DJ's description; 6'3 or 6'4, about 230 lbs. with dark skin. He also wore a red suede sweatshirt, which was telling in itself, considering that the man was a Blood.

Popcorn started drying off the top of his car, but Brandon could see that he was nervous by the way he kept sneaking quick glances in his direction. Brandon deliberately made Popcorn assume that he was running a check on him by looking at his license plates and keying the mike on his CB. "Sergeant Johnson, I need to run a check on a A-ALPHA - G- GEORGE - B- BRAVO 9- NINER- 9- NINER." When he released the mic button, anyone more than two feet away from his car would just be able to hear unintelligible garble. But to a man with two kilos of cocaine in his car, that garble was terrifying.

Brandon looked around to make sure that the car wash was empty. Then he took a deep breath, grabbed the Glock with his right hand and stepped out of the car. As he walked around the front of the Crown Victoria, he raised the 9mm and pointed it at Popcorn and said with authority and force, "Freeze, motherfucker! Put your hands out where I can see 'em!"

Popcorn dropped his towel and stood straight and still. "I didn't do nothin', officer."

Brandon ignored him as he rushed up and put the barrel of the gun against the big man's spine. "Put your hands on the trunk of the car and spread your legs, you know the routine!" Popcorn complied hurriedly.

"Don't move!" Brandon said, as he used his left hand to frisk the gang banger. He started under the man's left-arm and around the front of his waistband. Then he went to his front left pocket and felt a large knot. Brandon reached into the man's pocket and pulled out a large roll of money held together with a rubber band. He placed the roll on the trunk of the car and bent down to rub his hand around each of the man's ankles. When he stood up he switched the gun to his left hand and repeated the process on the man's right side. This time he found the guys car keys and sat them next to the money on the trunk.

Keeping the Glock in the man's back he barked, "Check this out Popcorn. The Gang Task Force Unit wants to talk to you about something. I was told to secure you until they reach the scene."

"What they want to talk to me for?"

"I don't know and I don't care." Brandon removed a set of handcuffs from his black utility belt. "I'm going to place the cuffs on you for my security until they arrive." This was said so that Popcorn wouldn't resist when he tried to put the cuffs on him.

"They know that I'm not gonna tell 'em nothin'. This is bull-shit!"

"They just want to talk, that's all. Otherwise I'd be taking your ass downtown." As Brandon said this, he reached up and took a hold of the man's right wrist and brought it around behind his back. He holstered his gun and snapped the cuffs on the man's wrist. Then he grabbed the man's left wrist firmly and cuffed that one too. Now that he was secured he felt better. This was a big ass dude. If he had given any resistance he would've had to shoot his ass right here.

Brandon grabbed the man by the elbow and said, "Let's wait in the air-conditioning. It's about 80-degrees already." Brandon wanted the big man to feel that everything was cool. Popcorn complied and walked to the car. Brandon helped him in and put the seat belt on him, then he went around the car and let the windows up and turned the air conditioner on.

Quickly, he walked back to the trunk of Popcorn's car and removed his leather gloves to reveal the latex gloves underneath. He shoved the large roll of bills into his pocket and took the car keys off the trunk. When he popped the trunk, he immediately saw the large grocery sack full of groceries. He dumped the sack out into the trunk. Out came eggs, milk, pancake mix, a couple packages of steaks, and two brick like packages of something wrapped in tape. He threw the bricks back into the sack and rolled it down, took the sack out and closed the trunk. He then walked to the passenger side and got in the car. He felt under the driver's side seat and pulled out a Glock very similar to his own. He put the gun back and turned his attention to the glove compartment.

Jackpot! Brandon grabbed the man's wallet and looked through it until he found Popcorn's driver's license. He matched the driver's license to the address on the registration paper, 330 E. Wintergreen, Desoto, TX. He quickly memorized the address. DJ had told him that most large dope dealers had two or three places to lay their head or stash their money. This would help him narrow it down a bit. Brandon locked up the car and returned to the Crown Victoria. He threw the sack containing the two bricks in the trunk. When he got back in the car, Popcorn was asking questions that were going to be ignored for the time being.

After the pig had put him into the police car, Popcorn saw the muthafucka open his trunk. He knew the pig had found the bricks of cocaine, but he wasn't too worried about that. He was just minding his own business and washing his car. What the pig had done was called "illegal search and seizure". His lawyer would get the case thrown out, he was sure about that!

As Brandon drove out of the car wash, Popcorn kept asking, "Man, where are we going? I thought that we were waiting for the

Gang Task Force. Why are you turning left? Downtown is to the right! What the fuck is going on, man? Talk to me!"

About a mile up the road, Brandon turned into a residential neighborhood. There were kids riding bicycles and roller blades up and down the sidewalk while the adults mowed the lawns in their yards. But Brandon blocked all of that out and concentrated on what he had to do.

Popcorn noticed that now this pig had turned into a neighborhood. What the fuck is going on? Then recognition dawned. This is a dirty cop! He just wants my dope! Well, if that's all he wants, then he can have those two bricks. He didn't need the hassle of a new case anyway. Why is he pulling over next to this park? Is he going to let me go, and make me walk back to my car? "Man, what's up with you fool? Keep the dope, I ain't trippin'! Just let me bounce."

The pig put the car in park and smiled at him. Then the pig reached into a pocket next to his knee and removed a straight razor; the kind they use in barber shops. Shit! "What the fuck are you going to do with that?"

Brandon had read that people were more afraid of getting cut than they were of getting shot. And being a man himself, he knew where the most fear lie. So he answered the man's question with one of his own.

"Well Popcorn, it's like this, dog. Where is your stash house? I want all of the cash, player. You can keep the dope. And at the same time, you can keep living. It's up to you. I don't play and I don't have time for your bullshit!"

"What you sayin'? This is a jack move? Man, fuck you! I don't have no cash, you already took my roll and keys. Fuck you!"

Brandon sighed and said, "Suit yourself man, or should I say '*wo*-man'? Because I'm about to turn your punk ass into a bitch!" Brandon reached over and sliced open Popcorns sweat pants down the front. Then he reached inside with his gloved hands and extracted the man's penis. He placed the sharp edge of the blade against the underside of the man's meat and applied pressure. Popcorn screamed like the female that he was about to become.

"Man, what the fuck! What the fuck! Please don't cut me! Oh shit, please don't cut me, dog!" he begged. "What you want, man?"

"I told you what I wanted," Brandon said, calmly. "Now player, what's it going to be?"

"Alright, alright! Just take the razor away!"

"You don't run shit here player. I'll take it away when you give me what I need." Brandon applied pressure. "Now give me the address to the stash house."

"Three-thirty East Wintergreen. I have $50,000 in my dresser. It's yours. Just take the knife away!"

"Wrong answer!" Brandon yelled and slowly let the blade bite into Popcorns penis. He removed the blade and held it up to the screaming man's face to show him the blood.

"Oh-h-h, my God! You done cut my shit off! Oh, my God!"

"Shut the fuck up, punk, I ain't cut it all the way off--yet. You can still get it sewed back on if I do." Brandon put the razor back under his meat. "Now try again, bitch, 'cause this time your shit is coming off!"

"Okay, okay! I have an apartment over by the Southwest Center Mall. Eighty Eighty-two Marvin D. Love Freeway, apartment 1110!" he cried.

Brandon used the man's pants to clean his blade. Then he replaced it and pulled away from the curb. He knew where that address was, he just had to locate the apartment.

Brandon ignored Popcorn's crying ass all the way to their destination. He looked pathetic, but Brandon had no remorseful feelings about what he did and what he would have to do later. As a kid he could always turn his heart into ice when he got into a fight. When he tried out for the football team, he quickly found out that his cold heart helped him to excel within the violent sport. DJ knew that he possessed the temperament to perform this task. Brandon had always been the leader between the two as boys. That's why DJ came to accept Brandon's refusal to be his crony. DJ understood that Brandon had to make it on his own terms.

Brandon pulled into the apartment complex at 11:20am. It seemed relatively quiet on a Saturday. There were kids out doing the same things as the kids in the neighborhood he'd just left. There were a few kids riding bicycles and a group of little girls were playing jump rope. He quickly located the apartment building 8082 in the back of the brown brick apartment complex. From the number of windows in each unit, he figured that he would be going into a two-bedroom apartment.

Brandon killed the engine and got out of the car. He walked into the breezeway of the apartment building and quickly found apartment number 1110 to his left. He started going through Popcorn's key ring looking for the keys that looked promising. He was working on the top lock and was rewarded on his second attempt. He gently twisted the knob and drew his Glock. Brandon entered the apartment gun first.

The living room area was to his left and the dining room was to his right. He could tell right away that the place was tastefully furnished. The couch and love seat were black leather. A big flat screen television hung on the wall next to the door, and a stereo system sat in front of the window on the far left of the living room. He quickly walked through the apartment. The kitchen was to his right. Further up the hall was the first bedroom. It was clean. He checked out the bathroom, clean. Brandon took a couple more steps and entered the master bedroom, clean. Once he was satisfied that the apartment was empty, he holstered his gun and went to fetch Popcorn.

Popcorn didn't give him any trouble on their walk from the car. Once he got Popcorn inside he dropped the big duffel bag and turned to Popcorn. He wasn't going to show him any mercy as he raised the Glock.

"Where's the stash, punk ass bitch!"

"The master bedroom...in the closet," he mumbled.

Brandon took him by the arm and pushed him out front to lead the way. Brandon followed Popcorn into the master bedroom and made him lie face down on the red bed spread before opening the closet. There were a few sweatshirts and a few pair of Nike sneakers in the closet, not enough clothes for a guy who distributed to as much territory as he did. The safe was a big black sucker. It was pushed against the wall on the right side of the big closet. Brandon turned to Popcorn.

"What's the combination?"

"Come on man, don't do this, dog! Let me make it. I'll give you some dope or something."

Brandon took out his Glock and held it up in the air, threatening to pistol whip him.

"What's the motherfuckin' combination?"

"Thirty-six, thirty-four, twenty-six," Popcorn hurriedly replied.

Brandon bent down and tried the combination and popped it on the first try. When he pulled the door back, he gasped. "Damn!" This was the most money he had ever seen. He quickly ran into the living room and retrieved his big duffel bag. When he returned, he dumped all of the stacks of cash into the bag. Once the safe was empty, he stepped out of the closet and looked around the room.

There was a brown dresser with a huge mirror to his left but there wasn't anything on the dresser. The bed was to his right. On each side of the queen sized bed was a night stand, and there wasn't anything on the top of them either, not even an alarm clock. Then it hit him. He knew something wasn't right about this place.

Brandon walked into the kitchen. There was a freezer that sat in the back of the kitchen. It was about four feet tall with a white base and a brown lid. But first he turned his attention to the refrigerator. All that it contained was mustard, mayonnaise, and ketchup. There were no perishables inside. This place was just used as a stash house. Popcorn didn't lay his head here like he had first thought. Brandon walked to the freezer and raised the lid. He went back into the room and retrieved the big duffel bag. When he got back to the freezer he threw the contents into the duffel bag on top of the money. He counted 20 bricks of cocaine. Brandon set the bag down next to the door, then he reached into his pocket next to his left knee and retrieved the .22 pistol and screwed on the silencer.

When he walked into the bedroom he sat the gun on the bed and removed the gray duct-tape from his pocket to tape Popcorn's hands above the handcuffs.

"What you doing, man? You've got all my shit. Now get the fuck out!" Popcorn screamed.

Brandon ignored him as he removed the handcuffs and placed them back on his utility belt. Then he rubbed Popcorns wrists where the handcuffs had been, in hopes of getting the blood flowing enough to hide any bruises that he may have caused. He wanted to make this case as hard as possible to solve for the authorities.

Brandon got up off the bed and placed the barrel of the .22 directly in the back of Popcorn's head. The last thing the man heard was a "thump" sound. Brandon retrieved the shell and flushed it down the toilet three times to ensure that it was long gone, then stepped back and surveyed the room. He wanted to make sure that he hadn't dropped anything.

Once he left the apartment with the bulging duffel bag, he headed straight for his trunk at a casual stroll. As he lowered the bag into the trunk, he used his shades and baseball cap to shield his eyes and face as he scanned his surroundings. Everything looked as it should be; quiet.

When Brandon left the apartment complex he drove directly to the storage facility. After pulling the Crown Victoria into the shed, he changed into a white T-shirt and removed the utility belt and holster. He put the Glock in the small of his back and locked up the shed before he walked home. When he got home he jumped into the Corvette and retrieved the duffel bag from the trunk of the Crown Victoria. He just didn't feel comfortable at the thought of packing a bag full of money and drugs up and down the street on his back. But once he had it safely stored in his room, he lay down to wait for night to fall.

At 1:00 am, he left the house dressed in all black with a black backpack that contained his boots and Dickey pants from earlier that day. Before he left his parents' yard, he retrieved a gallon jug of gasoline and a rag from the bed of his dad's utility truck. He carried the gasoline to the storage facility and put it in the front seat of the Crown Victoria. Brandon drove to the old Highway 75 underpass. He tossed the gun belt into the Trinity River that flows under the highway, along with the handcuffs and the .22 with silencer. He then drove to a neighborhood park called Fruitdale and wiped down the car with his rag to erase any fingerprints that may have been left inadvertently. Brandon retrieved the gasoline and doused the car's interior and trunk area. Then he stepped back, struck a match, and tossed it into the Crown Victoria.

As he jogged home he did a mental run down of the day's activities. All that he had kept was the 9mm Glock, three sets of handcuffs, the money and the dope. He had one more order of business to take care of before he turned his attention to investing his money. He had to get rid of the dope.

Chapter Nine

DJ & Shon

"She doesn't have any real friends here in Texas, DJ. You and I grew up here, so it's easier for us. But when you move to a different state, I guess it can get kind of lonely," Shon said.

"Well she wouldn't be lonely if she hadn't burnt off the night we met. It wasn't Tank's fault that Stephanie was so happy to see him that she squeezed his ass in front of all those people."

"I know, I know," she laughed. "I tried to explain that to her stubborn ass and get her to call him, because I could tell that she's still thinking about him. But she denies it and refuses to even discuss calling him, DJ."

DJ and Shon were on their fourth date in as many weeks. They were having dinner at an Italian restaurant called the Olive Garden in an upscale suburban neighborhood called Mesquite. Shon had chosen this particular restaurant. She was turning him on to new things and taking him places that he wouldn't have gone on his own. She was fast becoming someone special in his life. But he was so damned busy lately that he had been forced to cancel two dates with her already. So when she insisted on this date, DJ made sure that he didn't disappoint her. *She was so beautiful* he thought, as he checked her out from across the table. They both agreed to dress casual tonight. Shon wore a blue Tommy Hilfiger polo shirt and Tommy jeans that followed her every curve, enhancing her sex appeal to perfection. DJ had finally decided on a white Sean John button down with brown slacks. The Platinum chain was left at home. He never revealed his true occupation or his wealth to squares, professionals, or working class women. Not, right away, anyhow.

DJ could tell that something had been bothering Shon, as she picked over her fried squid. She had insisted that he call the dish by its Italian name, Calamari, but it had been hard for him to pronounce, so he had changed the subject and asked about her friend, Tabitha. As it turned out, Shon's concern for her friend was the problem all along.

"Tank's been real busy the last few weeks. He's trying to find adequate rental space for the shop that he wants to open." DJ took a sip of the white wine that Shon had insisted he order with seafood pasta. "But I'll talk to him and see if she's on his mind."

Actually, him saying that Tank was busy was an understatement, to say the least. DJ had paid his friend $220,000 in cash for the 22 kilos that he lifted off Popcorn. Hell, at $10,000 a piece he couldn't afford to pass that up. He usually paid $15,000 a piece from his connection in Houston. Tank was saving him $110,000 dollars. DJ was going through an extra five kilo's every few days after taking over Popcorn's clientele.

But Tank had been missing in action lately. When they talked over the phone a few days ago, his friend was busy lining up vendors, getting business cards made, buying radio advertisement, and looking for employees for a store that he didn't even have yet. DJ had told him to get a damn cell phone, but Tank had yet to call him with the number. DJ would talk to him about Tabitha as he had promised. But Tank could be just as stubborn as Tabitha, if not more so.

●●●●●●

Tabitha sat up. She had been tossing and turning for an hour now. She was just too restless today. She looked around her apartment for something to clean, but it was spotless. The only chore left for her to do was the laundry, and she was regretting it because it meant a trip down to the laundry room. Tabitha had found out that late October's in Texas could produce some very cold days. Her friend Shon kept telling her that 55 and 60 degree weather wasn't cold, but Tabitha had grown up in Southern Louisiana near the Gulf of Mexico, so sixty degrees was cold to her, she didn't care what Shon said.

Tabitha got off the sofa and walked upstairs to her bedroom and pulled on an old L.S.U. gray sweatshirt and matching sweatpants that she had kept from her college days. She looked at her queen sized bed and considered washing her bed linen, ultimately deciding that it could go another week before she washed them again. Who was she fooling; a man hadn't been in her apartment in the four months that she'd lived there. Hell, her sex life was so non-existent that she slept alone on the couch most nights anyway. It wasn't that she never met men, she just hadn't met a man lately that appealed to her enough to take a chance on a commitment with. When she'd meet a man, she quickly evaluated whether or not their chemistry was compatible through conversation. Lately no one did it for her. And with a sex drive as high as hers, she was frustrated.

As Tabitha got her clothes out of the dirty clothes hamper, her thoughts turned to Shon and DJ. She was so happy that her friend's relationship was working out. They had been dating for four months now, and all Shon did was talk about how happy she was. She walked around with a permanent smile on her face. Tabitha tried not to be jealous, but damn it was hard sometimes. And that's just keeping it real.

Tabitha snatched her laundry detergent off the floor and threw it in the laundry basket. After she put a handful of quarters in her pocket, she set off for the laundry room behind her apartment building. The complex had four laundry rooms that were virtually all the same. They each provided residents with six coin operated washers and dryers. As Tabitha entered the laundry room, she noticed that two of the washers were already in use, and from the looks of it, they were on the spin cycle. She chose the two empty washers next to the pair already in use. From her experience within the last months, they were the best of the six. She filled one washer with her colors and the other with her whites. As she was putting in her soap powder, the two washers next to hers stopped.

Tabitha dug off into the pockets of her sweat-top and withdrew a handful of quarters. As she was placing her quarters into the coin receptacle she noticed someone in the doorway through her peripheral vision. When she turned to see who it was, she was so startled she dropped her quarters all over the floor.

Chapter Ten

Brandon

"Damn!" Tabitha bent down to retrieve her quarters. "Look what you made me do!"

"I apologize. I didn't mean to frighten you." Brandon bent down to pick up a quarter that had rolled in his direction.

"Stop! I don't need, nor do I want your help, Brandon Elliott, or should I call you Tank?"

Brandon bit his tongue so that he wouldn't say something that he might later regret. He liked this woman a lot and if she would lighten up a little, he was sure that she would like him too.

"Tabitha, we got off to a bad start. I didn't do anything to encourage what happened at the club that night." Brandon leaned against a washer and crossed his arms. "And I've been thinking about you off and on ever since. I just can't get you out of my mind. What I'm trying to say is that I'd like another opportunity to get to know you. Because I want you to get to know me."

Tabitha picked up the last quarter and rose to face him. He was wearing a sweatshirt just like her, except his was burgundy with gold letters that read U.S.C. Athletic Dept. on the front.

"I felt totally disrespected that night, Brandon." Tabitha started feeding quarters into the coin slot of the washing machine again so that she wouldn't have to look at him. "No, I felt humiliated. Here I was prejudging DJ, thinking he was the player, when all along, I was the one with the wolf. DJ's been the perfect gentleman ever since he met, Shon." She slammed the lid down on the washers to start the cycle.

"I'm not a wolf, Tabitha. What do you want me to do? I apologized, and I'll do my best not to ever put you in that situation again. But I like you, Tabitha, I like you a whole lot." He'd decided to lay his cards on the table.

Tabitha sighed. "Brandon, I have to be honest. I like you a lot as well. Maybe I like you a little too much. And that's what I'm afraid of. I don't have time for games in my life. I would love to find a man that I can do things with, but I need a man that I can feel at peace with, because I have peace in my life now. I don't want the aggravation that an indecisive man will bring."

Brandon gently took both of her hands into his. "If you want a friend, then I can be your friend. But if you want a man, I'd much rather fill that open position in your life. Just have dinner with me tomorrow at my place, and we'll take it one day at a time," he said.

Tabitha looked him up and down. "Where is your place Brandon Elliott? And why are you in the laundry room anyway?" She was afraid that she already knew the answer to her question.

"Well, my apartment is in a building over from yours. And I'm in the laundry room because those are my clothes that just stopped spinning."

She smiled and said, "I figured as much. Why don't you put your clothes in the dryer and we can sit here and discuss what you're going to cook for me tomorrow night, Mr. Elliott.

"You took the words right out of my mouth, Ms. Smith," Brandon said, as he started transferring his damp clothes to the dryer.

When he finished they sat on top of a washing machine and talked until their laundry was finished. After they had helped each other fold their clothes, Brandon walked her home.

"I guess I'll see you tomorrow night," she said.

"Can I have a little kiss to hold me until tomorrow night?" he asked as he leaned into her.

She smiled and offered her cheek.

●●●●●●

After Brandon got home with his laundry, the first thing that he did was check his caller I.D. He had received one call, and that was from DJ. Brandon walked around the black leather love seat and sat on the matching sofa. His mind was already focused on the job that he planned to do.

There was a contract on the head of a cat that called himself "Sweety Boy". The job paid $20,000, and with DJ's persistent encouragement he agreed to do it. DJ said that Sweety Boy had come from a small town, but when he arrived in the big city, he came with some vicious pistol play. He had shot several low-level distributors and corner hustlers in several very successful robberies. Sweety Boy would either shoot his victims in the leg or pistol-whip them. Then he'd take their money, jewelry and cocaine. *He should have killed them,* Brandon thought. Sweety Boy's lack of professionalism was about to get his ass killed.

The distribution of drugs is like any other business. Those low level distributors had distributors on a higher level. The higher level distributors had suppliers. DJ and his competitors were the suppliers in Oak Cliff, and they were the one's putting out the contract to protect their distributors. DJ had also said that Sweety Boy was being blamed for Popcorn's murder, but as long as DJ was the only one besides himself who knew the truth, Brandon didn't give a damn who got blamed for it.

He picked up the telephone to call DJ.

"Who this?"

"It's your brother," Brandon replied.

"What up?"

"You got my tool box?"

"Word."

"Meet me at the old good place on L at nine tonight."

"Word."

"Peace out!" Brandon said, before he hung up the phone.

They rarely talked over the phone because of the business that DJ was in. You could never know when or if a government agency had your phone tapped, so when they did talk, it was usually in code, especially when they were doing dirt. The phone companies automatically recorded conversations when certain words were spoken into the receiver, such as "heroine", "bomb", "kill" and probably several more that he didn't know about. DJ had said that his "tool box" was ready, which meant that DJ had obtained the .22 semiautomatic pistol along with any biographical information that he could find on the target. The reference to the meeting place was also in code. The good place on L was a fast food restaurant in a shopping center near their old neighborhood on Ledbetter Rd. The restaurant used to be called "Good Luck" until Asians bought the owners out and changed the name.

When Brandon arrived at Ledbetter Shopping Center, he wasn't surprised to see that the area was crowded on a Saturday night. The shopping center sat on three acres. Good Luck sat in the middle of the lot, and an assortment of small businesses were aligned along both sides of the shopping center. DJ had his Benz backed into a parking space in front of Big Boys Beauty Supply talking to one of his ex-girlfriends from high school, named Vicky. Her parents owned the popular beauty supply.

Brandon tapped his horn and motioned for DJ to follow him. They cruised around for a few blocks and were quickly immersed inside their old neighborhood.

Brandon parked under a streetlight and climbed into the passenger side of DJ's car. DJ passed Brandon a thick newspaper. Brandon opened it and saw that it concealed a fat manila envelope.

"I can only front you $10,000. You'll get the rest when you finish the job."

"What? You think I can't handle the job? You doubting me now?" Brandon asked.

DJ threw his hands up. "Anything could happen, Tank. Business is business, man, you know that." DJ ran his palm over his face, "Just do it my way, please, and be careful. This cat is bad news."

Brandon didn't press the issue. He just stepped out the Benz and climbed back into his Vette. When he got back to the apartment complex he noticed that Tabitha's lights were still on. Brandon parked his car and sat there for a minute trying to fight down the desire to knock on her door.

Since he had come home from college he'd had a few one-night stands of passion that he never would repeat with the same woman again. Brandon's mind was focused on achieving his goals. DJ and Shon had constantly encouraged him to call Tabitha for the last three or four months now, but he would always decline to do so. Then his matchmaking mother had informed him one day that she had an apartment for him. It just happened to be right by Tabitha's. He had been able to avoid her until today.

Two months ago, he opened Elliott's Car Stereo and Cellular Phone Store down the street in Spring Valley Shopping Center. At first he didn't think that he had the time that it would take to nurture a relationship with a woman like Tabitha. But his shop was running smoothly thanks in large part to the competent and efficient employees that he was lucky to find. Now, his thoughts had turned to the future.

Brandon wanted a woman to share his dreams with and a woman that would allow him to help her fulfill all of her dreams. Tabitha could be that woman, if she would just stop playing the role of the independent woman. He knew that she was feeling him. When they were in the laundry room, the sexual tension had gotten so thick that you could damn near smell it. Yeah, Brandon was feeling this woman and it was time to show her just how much.

Chapter Eleven

Tabitha & Brandon

After Tabitha put away her clothes, she sat down and ate a bowl of Frosted Flakes. She then went up the stairs to take a hot bubble bath. After lighting her cinnamon scented candles all around the bathtub, she threw in the latest CD by Eric Benet and eased into the steaming hot water to soak.

Tabitha could feel the muscles in her legs and back relaxing as the hot water performed its magic. She closed her eyes and thought about how good Brandon had made her feel earlier with only his conversation. They definitely had good chemistry together. And he looked so damn good! Tabitha squeezed both of her legs together and gently ran her hands over her breasts. She tweaked her nipples and made them stand at attention. It had been too long since she had a man to pop her back, she thought. Tabitha was interrupted by loud knocking at her door.

"Who is it?"

"Tank... I mean, Brandon!" He had been sitting in his car alone with his thoughts when he saw her lights go out. His mind was made up then. He had to see her.

Brandon could hear her unlocking the door and removing the safety chain. When she opened the door he could see that she had been in the bath or shower because she was still wet. She had thrown on a very short pink terry cloth bathrobe in her haste to answer the door. Brandon could also see her nipples pressing provocatively against her robe.

"Brandon, is something wrong?" she asked nervously, as he stepped into her apartment forcing her to take a step back.

Brandon took her hands and put her finger up to his lips and softly kissed them. In the same motion, he used his foot to close the door.

"I just can't get you off my mind, Tabitha. So you tell me, is something wrong with that, baby?" he said softly. Brandon pulled her into his arms and looked into her beautiful eyes. "No woman has ever made me feel the way that you do."

He brought his lips down to hers in an attempt to taste her lips for the very first time. Tabitha willingly gave him her tongue. Brandon pulled it into his mouth and sucked her tongue like he wanted to keep it forever! Her body molded perfectly into his. Brandon's kiss was making her feel like he was absorbing all of her strength and wiping away any thoughts of resistance. He broke the kiss and slid his lips down to her neck. Simultaneously he used his hands to open her robe to explore all of her valleys and peaks. Tabitha moaned as his hand found her to be wet and ready.

With no warning Brandon dropped to his knees and covered her mound with his open mouth and sucked her juices into his body. She grabbed his head as he gently nursed her clitoris with his lips. She lewdly gyrated her hips. "Oooh, shit, baby! Yes, Brandon, suck it baby, suck me-e-e!" she moaned. Tabitha was on fire! It had been so-o-o long. Brandon worked his mouth on her.

"Oooh Brandon, ooh baby I'm coming, I'm comiiiing, Brandon!" she screamed, holding his head tighter while he continued to suck her pussy through her climax.

Brandon had held her ass in his hands and rode with her, keeping her from falling down in exhaustion after she'd come. He rose from his knees and she kissed him, allowing him to put his tongue in her mouth. Tabitha willingly tasted herself, and for some reason she held no inhibitions with this man.

But now that he had given her pinned up sexual frustration a little relief, she was rapidly getting her head back together. Reluctantly she broke the kiss and gently pushed Brandon away to break contact. She had felt him against her stomach and he seemed to be as hard as steel. It took everything that she had to restrain herself from reaching out to touch it. But Tabitha instinctively knew that she couldn't allow him to seduce her on his terms. She had to gain his respect first. And from experience, she knew that nothing made a man respect a woman more than withholding from sex. She just hoped that she could withhold her damn self!

"Brandon, I'm not ready for this," she said, turning around and closing her robe.

Brandon walked up behind her and made an attempt to hug her from behind, but she pushed his hands away and walked further into the living room.

"What's wrong, Tabitha?" he asked, while wiping her wetness from his face.

"We're going too fast, that's all." Tabitha went to stand on the opposite side of her coffee table and used it as a divider, "I'm extremely attracted to you. But I don't want our relationship to just be based on sex. Please don't be angry with me, Brandon. I promise that I'll make it up to you when I feel that the time is right."

Brandon felt rejected, but he understood where she was coming from. "Alright, Tabitha, take your time, but I'm going to hold you to your promise. Now quit hiding behind that coffee table and come here." Brandon held out his arms and she walked into his embrace.

"I just want us to take our time. I'm not going anywhere. I need some stability in my life and in my man. But I need someone who feels the same way, Brandon. Can you understand that?" She looked at him, hoping that he understood.

He squeezed her tight and whispered, "You're right baby, there's no need to rush anything." He held her at arms' length. "So are we still on for tomorrow night?"

Tabitha punched him in the chest. "You bet we are, Mr. Elliott, and I can't wait to taste your Southern cuisine.'"

He smiled and took a look around her apartment. She had a lot of bright colors, he thought. There was a light blue sofa, with live plants and blue lamps with yellow shades that matched two paintings on the wall behind the couch. Her chrome stereo system matched the chrome around the glass coffee table. Nice!

"Good night, Brandon." She opened the door for him.

"Good night, Tabitha."

Chapter Twelve

Brandon

Brandon stopped by his car and retrieved DJ's package before he went home. When he entered his apartment all thoughts of Tabitha were erased from his mind. He tossed the package on the sofa and went to his hall closet and retrieved a pair of latex gloves and a couple of oily rags.

Before he opened the package he spread a rag out on the carpet and put on his latex gloves. He removed the .22 semi-automatic, the silencer, and a box of shells. He placed these items on the oil cloth, then removed the bundle of money and tossed it down on the glass coffee table. The last item to be removed was a manila folder about an inch thick with a rubber band around it to secure the contents. Brandon removed the rubber band and sat back on the sofa to read about Sweety Boy.

DJ was able to provide him with the man's arrest record, as well as his parole provisions. His real name was Willie Davis Jr. His vitals reported him to be in good health. He was 5'8 and 175 lbs. when he was paroled from prison a year ago. He had been arrested several times for domestic violence, burglary and assault. But Sweety Boy was sent to prison for a conviction of robbery. He had served four years on a five year sentence. According to his parole papers, his listed address was 1226 Highland Hills Apartments, Number 125. Perfect! Brandon had lived in this same apartment complex when he was younger. It was a huge complex that probably sat on fifty acres or more.

Brandon took a minute to study the photo that was attached to the parole papers. He was a mean looking, bald headed, brown skinned man. There wasn't any facial hair in the photo, but he'd heard that the Texas Department of Corrections made their inmates remove all facial hair.

Brandon memorized all the information that he needed and took everything on Willie Davis to his kitchen sink and burned it. The last item that he burned was the man's picture. Once he was satisfied, he washed the ashes down the drain, dried his hands and went to put on his latex gloves.

He took the second oilcloth and wiped down nine shells and fed them into the clip, wrapped everything up and placed the bundle in top of the hall closet. He looked at his Rolex and saw that it was 11:10 pm. If he hurried, he could make it to a Super Wal-Mart store to get what he would need for the job tomorrow. Brandon snatched his keys and rushed out the apartment.

●●●●●●

At 9:30 Sunday morning, little Kenisha was riding her bicycle up and down the sidewalk in front of her apartment building. She was six years old, and her mom had told her that when she turned seven on December 26th, she would take the training wheels off her bike. Big girls didn't need training wheels. Her mom didn't usually agree to let her ride her bike this early, but she had company last night. They were drinking something called Hennessy and smoking on a nasty smelling cigar. So this morning her mom didn't feel like fussing at her when she kept asking to go outside. She just wanted Kenisha to stop talking so loud.

Kenisha had knocked on her friends' door upstairs, but Chrissy and Starlett's mother wouldn't let them come out to play with her, so she would just have to have fun for her friends too.

She stopped her bike and watched the nice man walking towards her hallway. Her mom told her to call him Mr. Maintenance Man. He always came to fix stuff in her mom's bedroom at night time, but today he was fixing stuff for that mean man that lived across the hall from her. She knew that he was going to fix something because he had his big belt full of tools and stuff. Kenisha watched him knock on the door. She wanted to tell him that her mom said to stay away from the mean man because he did drugs. But before she could make up her mind, the mean man opened the door.

●●●●●●

Brandon could hear movement on the other side of the door before he knocked.

"Who is it?" the deep voice growled.

"Maintenance man!"

"I didn't call no maintenance man!"

"Sir, I have to go around to all the apartments and get the serial numbers off the appliances in the kitchen. The apartments are going through an emergency audit," Brandon said. "It'll only take a minute."

The man unlocked the door and stepped back allowing Brandon to enter the apartment. He ID'ed him as Sweety Boy right off. As Brandon entered the apartment and headed for the kitchen, the stench of the filthy apartment hit him like a punch from Mike Tyson. *Damn!* But he recovered quickly. As he walked through the living room he noticed a 9mm Barretta on the coffee table next to a steaming crack pipe, and about two ounces of crack cocaine that sat on top of a white plate.

The kitchen was to the left of the door on the other side of the bar. When Brandon walked into the kitchen he could see Sweety Boy within his peripheral vision checking him out, so he continued on straight to the refrigerator. Using his leather gloved left hand he opened the refrigerator in search of the serial number to record on his clipboard. Brandon had chosen a blue Dickey long sleeve shirt and matching pants for this job. He also wore a brown leather tool belt with a few screwdrivers and a hammer to enhance the authenticity of the character that he wished to portray.

Brandon could hear a cigarette lighter striking in the living room. When he closed the empty refrigerator, he turned and went to the filthy sink. Roaches crawled all over the nasty food encrusted dishes, running from plate to plate. Brandon looked across the bar and into the living room. Sweety Boy had gone directly back to smoking crack. Brandon looked around the apartment at the trashy furnishings. It was the kind of stuff that you would normally find in a cheap hotel.

Sweetie Boy blew out his crack smoke and turned to see the maintenance man staring at him from the kitchen. He held up the crack pipe and asked, "You want some? No? Then what the fuck are you looking at then?" Sweety Boy reached for his 9mm next to the plate of crack. He knew that crack made him paranoid, but this cat was watching him when he should've been working.

"I'm not looking at nothin'! I was just waiting for you to finish so I could tell you that I just need to get this number off the garbage disposal and I'll be out of your way."

"Well, hurry the fuck up and get the fuck out! I shouldn't have let your nosy ass in anyway." Sweety pointed the gun at him, "If you tell that nosy ass manager my business, I'm coming to find your punk ass! Believe that, podnah!"

"Say man, I ain't seen shit!" The maintenance man ducked down under the counter. "Just let me get this serial number and I'm out."

Sweetie Boy set the gun down and saw the big slab of cocaine on his plate and forgot all about the maintenance man as he prepared his pipe for another hit.

When Brandon was safely squatting down behind the counter, he raised his right pants leg and removed the pistol that was secured with an ankle holster, then removed the silencer from his utility belt. He hastily screwed the silencer onto the barrel of the pistol and gently set the gun down on the floor. The leather gloves had proven to be too bulky for the small pistol, so he removed them to reveal the latex gloves that he wore underneath. After stuffing the leather gloves into his utility belt, he retrieved the pistol and waited until he heard the strike of Sweety Boy's lighter.

Sweetie Boy had been getting high for two days straight. Just as long as these punk ass so called drug dealers had dope, he was going to continue to get high for free. Sweety Boy took a big ass hit off his crack pipe. He knew that it was good dope because he was seeing stars and hearing ringing bells and shit as he held in the smoke. When his lungs were full, he slowly removed the pipe from his mouth and opened his eyes to see the maintenance man standing over him with a long ass pistol in his face.

"What the fuck!" Sweety Boy choked and coughed the smoke up out of his lungs, while leaning back on the couch and throwing his hands out in front of his face. "Man, what in the hell are you doin'?" he sputtered.

"Put your hands behind your head and enter-lock your fingers, now!"

Sweetie Boy quickly complied to the demand. Brandon bent down and snatched Sweety Boy's pistol off the table and placed it in the small of his back. Then he pulled the wooden coffee table out of his way.

"Slowly, very slowly, I want you to lie down on the floor and put your hands behind your back." Brandon kept the pistol aimed at the man's heart as he took a step back to give Sweety Boy room.

"What did I do? You the law?"

"Shut the fuck up and do what I said, before I bust a cap in your ass!" Brandon hissed.

Sweetie Boy slowly slid off the couch onto his knees.

"Now lay down and put your hands behind your back."

"Alright, alright, just don't shoot!"

When Sweetie Boy was flat on the floor with his hands behind his back, Brandon placed his boot on the back of the man's neck and pressed down. "Don't you fuckin' move!" he ordered.

With his left hand, he removed a set of handcuffs from his utility belt and placed them on the man's wrists. Then he removed the duct tape and covered his mouth. He had to check out the apartment to make sure that they were alone.

As he crept down the hallway, the first door that he came to was the bathroom. With a quick glance he was satisfied that it was empty. Then he turned his attention to the bedroom. Brandon held his gun out in front as he entered the funky ass bedroom. It contained a queen sized bed that sat in the center of the room with a piss stained mattress. Sweety Boy also had an old scratched up dresser against the wall. Apparently, a dresser and a bed were all that he cared to have, because the only other thing in the room was old fast food trash. The guy lived like a pig.

On his way back to the living room he thought about what he was going to do to this man. When DJ had first offered him the contract, he had tried to apply stipulations that he just couldn't accept. They had originally wanted Brandon to bring them Sweety Boy's head in a sack. DJ had made an attempt to justify his associate's request. They wanted to send a message to all other would be jackers. So to secure the contract, Brandon had assured DJ that he would send a message. But he wasn't about to roll around in his car with another man's head. Not for twenty thousand dollars he wasn't!

Brandon wrapped the gray duct tape around Sweety Boy's wrists, just above the handcuffs before he removed them and put them back into his utility belt along with the tape. Then he removed Sweety Boy's gun from the small of his back and put his own weapon in its place. He sat Sweety Boy's pistol on the floor and looked down at the man as he wiggled and glared up at him with bug eyes that were enhanced by the use of cocaine. Sweety Boy wasn't wearing any clothing except for some dirty ass boxers and a pair of gray socks. He was sweating profusely, which made it difficult for Brandon to lift him up and throw the man over his shoulder.

Brandon carried him into the bathroom and laid him down in the filthy tub. Sweety Boy was mumbling something, but Brandon ignored him. He reached into the small of his back and cocked his pistol before shooting Sweety Boy behind his ear. Brandon stepped back and watched Sweety Boy's body as it went into spasms. Once he stopped jumping around, Brandon retrieved the spent shell from the floor and flushed it down the toilet, then flushed it three more times to ensure that it was gone forever. He raised his left pants leg and removed the 12 inch hunting knife from the scabbard strapped to his shin and held it up to the light. It was titanium steel with a sharp edge on one side and a serrated edge on the other. It was primarily used by hunters to cut through wood and bone.

Brandon placed the sharp tip of the knife under the man's chin at the base of his neck where his chest met. He applied pressure to the handle of the knife and heard a little "pop" when the tip of the knife penetrated through the wind pipe. Brandon applied more pressure and used the serrated edge of the blade to saw through the chest cavity and stomach. He removed the knife and set it to the side. Then using both hands, he stuck them inside the man's chest cavity and ripped the entire body cavity open, breaking the man's ribs in the process.

"Shit!" he yelled in disgust.

Brandon turned on the hot water and the shower valve, aiming the shower nozzle at Sweety Boy's chest. The hot water would shrivel his organs. Hopefully that would be enough for DJ's associates. The man would look like a mummy by the time his body was discovered. Brandon rinsed his hands and the knife, then replaced it along with the pistol in their holsters. He turned on the vent and closed the bathroom door. Finally, he used the duct tape and sealed the outside of the door jam to keep in the smell for a few days as the body decomposed.

On his way out, he readjusted the temperature in the apartment by turning the gauge to 50 degrees. At the door he put his shades and gloves on and pulled his baseball cap down low.

As he was walking away, a little girl on a bicycle waved at him and said, "Bye, Mr. Maintenance Man! My mommy's asleep!"

Brandon waved at the little girl and went the opposite direction. "I wonder what that was all about?" he said, under his breath. When he looked at his watch, he noted that the job had taken forty-five minutes to complete.

Brandon parked his car in a residential neighborhood about a half a mile away from the apartment complex. Once he reached the Vette, he drove directly to Old Highway 75. He got out of the car and threw the knife and scabbard, the pistol and silencer, along with the handcuffs into the murky water of the Trinity River. As he pulled away, there was a smile on his face. Brandon was going grocery shopping so that he could prepare the best meal of his life.

He was having dinner tonight with the most beautiful girl in the world.

Chapter Thirteen

Brandon & Tabitha

Tabitha was sitting across the dinner table from Brandon. They had finished eating two hours ago, but they were enjoying their conversation so much that they weren't aware of it. When she showed up at his door wearing a black silk Donna Karan dress with matching shoes, she was nervous as hell. But he quickly eased her fears by constantly showering her with compliments.

She was glad that she had kept her date with him. This had given them a chance to really get to know each other. After Brandon had left last night, she had gotten back into her bubble bath and made her mind up to give love a chance.

Brandon had filled her stomach with some delicious seafood gumbo and a nice Zinfandel. They needed two bottles to help cool their palates. At first she didn't believe that he'd prepared the home-made meal himself. Being from Louisiana, Tabitha recognized the hot spicy flavor of fresh seafood gumbo. But he showed her a receipt from his shopping trip earlier in the day, and sure enough, he had purchased all of the ingredients.

Tabitha had also been surprised to find that he lived so extravagantly. Brandon's apartment was really impressive. There was a flat screen plasma television with a matching state of the art flat stereo system that was currently spinning "Don't Say Good Night," by the Isley Brothers. He had a glass dining room table with its miniature match in the living room as a coffee table. Brandon could see that she was impressed, so he had given her a small tour. His apartment was a loft style one bedroom like hers. They climbed the stairs to view the bedroom, and it too was nicely decorated. There was a king sized four poster redwood bed with matching dresser and night stands. The beige lamps matched the beige silk bedspread and the beige carpet.

Brandon had good taste in furniture and clothes. Every time she saw him, he looked good. But tonight he looked edible and she was thinking about doing just that! He had a fresh bald fade and his mustache and goatee was trimmed to perfection. The tight fitting brown sweater that he wore tonight showed off the nice definition in his chest, shoulders, and arms. He had on cream colored slacks with a brown belt, and brown, square toed Prada shoes. The only jewelry that she could see was a gold diamond faced Presidential Rolex.

Tabitha was listening while Brandon talked excitedly about opening a second store in the Oak Cliff area of Dallas before the New Year. They were holding hands from across the table as they talked.

After she'd arrived, Brandon hadn't been able to keep his hands off of her. That's why they weren't sitting next to each other now.

"I want to open a store on Camp Wisdom Rd. or Ledbetter Rd. in Oak Cliff, and I want it to be a bigger store that offers more services to my customers."

"Was this your dream when you were a freshman in college, Brandon?"

He shook his head at her. "No. As a freshman I had dreams of playing football professionally in the NFL. But I broke my collar bone as a junior."

"Couldn't you still have gone pro?"

"Well, I played fullback in college, and at that position your shoulders take a pounding. The pro scouts didn't feel that my shoulders would be able to absorb the pounding long enough to see me through a professional contract. But I didn't learn all that until my senior year." Brandon refilled their wine glasses before continuing, "I chose to become a business major because I planned to become an entrepreneur after my professional football career was over. When I learned that there wasn't ever going to be a professional career, I switched gears, and here I am."

She nodded her head as if she understood and asked, "So where do you see yourself in five years?"

"Are you speaking in terms of my personal life or professionally?

"Both," she said.

"On a personal level, I would love to be married and working on a kid or two. I'm very family oriented. I guess it's because I always admired that my great-grandparents, my grandparents, and my own parents never divorced or left one another. I'd like to carry on the tradition.

As far as being an entrepreneur, I hope to have at least ten stores within the next five years. But I also have another business venture that I'm contemplating. I'm just waiting for everything to come together."

Tabitha hadn't known that Brandon was so damn mature for his age. Most men ran from commitment. In her eyes, she held a whole new sense of respect for this man.

"You really want a family, Brandon?" she asked softly.

His facial expression became passionately serious at Tabitha's question. It was as if he had become heated that she might doubt him.

"Tabitha, along time ago I realized that I was wiser than most of my peers. I don't play games with people and my word means something to me." Brandon released her hand and slapped his palm across his heart.

"I need one woman that's down for me. I need to know with out a doubt in my mind that she'll be there in good times and in bad times, because life isn't easy. There will be bad times. I'm not perfect, Tabitha, but I'm real! If you want to take a chance on love and allow me to be your man, I will always treat you like you're my queen. But I'll expect to be treated like a king in return. I need a woman that knows how to act like a lady in public. But at the same time, she has to be willing to get down for hers in my bedroom." Brandon took both of her hands into his and maintained eye contact.

"I want to be your man and I want you to be my woman. As your man, I promise to protect you and provide for you, as you need me to do. Let's be clear here, Tabitha. I won't fuck over you, baby. My dick, my money, and my love will only be given to you as my woman, and I would like the same respect from you. I've never felt this way about a woman. But my heart is very receptive to you. And if this is love that I'm feeling, then I'm with it, because the feeling is just going to grow and grow, baby!"

Tabitha held his gaze for a full minute. She was utterly speechless. No man had ever asked her to be his woman quite like this. She believed every word that he said. And with that revelation a weight was lifted from her heart and mind.

This was a man--a responsible man that wanted to be her man. Call it female intuition, but some how she knew that he wouldn't ever let her down. So if he wanted her, then she would be there for him in every way. And she knew the perfect way to prove that she was his woman.

Tabitha stood up and seductively walked around the table, never breaking eye contact with her man. "Come here," she whispered.

Brandon allowed her to lead him into the living room. She stopped in front of the big leather sofa and softly kissed his lips. She pressed her finger to his full lips and whispered.

"Shhh, let me become your woman, my way." Tabitha sat down on the sofa and unbuckled his belt. She pulled down his pants along with his boxers, and slowly rose to view her prize. Her eyes were bright as she took his circumcised dick in her hand.

"Brandon, is this all for me, baby?" She ran her tongue around her succulent and juicy lips. He was big and hard. *I'm going to enjoy this*, she thought. Tabitha used her other hand to weigh his balls. She took half of him into her mouth and softly pulled until she had the head between her lips. Then she grabbed the cheeks of his ass and slowly pulled him into her throat to hold him there.

"Oh shit! Damn girl, shit!" he cried. When she released him from her throat, Brandon put his hands in her hair and rode her as she bobbed up and down with her mouth, sucking harder and harder.

She did this for ten minutes before she pulled him out of her mouth to rest her jaws. She jacked him off trying to pull her prize up from his balls. As she jacked him she raised his dick up and put one of his balls in her mouth and started moaning.

"Oooh Tabitha, ooh baby, don't stop, please! Shit, suck it baby, just don't stop please!" he begged.

She didn't stop. Not until her man was satisfied she didn't.

Chapter Fourteen

Tank & DJ

It was a beautiful spring morning that they would never forget. Brandon was riding with Tabitha in her Camry on their way to Parkland Hospital. As Brandon rode in the passenger seat watching the scenery pass him by in a blur, he kept hearing his mother's voice over and over in his head.

Brandon had spent the night at Tabitha's apartment so his mother was unable to reach him right away. It had taken her an hour to find his cellular phone number. He rolled over and snatched the phone off the nightstand, and barely had a chance to say hello before his mother was telling him that DJ's mother, Mrs. Jackson, had called crying with worry because DJ and Shon had both been shot while leaving a restaurant last night! Brandon was so shocked that he couldn't say anything at first.

She went on to say that they both had gone through surgery and were now in the intensive care ward of the hospital. When Brandon was able to speak he asked his mother which hospital, then he hung up the phone and turned to see Tabitha looking at him worriedly.

"DJ and Shon got shot last night!" he threw the covers off his legs. "Lets get to Parkland, baby. They're in intensive care, so come on!" he said, as he climbed into his jeans and T-shirt.

While Tabitha got dressed he went into the bathroom to brush his teeth and wash his face. But he really needed time to think. Brandon had a pretty good idea who shot his friends. Last year during a Christmas party that DJ and Shon threw, one of DJ's adversaries from East Dallas slapped Shon on the ass. DJ had pistol whipped the man in front of the whole party, so for the last five months, there had been tension between hustlers from East Dallas and Oak Cliff. DJ had told Brandon that he was expecting some type of retaliation to come his way, but he figured that one of his gambling houses would get burned down or shot up. Not this, Brandon thought. *Not this!*

After rushing through the sliding glass doors, they walked directly to the information desk. They could see a pretty woman talking on the phone. When she noticed their hurried approach, she hung up the phone and asked, "How can I help you?"

"We're looking for the room of two family members, DeJuan Jackson and Shondalyn Edward," Tabitha said, nervously.

"Just one second," she said, as she hit some keys on the computer. "They're on the fourth floor in room 415."

"Thank you," they said simultaneously before rushing to the set of elevators.

"This way," Tabitha said, as she led the way to room 415. They entered the room and stopped in their tracks. Shon was in the first bed, lying on her back with tubes in her nose and arms. Standing next to her bed with a worried expression were Shon's parents, Mr. and Mrs. Edwards. They looked up when Brandon and Tabitha came into the room. But it was clear where their concern lie. Tabitha went to Mrs. Edwards and Brandon could hear the two women crying as he crossed the antiseptic smelling room to reach DJ's bed. Brandon placed a comforting hand on Mrs. Jackson's shoulder as she sat watch over her only son.

"Brandon, look what they did to my baby!" she said, with tears in her eyes.

He bent down and kissed her on the cheek. Brandon noticed DJ's eyes flutter as if he were trying to clear his vision. He walked around Mrs. Jackson and leaned over DJ's mouth hoping that he could talk.

"What's up, homeboy?" Brandon asked softly.

"Hun'red-thoushan' fo Bombe hed. Kilt me babe," DJ slurred.

There was a bandage around his neck, so Brandon assumed that he either was shot in the throat or the neck area. But until he could speak with DJ's doctor, it probably wasn't good for him to talk.

"Listen, DJ. Shon is fine, man. She isn't dead, alright? We'll talk when you get better."

"No! He kilt my babe! I woun hees fukin hed. Do thes fo me Tank Pleees!" DJ passed out from the tremendous effort that it had taken for him to give Brandon his message.

Brandon kissed Mrs. Jackson again and walked over to check on Shon. After meeting her parents, Tabitha led him out of the room and into the hallway. He could tell that she was pissed.

"I kept quiet all the way over here Brandon hoping that you would open up and tell me what was going on." She put her finger in his face. "Because I know that you know something!" she hissed. "The police told Shon's parents that DJ was known to them to be a major player in this city's night life, whatever that means. They also said that there's a feud brewing against drug lords in East Dallas and Oak Cliff." She wiped tears from her eyes. "Now, I know that Shon is a big girl. But if you knew that her life was in danger by DJ's stupid drug life, you should have said something to me so that I could have warned her!" Tabitha pointed at the room. "Now she's laying in there with bullet holes in her body, and she lost the baby too!" She fell into Brandon's arms with racking sobs. "Shon wanted that baby so bad! She was so happy!"

Brandon let her cry. The more that she cried, the angrier he became. BomBay would pay for hurting his friends. And he would pay with more than his life!

Chapter Fifteen

Brandon

Three weeks after DJ and Shon had been shot their doctors were allowing them to come home. Brandon would only go and visit his friends every few days. The shooting had captured the attention of the media, which in turn spurred the Dallas Police Department to step up in their efforts to squash the conflict before a war was launched between factions from East Dallas and Oak Cliff. But without DJ's cooperation, the authorities' hands were tied. And DJ wasn't cooperating at all. He had his own plans. In fact, the only thing on his mind was enacting revenge against BomBay.

Because of the high police traffic in and out of DJ and Shon's room, Brandon decided that it wouldn't be prudent to visit everyday. Tabitha had gotten upset at him for not visiting more often, but he couldn't tell her about his reservations of being placed under scrutiny for any reason. He had led her to believe that he knew very little about DJ's drug business.

After the Sweety Boy job, Brandon had taken out two more contracts. In a year he had made over $400,000 in undeclared income that he stored away in several safety deposit boxes. In college, he had been taught to invest his money and let it grow for him. But he was not yet ready to do that, except for the money that he used to open his first business. That investment was so successful that he had been able to re-invest the profits in opening his second store in Oak Cliff without touching the cash in his safety deposit boxes. Brandon had an idea to launder his money and DJ's too, but he wanted to give DJ time to recover from his neck and leg wounds before he made his best friend an offer that he couldn't refuse.

Brandon's thoughts turned to the love of his life. They had been together for less than a year and he was thinking about asking her to marry him. It was becoming more obvious everyday that she wanted to shack up. She gave him subtle little hints that he pretended not to catch. Brandon was old fashioned in a lot of ways and he knew it. So shacking up wasn't something that was high on his list of things to do.

Their sex life was incredibly erotic. They had ass slappin-head board banging-hair pulling-call the police and fire department sex! It was hot and ruff. No woman had ever excited him in the bedroom, as well as stimulate his mind and emotions at this level, and tonight he would direct all of his attention to pleasing her. They had plans to just kick back over a pizza and enjoy each other's company.

The antique wall clock in his office read 3:15. His Spring Valley store closed at 6:30, but he'd be long gone by then.

His pretty little store manager, Nia, stuck her head in the door with an agitated expression on her face. "Mr. Elliott, I have a problem out here."

"Alright, I'm on my way," Brandon said as he rose and came around his big desk.

There were two departments to Elliott's Car Stereo and Cellular Phone: The Customer Service area contained cellular phone and car stereo displays as well as accessories. The second department contained two bay garages that were used to install car stereo speakers, DVD's, and any other electronic gadgets that a customer may want in their car.

Brandon found Nia in the bay area talking with a well-dressed man that was obviously pissed off. He was practically screaming his lungs out as he pointed a finger at a candy red

Mercedes Benz S 500. Brandon instantly recognized the man from DJ's Christmas party. He remembered him because he could never forget the look of fear on BomBay's bloody face after DJ hit him upside the head with his nickel-plated Colt 45.

As Brandon approached his furious customer, he had to mentally restrain his temper so as to remain under control. He was furious for the harm that this man had caused, but he took pride in the way that he could mask his true feelings in most situations. Just as a chameleon would lie in wait to pounce on its unsuspecting prey, he too would wait until another day.

"Is there a problem, sir?"

The man looked Brandon up and down with a grit on his face as if he wanted to spit on his tailor-made suit.

"Yeah, it's a problem!" I'm pissed the fuck off and I'm about to take it out in somebody's ass if it don't get fixed, right mutherfuckin' now!"

Brandon slowly raised his hand in a non-aggressive manner and rephrased his question.

"What seems to be the problem, sir?"

BomBay opened the door to his car. "Look what that bitch did! She smashed up all four of my TV screens. Two in the front and two in the back. These mutherfuckers cost me $1,800 with installation. And when I got 'em, this bitch here gave me a warranty!" BomBay sneered at Nia, "Now the little bitch is trying to weasel out of the deal by telling me that my woman's destruction of my property isn't covered on my warranty!"

Brandon wanted to kick his pinstripe suit wearing ass for disrespecting Nia with his foul gold teeth filled mouth! But he found satisfaction in the thought that this little man would die before the one year warranty expired on the new TV monitors that he would receive. Brandon didn't even bother to assess the damage.

"I want four new TV monitors installed in this gentleman's car at no charge by the end of the day. Make sure there isn't any other damage with our merchandise. If there is damage, I want it replaced free of charge." Brandon turned from Nia and offered his hand to BomBay. "What is your name sir?"

The man took Brandon's hand. "George Addison, but people call me BomBay. As a matter of fact, you look kinda familiar. Have we met before?"

"Not that I recall sir. But I would like to apologize for any inconvenience that my young manager may have caused you. I can tell that you have a good head for business. I would love to have a head like yours someday," Brandon said.

The inside joke passed over BomBay's head. He mistook it for an honest compliment as he beamed at Brandon, displaying all his gold teeth.

When Brandon got home, he took a long relaxing hot shower. When his muscles were sufficiently relaxed he got out and slipped into a pair of black silk boxers with matching tank top and slippers. He went downstairs and threw in a Brian McNight CD, and let the music take him away as he sat on the sofa to meditate.

He hadn't been sitting there five minutes when he heard a key enter the lock in the door. Tabitha peeked her head in and said, "Hey baby, I'm home!"

That was another subtle hint, he thought. "Hello, babygirl! Come and give me some suga. I missed you today."

Brandon noticed how sexy she looked in her tight gray sweatpants and one of his Polo T-shirts, as she twisted her hips seductively into the living room to sit in his lap.

"Uumm!" he moaned as he pulled her tongue into his mouth.

Tabitha broke the kiss and wrapped her arms around his neck.

"Are you hungry, baby?"

"I'm always hungry for you."

"Do you feel like giving me a massage then?"

Brandon smiled. Their massages always led to sex.

"No doubt. Which flavor of oil do you want?"

"Let's try that vanilla. We used cinnamon last time and cherry before that," she said.

When they got upstairs, Tabitha went to fold down the bedspread while Brandon retrieved the oil from the bathroom. When he came back, she was already lying in the middle of the bed, nude and on her stomach. Brandon took one look at her plump golden brown ass cheeks and quickly stripped out of his clothes to climb into the king-sized bed and straddle her butt. Tabitha had her arms fold with her chin resting on her hands as Brandon leaned over and kissed her cheek. Then he poured oil into his hands and vigorously rubbed them together to make the oil warm. He started at her neck and gently but firmly worked the kinks out of her back. She was softly moaning as his strong hands gradually worked down her spine.

After Brandon reached her butt cheeks, he applied more oil to his hands. Tabitha enjoyed it when he massaged her ass cheeks, and her increased moans were a testament to her appreciation. When he got to the lower part of her ass, he would simultaneously use one hand to massage her butt and the other to work the upper part of her thigh. As he massaged her upper thigh he would use the side of his hand to rub up against her pussy. The accidental grazing continued until he could feel her wetness on his hand. That was the signal that he was looking for.

Brandon climbed in between her legs while she raised up to all fours. He reached down and rubbed his hand back and fourth a few times before he lined his hardness up with her softness and entered her to the hilt with one slow stroke. Brandon remained inside of her for a few seconds so that she could have a chance to get use to his size, then he slowly withdrew until only the head of his dick was still inside. Using one of his hands to hold her hip and the other to grab a handful of her hair, Brandon grit his teeth and slammed into her as hard as he could.

"Uughh!" She grunted at the force of impact.

Brandon began to long stroke her hard. He gradually increased the speed of his hips as she cheered him on.

"Ooh Brandon! Uhh, fuck meee! Yees, yes, like that! Harder, just throw it harder baby!" she screamed.

Brandon pushed her head down into the pillow and used both hands to squeeze her butt cheeks as she ground her ass back on his dick. When he felt his climax rising, he pulled out and jumped off the bed, wet with sweat.

Tabitha collapsed and rolled over onto her back, lewdly spreading her legs. She knew why he quit. She'd already come twice. One more should do the trick, she thought to herself. She had to teach him a lesson. She reached in between her legs and stroked herself. "Come get some of this."

Brandon looked at her in amazement. Her provocative attitude was a turn on. Damn he loved this woman!

He crawled in between her legs and ran his tongue over her clitoris in slow, long strokes. She was so hot that she clamped down on his head with her big thighs and screamed in orgasm. When he was finally able to extract his head, he laughed and climbed on top of her, simultaneously raising her legs up and placing them on top of his shoulders.

Brandon's dick seemed to have a mind of its own as it found her warm and wet slit. He reached down with both hands and squeezed her ass cheeks while he slammed into her, long stroking. In turn, Tabitha grabbed his ass and pulled him down to her on every down stroke.

"Fuck me! Fuck me harder, baby! Oh, ooh yees, like that!" she screamed, as the headboard slammed into the wall with each thrust from his hips.

"Baby, baby! I'm comin', baby, I'm commmin'! Oh shit!" she screamed again, short of breath.'

Brandon kept stroking after her orgasm.

"Wait, baby! Wait! Stop, Brandon!" She pushed at his chest.

He gradually slowed down and rolled off her, breathing hard with a look of concern on his face. "What's wrong?"

Tabitha rolled out the bed to stand on her wobbly legs. *He had certainly put in work today*, she thought.

"What's wrong? Where are you going? I haven't got mines!"

Tabitha giggled as she walked to the bathroom. "Well I did. At least three or four times."

"What about me, baby?" he cried.

"Maybe next time." Tabitha went in the bathroom and locked the door.

"Fuck!" Brandon slammed his fist into the bed. Tabitha was paying him back for the quickie that he had insisted on yesterday morning. She hated quickies.

"Damn! Fuck!" he yelled.

Chapter Sixteen

Brandon & DJ

DJ had been home from the hospital for three days before Brandon decided to make an appearance. He looked surprisingly well for a man that had been shot. Except for the bandage on the side of his neck and a slight limp, he looked just like the same DJ.

Shon was recuperating at her parents' house. The bullet had entered through her back, slightly grazing her kidney. It continued on and made an exit on the side of her stomach. The trauma and loss of blood was the primary cause of her loosing the child.

DJ and Brandon were sitting by the pool enjoying the beautiful sunshine. He claimed to believe in the healing powers of the sun.

DJ picked up a briefcase and gave it to Brandon.

"What's this?" he asked, while opening the briefcase.

"It's a $100,000 up front, the entire payment. What do you need to take care of this job?"

Brandon closed the briefcase. "It depends on the stipulations."

"Stipulations! Stipulations? I want his fuckin' head in a motherfuckin sack! Those are the stipulations. I respect the game man. He could have shot me and I might have let it go. But to shoot my woman and kill my child!" he pointed a finger at Brandon, "That, I can't let go. She was four months pregnant, man!"

"I would do this for free..."

DJ cut him off. "I insist on paying you for this job," he said.

"Let me finish." Brandon said. "You told me once that if I was going to be in this game, then I would have to respect it. It's never personal, it's about business and that's how I've decided to approach it. This is my last contract. So with that in mind, I except the stipulations of the contract by excepting this money." Brandon took a sip of his lemonade. "After this job is completed man, I'm out of this business, DJ. I don't enjoy killing people, man. I'm just able to detach my mind and emotions away from the act when I do a job. I started this shit because I had a burning desire or impatience to have nice things at a young age. But now that I'm in the position to have those things, it would be stupid of me to continue."

Brandon looked DJ in the eye and continued. "When I came home you asked me to help you clean your money. Well, I can do better than that dog. I have over $500,000 now, DJ. I know that you have at least a million put up. I'm going to turn you into a legitimate businessman, DJ. When this job is over I'm going to the Cayman Islands to start an offshore corporation that will pay us a salary and allow us to spend our money freely. It's time that I put my education to use. You put me in the game that I'm in and I want to show you my appreciation for doing that.

"Our girls are accountants, dog. I know that you love Shon and I love Tabitha. Lets gone and marry them and bring them into the company with us. They know all kinds of shit about taxes and tax laws."

"Marriage? Who said anything about marriage?" DJ asked.

"Just think about it, will you please! But that's not going to be the most important decision that you'll have to make."

"Shit! Sometimes I'm glad that you went to college. Other times I think college fucked you up, because you think to damn much." DJ sighed. "So tell me already. It's obvious that you had this planned while I set up in the hospital."

Brandon looked at DJ with a deadly expression. "I can't help you become legitimate if you still have your hands in illegitimate shit. You have to let the dope and the gambling houses go, DJ. I'm trying to become a legitimate businessman. I can't have you as a partner if you still have the baggage of the street life. You owe it to Shon, your child, your mother and yourself to at least give it a try. Because it's very rare that you ever see a street hustler live to a ripe old age. Street life leads to death, prison, or both. If you go to prison and don't heed the warning that it was meant to be, then in my eyes, that person is foolish. The same can be said of a millionaire street hustler who just got shot."

DJ touched the bandage on his neck. "Don't you think that I've thought about getting out? Do you realize how many people count on me?"

"DJ, you're like a brother to me and I love you man. If you just give me a chance, I promise that you'll live to thank me. But ultimately it comes down to this. Either you're with me," Brandon pointed his thumb towards the street. "Or you're with them. I'm not going to wait for you either. A week after I hand you BomBay's head, I'm leaving for the Cayman Islands. I'm going to make two extra reservations for you and Shon. If you decide that you're with me, then give me a call." Brandon stood up to leave, "Otherwise, don't bother, DJ."

As Brandon started to walk away, he turned back in afterthought. "Oh yeah. I'll need a clean house with a garage and a big work table. I want a 9mm with a silencer and any background information that you can find.

Chapter Seventeen

Brandon

Brandon was still upset at DJ when he entered his apartment. He was surprised to see Tabitha sitting on the couch reading an *Essence* magazine because she was supposed to be spending the day with Shon. He quickly wiped thoughts of DJ out of his mind to focus on his woman.

"Hello, beautiful!" As Brandon walked into the living room, he set his briefcase down and gave his woman a kiss.

"Hello yourself, handsome!"

"How's Shon feeling?" he asked, as he sat down next to her.

"She's getting better. There's still some discomfort but she'll be alright."

"What's up for tonight?"

"How about a movie? I was looking in the paper and there's a new Jennifer Lopez movie out that we haven't seen yet. You know how you like to look at her ass," she teased.

Brandon laughed. "Her ass can't touch your brown round. And believe me when I say that you unequivocally have more bounce to the ounce. I'll take you over J-Lo any day, and if you'll come upstairs I'll show you what I'm talking about," he said.

Tabitha pushed him away. "Go upstairs by yourself and take a cold shower. You know that I caught my period yesterday."

"You're a lucky girl, because I just might have hurt your back or something today." Brandon got up to go take his shower.

"Yeah right! You know I'll wear your ass out!" she boasted, throwing a pillow at him as he went up the stairs. "Hey, it's about 7:15. We can catch the 9:30 show tonight."

"Whatever, it doesn't matter to me," he yelled over his shoulder.

Tabitha picked up the *Dallas Morning News* and found the crossword puzzle. "Now I need a pen." She said absentmindedly.

She saw Brandon's briefcase at the end of the couch. After she sat back down and placed it on her lap, she popped the latch. What she saw inside made her grab her heart. Tabitha had never seen this much money before in her life. She picked up a stack of bills and flipped her thumb through the hundred dollar bills. She quickly counted the bills in her hand. There were fifty one hundred dollar bills in the stack. Then she counted the number of stacks and quickly calculated the total amount. She hurriedly closed the briefcase and ran up the stairs.

Brandon was drying his hair and his face as he walked toward his dresser. When he removed the towel to maneuver around the four poster bed he stopped in his tracks.

"What is this, Brandon Elliott?" Tabitha was in the center of his bed surrounded by stacks of money. "Where did you get all this money?" she screamed.

He stared at her defiantly for a second before continuing on to the dresser in search of clean underwear.

"Answer me! Where did this money come from? Please tell me that you're not a drug dealer. Please tell me that you're not like the person that almost killed my friend!"

Tears ran down her face. She knew that it made sense for him to be a dope dealer. He had too many expensive possessions for someone who had a stereo business for only a year.

Brandon knew that he couldn't tell her what the money was for or make her understand why he had it. The world that they lived in was conditioned to seeing violence on television, movies, and reading about it in books and newspapers. But Joe Blow Citizen didn't want a killer knocking on his door and eating at his table. He would tell her what she needed to hear. She thought that she wanted the truth, but she couldn't handle the truth. Brandon slowly selected his underwear before he turned to confront her.

"Tabitha, do you recall the conversation that we had a little while back? I told you that my business was my business and if I wanted you in it, then I'd put you in it." Brandon was slowly advancing towards the bed. "I also recall telling you that I don't play games and that I would be true to you and treat you like a queen. I've kept my word to you, Tabitha, so don't come in here questioning me and accusing me of something unless you have all the facts!"

"I didn't accuse you of anything!"

"You just called me a dope dealer. And unless I'm mistaken, I paid my own bills last month. Before I allow you or any other woman to dictate how I earn a living, I'll walk away from the relationship." Brandon sat down on the bed. "Just this once, I'll allow you to stick your nose in my business."

Tabitha sat back against the headboard and crossed her arms over her ample breasts. "Do you sell drugs, Brandon?"

"No, Tabitha, I don't sell drugs. I tried it once but I quit." Brandon looked her in the eye. He saw his opportunity to bring her into the fold of his business.

"Baby this is DJ's money. He gives it to me so that I can launder it through my stores. I charge him a percentage for my services. I'm no angel, Tabitha and I never claimed to be. I like nice things and this was an opportunity that I couldn't pass up," he said.

Baby, what if you get caught?"

"I'm not going to get caught because this is the last briefcase. I've made enough money now to start a new firm. As a matter of fact, baby, I could really use your help."

"My help? Doing what?"

"I want to hire you and Shon as accountants."

"Me and Shon? What type of accounting will you need?"

"I'm starting a tax-lien brokerage firm. The city, the state, and the government all hold public auctions for tax lien certificates. What I have in mind for you and Shon is to attend these auctions to purchase delinquent property tax bills. Our company will collect the penalties and the interest that's accrued as a result of the homeowner, and sometimes business owner's, failure to pay their taxes on time. When the taxes are paid, it's paid directly to the company that holds the tax-lien certificates. Sound good so far?"

He held up his hands. "Wait, there's more. To avoid loosing their property, the original owner, which in most cases will be a bank or mortgage company, must pay the lien, plus a penalty which provides for an interest payment to our firm. If they can't pay within a set time, we can take the title for the property. But that will rarely happen. I'm starting the firm in a few weeks. I'll start you and Shon out with $75,000 a year, plus a company car with a booming system, courtesy of Elliott's Car Stereo."

Tabitha leaned forward and hugged Brandon in excitement. "What's the first step, baby?"

"We'll have to take a trip to the Cayman Islands to meet with a banker and a lawyer. I need you to make reservations on a cruise ship one way for me, you, DJ, and Shon. We'll catch a plane back home. But find a cruise that leaves in two or three weeks. We need to give Shon and DJ a chance to heal. I'm going to be very busy in the next few weeks, so you probably won't get to see me for a few days from time to time."

"Alright, baby. Do what you have to do. I trust you. And you know what else?"

"What?" he asked.

"I love you too." Tabitha looked down at the pile of money. "I know that I'm on my period. But...uh...lets spread this money out on the bed."

"For what baby? You just said that you're on your period."

"Well… there's nothing wrong with my mouth is it?"

"You sho'll right!" Brandon jumped off the bed to strip.

The following week, Brandon spent his days in the store and his nights alone working at his PC. He searched his computer for a listing of corporate attorneys until he found one to help get the proper paperwork filed to start their offshore firm. Brandon listed himself as C.E.O. and DeJuan Jackson as President of E & J Investment Group. Their attorney would arrange for them to receive a yearly salary of $200,000. Tabitha and Shon would be placed on the books as executives. Brandon's attorney assured him that if anyone ever did a cursory investigation they would never be able to determine the true owners of their investment firm. He also assured Brandon that he would set up a board of directors that would essentially be made up of ghosts. They were all to be listed as employees with credit cards and expense accounts. As the company's profits grew, so too would their salaries.

Brandon shut off his PC and picked up the telephone. He hadn't heard from DJ since last weekend and he was a little concerned about that. DJ's capital was essential for them to reach the level of financial security they desired. He just hoped DJ took his little heart to heart talk seriously.

"Hello!"

"What's up, man?"

"I tried to call you, but the line was busy," DJ said.

"I was probably on the computer. How's your wounds healing?"

"I'm cool. I got a package in the mail for you today. When can you come and get it?"

"Man, you live on the other side of town. Meet me half-way."

"I don't feel to good, dog." DJ whined.

Brandon laughed. "Get off your ass and move around. I need to holla at you anyway."

"For real, Tank. I just took my medication and this shit is making me sleepy."

"Alright. Damn! I'll be there in a minute, cry baby."

"One!"

"One!" Brandon hung up the phone and slipped on his slacks and climbed into a pair of jeans with a black wife beater before grabbing his car keys.

There were several cars parked in DJ's circular driveway and along the street out front when Brandon pulled up. He picked up his cellular.

"Hello!"

"What the fuck are you doing, having a party?" Brandon asked incredulously.

"Hold on, dog."

Brandon could hear DJ moving away from a rambunctious group of people. "Tank?"

"Yeah. What's going on in there?"

"I'm having a little meeting. I'll tell you about it when you come in."

"I'm not coming in there. We need to take care of serious business, and I'm not trying to meet no new faces. Bring your ass outside with the mail." Brandon disconnected the line.

A few minutes later DJ hobbled out the front door wearing a purple suede LA Lakers sweatsuit. Pretty soon Brandon would have to talk to DJ about toning down his flamboyant attire. Leaning across the console, he pushed open the passenger side door so DJ, could climb into the car.

"Here, take this." DJ handed him a brown paper bag.

"Why didn't you tell me you had company?"

"They didn't show up until we got off the phone."

Brandon looked around and counted seven cars besides DJ's. "What they want?"

"Stop asking so many questions and let me ask some, because this is some serious shit."

"What?" Brandon asked, confused.

"This getting out the game and starting a business shit is what." DJ pointed at his house. "They're pissed because they don't have any more product and I don't have any more to sell 'em because you have a big money scheme and I'm not sure I'm with it! With out me, they won't be able to feed their families or pay their car notes and shit!" DJ said angrily.

"Man, fuck them! Tell those sons-a-bitches to get a job! They don't give a fuck about you and I don't give a fuck about them!" Brandon pointed towards the house. "How many of those motherfuckers came to visit you and Shon in the hospital, huh?" Brandon cupped his hands over his ear. "Speak-up, I can't hear you, DJ!"

They were silent for a few seconds to allow their tempers to subside.

DJ sighed. "Tank, I'm just scared a little. No, scratch that. I'm scared a lot!"

"DJ, I've already started the ball rolling, man. I'm the C.E.O. and you'll be the president of E & J Investment Group. Just trust me, baby boy. Give me a chance to make all this hustlin' worth something. Don't give into those whinnying ass cats in there. Fuck negative peer pressure, dog! I went off to college and left you behind once. Don't ask me to do it again."

"Tell me about J & E Investments."

Brandon laughed. "E & J Investments, punk!"

He took the time to reassure DJ by explaining the basic concept of their new business venture and patiently answered his questions before opening the package DJ had given to him.

"Where is this address located exactly?" Brandon asked.

"It's across the street from White Rock Lake in Northeast Dallas. They have some really nice mansions over there."

"Across the street you say?" Brandon asked.

"Yep. Probably cost 250G's or more for a house that would normally cost half that anywhere else."

After DJ got out the car, Brandon stopped off at K-Mart to purchase a bicycle and a few accessories.

● ● ● ● ● ●

Early Sunday morning, Brandon was riding his new mountain bike along the rough cycling trails next to White Rock Lake. There were a few early morning runners and cyclists following the trails as well. Brandon blended in perfectly with his biker shorts and shirt. He even sported a cyclist's safety hat and goggles to authenticate the impression that he wished to convey.

As the sun rose, the bright orange light cast a beautiful warming glow off the shimmering waters of the manmade lake. Brandon noticed that several cyclists wore Walkman radios or CD players as they enjoyed their morning ride. But he preferred the music of nature as he listened to the water sloshing around before slapping violently against the banks of the huge lake, and the birds greeting him in song as he passed by their nests that sat high in the dark green trees.

Brandon wasn't so consumed with his love of nature to the point of forgetting what he came for. He wasn't cycling for pleasure. There was a job to do, and he'd been paid handsomely to perform, and perform he would.

A rock's throw away, through a line of trees, and across a two-lane road, sat several beautiful one and two level brick homes. Brandon had located BomBay's one level brick house over thirty minutes ago. He'd made two circuits past the house, and on each he'd taken in new information. He recognized the Mercedes in the driveway parked next to a customized Ford F-150 pick-up truck. On the second pass he noticed a small sign shoved into the grass in front of the house. From past experience he knew the sign was in place to help deter would be burglars by advertising the existence of an alarm system.

As he made his third and final pass a plan of attack had formed in his mind. Reaching his car, Brandon strapped the bicycle to the bike rack on the roof. Then he drove by the old wood frame house that DJ provided him for tonight's activities, to ensure that everything was straight. Once he was satisfied, he drove home to get ready and wait for darkness to fall.

●●●●●●

Brandon was sitting on the living room floor of his apartment removing all the reflective devices from his mountain bike when he heard Tabitha's key slide into the lock of his door.

"What's up, stranger?" she asked as she entered the apartment wearing a pair of tight jeans and T-shirt. They hadn't spent any time together in over three days and she was getting lonely.

"What's up?" he replied dryly.

Tabitha walked around the sofa to see what he was doing. "That's a nice bike. Why are you tearing it up?"

Brandon took his time about answering her question. He really didn't have time to spend with her right now. His mind was on the execution of this job and he resented her intrusion. The only way to get rid of her would be to piss her off, so he did what he had to do--he ignored her.

"What's wrong with my baby?" She came around the bicycle and tried to give him a hug. But he ducked under her arm and brushed her off.

"Tabitha, can't you see that I'm busy! Leave me alone right now. A'ight?"

Tabitha looked at him. "What is wrong with you?" she asked slowly.

Brandon sighed. She didn't get the hint, so he spelled it out to her. "I just told you. I'm busy! There's things on my mind that I have to deal with. Preferably alone."

"Well forget you then! I haven't seen your ass in three days and you cop an attitude when I come around." She walked to the door. "I don't need this shit! And work out your problems alone the next time your dick gets hard too!"

After she'd slammed the door, Brandon smiled. He wasn't too concerned about hurting her feelings. She'd get over it in a few hours and call or come back over in an effort to work it out. But he planned to be long gone by then.

Dressed in all black with leather gloves and a backpack, Brandon parked a half-mile away from White Rock Lake inside an upscale apartment complex. When he reached BomBay's house, he saw that the truck was missing from its spot next to the Mercedes. Using a rag, Brandon wiped down the bicycle of all fingerprints before leaving it up against a tree. If everything went according to plan, he would never see the bike again. Brandon checked the time and saw that it was 10:35. Hopefully he wouldn't have too long a wait, he thought as he crossed the road and ran in a slight crouch across BomBay's yard.

Thunder rolled through the night sky as Brandon settled down behind a waist-high row of hedges that ran down the front of BomBay's house. It started to rain as he removed the backpack and took out his pistol.

Brandon hadn't exactly worked out how he was going to approach his target. People had a tendency to react differently when a gun was shoved in their face. But having firsthand knowledge of the marks cocky arrogance, he decided not to take any chances with this man. Rolling down his stocking mask, he lay down on his stomach to wait for BomBay.

Every now and then to Brandon's chagrin, a set of headlights would turn onto the road only to continue past the house, raising his anticipation and making the wait more unbearable. The constant rainfall had turned the ground into a soggy mess, soaking through his clothes and giving him a chill to the bone.

At 1:35 in the morning, Brandon was wet, sticky and miserable. He was fighting the urge to lay his head down in the soft mud and go to sleep when a set of headlights turned onto the road and pulled into the driveway. The truck stopped about fifteen feet from him as the driver killed the engine and headlights. He waited until the door opened to illuminate the cab before easing into a crouch and charging from the hedge.

●●●●●●

With his hands full, BomBay's left foot had barely touched the ground when he looked through the opening between the door and the windshield at a dark figure emerging from behind his hedges, slipping and sliding. BomBay dropped the two sacks of money along with his keys to fumble behind his back for his pistol.

Brandon didn't have any traction when he attempted his charge from the hedges. As he hit the wet driveway, he slipped again and landed hard on his backside. BomBay almost laughed when he saw the jacker bust his ass. He knew that he had the advantage as he brought the nickel-plated Colt .45 up between the door and the truck cab.

Still on the ground, Brandon was a fraction of a second too late as he raised the silenced semi-automatic. Everything seemed to move in slow motion as he stared into the wide barrel of another man's gun for the first time. BomBay squeezed back on the trigger, and fear registered on his face when the big gun failed to buck in his hand. In his rush, he'd failed to release the safety. Brandon took advantage and quickly pulled the trigger.

"SPIT! SPIT! SPIT! SPIT!" was all he heard as bullets crashed through the windshield and the door of the truck. BomBay caught a slug to the neck and was violently spun around. As his gun clattered to the pavement he slowly fell to his knees.

Brandon ran to the truck and raised the man's arm and shot him twice in the heart. Hurriedly, he lifted the deadweight and shoved him inside the cab of the truck. As he was looking at the ground for the truck keys, he was aided by Mother Nature as lightening turned darkness into day. Brandon snatched up the keys and instinctively tossed the two paper bags into the cab. Backing out the driveway he flipped on the windshield wipers and breathed a sigh of relief. The hard part was over.

●●●●●●

The four friends were in the opulent dining room aboard the cruise ship *Alexandria*. After enjoying a huge buffet of crab legs, shrimp, and lobster, Tabitha and Shon excused themselves to go to the ladies' room.

Brandon set down his napkin and looked at his best friend. The last time that he'd seen DJ in a tuxedo was at their senior prom, and at almost 25 years of age, they still looked good. Their future was just beginning. Each one of them had come aboard the ship with $300,000 a piece, strapped around their waist in money belts that were now safely stashed away in their cabins.

"DJ, I know that it wasn't easy for you to walk away from hustlin'. But if you give me two or three years, I promise to make you a legitimate millionaire. Maybe even sooner."

"Yeah, yeah, I don't doubt it. I wouldn't have done it if I didn't trust you. You've always excelled in anything that you set your mind to do," DJ said.

"So what did you do with BomBay's head?"

"I buried it in the corner of my backyard. I'm going to buy a big ass dog and have him trained to shit in that one spot."

DJ thought back on the night that his best friend came to his door in a violent thunderstorm. He was dressed in all black and holding a leather bowling bag that contained the head he'd asked for. The memory gave him the shivers.

"What's up, dog? You've been acting morose all night," Brandon said.

DJ sighed. "I told you that a lot of people depend on me and I meant that. Walking away, I knew that my hustling ability and leadership allowed them to eat, so it was hard to turn my back.

Not to mention that my Colombian connection in Houston was pissed."

"You've made him a lot of money. What is he pissed about?" Brandon asked, angrily.

DJ took a sip of wine to clear his throat. "Brandon, on a good month I was buying 35 kilos every two weeks. That's over a million dollars a month that he wouldn't see anymore. Think about that for a second and maybe you can see why he's upset."

"What did he say?"

"Actually, he told me that I couldn't quit."

Brandon was on the edge of his seat. "What did you say?"

"I told him that I'm my own man and that I've made enough money from the game. It's time to go legit. So fuck off! Then I hung up the phone before he could say anything."

Brandon was quiet for a moment. Then he asked, "Do you think that there's going to be any repercussions?"

"Man, I really hope not. But the truth is... I don't know."

Brandon could hear the worry in DJ's voice.

"I don't know, Tank!"

Two Years Later

Chapter Eighteen

Brandon

Brandon was parked across the street from a seven year old $95,000 brick home in Mesquite Texas. Ever since he started the E & J Investment Group a little over two years ago he had spent countless hours driving around to view potential properties, a responsibility that he shared with his business partner DJ.

Once they agreed on a potential property that they wished to attain, their wives, Tabitha and Shon, would attend property tax-lien auctions in pursuit of securing the winning bid for the certificate note on the approved property. Then BC, the company's only employee who didn't share in the profits, would negotiate with the homeowners or lien holders to pay the delinquent note within a specific time frame. If they failed to pay within that time frame, the property became an asset of E & J Investment Group.

Everyone worked out of their own home offices, and they all enjoyed the luxury of a company Lexus LS 430. Brandon had been able to negotiate a two year lease agreement with a Lexus dealership in Dallas. Everyone stayed coordinated through the use of telecommunications in the form of home computers, fax machines, and cellular phones.

As Brandon sat in his car thinking, he was startled by the ring of his cellular phone.

"Hello! Yeah what's up? I thought you were going to check out that property in Lancaster, Texas."

"Yeah, I'm hungry anyway. I'll meet you there in about 30 minutes or so. If I'm late go ahead and order me the alligator tail for an appetizer. I'll see you in a little bit."

Brandon took one last look at the house and decided that it would be beneficial to try to obtain the note against the property. He made a mental note to e-mail BC and have him do a financial report on the homeowner. As he started the car, he was wondering what DJ had on his mind.

••••••

Tabitha was running late. She was leaving an apartment in Arlington, Texas re-adjusting the lapels on her Chanel suit. After she climbed into the Lexus, she fiddled around in her purse until she found her diamond studs. She put them back in her ears and freshened her lipstick before starting the car.

Shon was going to kill her if she was late again! The auction was being held at the Convention Center in downtown Dallas. They had approval to bid on three properties that were being offered today. Her husband expected results and he wasn't shy about voicing his displeasure when they failed to win a bid.

She was so blessed to have such a good man. Brandon was loving, romantic, faithful, generous, and an all around good person. He loved her and she loved him. Brandon gave her everything that she asked for. On a cruise ship a couple of years ago, Brandon and DJ had her and Shon out on the quarterdeck of the ship. Under a beautiful full moon, the two men had got down on one knee and asked for their hands in marriage.

Both Tabitha and Shon had been offered an identical five-carat diamond ring. They were married a couple of days later by the captain of the ship.

Since that time, Brandon had purchased them a beautiful two level brick home for $250,000 in a suburb called Ducanville. He'd bought her a convertible Mercedes-Benz SL 500 for her birthday in January, and she had all the major credit cards to shop till she dropped. She knew that any woman in her right mind would kill to have her life. Shit, her man too for that matter!

Tabitha thought she had the life that she always wanted. But lately she wasn't sure. She wasn't sure about anything any more. She was on a destructive course and she knew it. As she pulled into a parking space, she decided that the best course of action to take would be to discuss her feelings with Shon. Tabitha knew that she had to talk to someone, and the sooner, the better.

Chapter Nineteen

DJ & Brandon

DJ watched his best friend leave his car and head toward the entrance to the restaurant with fondness in his eyes. Tank was always dapper and clean cut. Today he had chosen a black Hugo Boss suit with Armani square-toed gators. Brandon's outfit actually mirrored his own, except DJ's Hugo Boss was brown. He preferred brown suits over black or blue because the color enhanced his yellow skin.

After Brandon entered the half-filled seafood restaurant, he noticed DJ sitting at a table in the back. His friend had been distant and preoccupied lately. Brandon figured that DJ and Shon were probably having some type of marital problems, problems that DJ would reveal to him after he got the situation under control.

"What's going on, dog?"

Sometimes Brandon and DJ liked to talk to each other as if they were still running around their old neighborhood.

"A hell of a lot, playa. Pull up a chair and let me put a bug in your ear," DJ said.

Brandon sat down and dug into the alligator tail that was a house specialty at Popedeauxs Seafood Restaurant.

"Good lookin' on the tails, fool."

"Slow down man. Didn't Tabitha cook breakfast this morning? Damn!"

DJ was joshing him. Tank always did like food a little too much. But he stayed fit by working out at least three times a week. That was probably a good thing.

Brandon chewed his food before replying in between bites. "No she didn't. She claimed that she was too tired. She's been tired a lot lately and I really don't see why." Brandon dipped a nugget in the hot sauce. "How's Shon? Is she tired a lot lately?"

"No, not really. We still fuck like rabbits every other morning. She's ready to try and have another baby and I'm encouraging her with my effort, if you know what I mean," DJ said, grinning from ear to ear.

"Here comes the waitress. Do you know what you want to order yet?"

"Yeah," Brandon said, as a pimply faced teenager came to take their order.

"How are you gentlemen today?"

"Fine."

"My name is Wendy and I'm your waitress this afternoon. I recommend the turtle soup, it's delicious and fresh."

"I'll pass on the turtle, but I will have the sea bass with a glass of white wine, please."

"Alright. And you, sir?" She wrote DJ's order and turned to Brandon.

"I'll have the lobster with a glass of white wine also, please."

"Thank you gentlemen. Will there be anything else? No? I'll be right back with your order." Wendy walked away.

"So, what's on your mind DJ? You said over the phone that you have a problem."

"Do you remember asking me if there was going to be a problem with my decision to leave the dope connection that I had in Houston?"

"Yeah, I remember," Brandon said, hesitantly.

"You know that I've stayed in touch with a few cats from the street, dog. And from time to time I hear a little somethin', somethin' about the Colombian in Houston, Fat Chris." DJ took a sip of water before continuing.

"Obviously, he's still pissed off at me for leaving the game. He lost the Dallas market for awhile. You can't just trust anybody with sixty or seventy kilos a month. The guy he eventually settled on was a stupid up and comer named Byron. The word that I hear is that Fat Chris is constantly threatening to put a contract out on him because he keeps coming short with the money."

Brandon couldn't see why Fat Chris' problem should be a concern to DJ, but he would humor him anyway.

"Why doesn't Fat Chris just cut this Byron loose?"

"Your guess is as good as mine. But I really don't give a damn what happens to Byron. I'm concerned with my own ass," he said.

"What are you talking about DJ? You've lost me somewhere."

DJ slowly blew out a breath. "Fat Chris isn't just talking about killing Byron. There's also rumors that he's thinking about placing a contract on my head too!

"Why?" Brandon asked.

"Because he's blaming all of his problems with Byron on me. Now, the way that I see it, I have a few decisions to make."

"What kind of decisions, DJ?" Brandon asked with trepidation.

"I can go back into the business and bail Byron out. I can go and talk to Fat Chris and try and work this thing out, or I can put a contract out on Fat Chris' ass. And I'm leaning toward doing just that!"

Brandon looked around to see if his friend had been overheard.

"Calm down. Just calm the fuck down, DJ! You are a legitimate business man now. And I'm aware that everything we've worked for is being threatened by this punk ass Colombian. But we'll try to solve the problem as businessmen before we do anything else!" he hissed.

DJ knew that Brandon was right. But he had also hoped that his friend would agree to killing Fat Chris. *Hell!* DJ thought. *If you have a best friend as a professional hit man, what good is it if you can't get him to kill your enemies?*

"Here you go, gentlemen" the waitress said as she placed their orders on the cloth covered table. "If you need anything else, just give a holler." Wendy sauntered off to another group of customers.

Brandon dug into his lobster while DJ waited impatiently. As he was taking a bite DJ cleared his throat to get his attention, stopping Brandon's fork in mid air.

"What?" Brandon asked.

"My problem is what! What are we going to do?"

"We're going to Houston so that we can have a sit down with this cat, Fat Chris."

"I want you to understand something," DJ said as Brandon enjoyed his meal. "I realize that I can't solve my legitimate business problems by killing. But Fat Chris isn't a legitimate business problem. He will have my ass killed just as sure as you're eating that damn lobster! But we'll do it your way for now and talk. I'll set it up tonight."

"You do that. I want to meet this Fat Chris. Because if he fucks with you, then he fucks with me," Brandon said, as his cellular phone rang.

"Yes?"

"Hi, baby!"

"Hi yourself. How did the auction go?"

"Great!" Tabitha said excitedly. "We won all three bids today."

"That's good, baby. I'm proud of you guys. But check this out. Me and DJ may have to take a trip down to Houston so that we can handle some business."

"What kind of business?"

He looked across the table at DJ. "There's a list of properties down there that we need to consider. They're having an auction down that way soon, so I don't know how long we'll be gone," he lied.

"Are you leaving tonight, or what?" she asked.

"What's today, Friday? No, we probably won't leave until tomorrow."

"Okay. Well, what time will you be home?"

"I don't know, baby. I have to go by momma's house later, and I still have a property or two to check out before I call it a day."

DJ was whispering at him and using sign language.

"DJ wants to know where Shon is. Okay, I'll let him know. Love you too. Bye, baby." Brandon hung up the phone.

"She's on her way home, dog."

When they were halfway through their meal, DJ said, "I'll try to set the meeting up for Sunday. Fat Chris is Catholic; he doesn't like to commit violence on Sunday." DJ smiled, but Brandon didn't see the humor in it.

Chapter Twenty

Shon, BC & Tabitha

Shon was on her way home to the beautiful mini-mansion that she shared with her husband. She couldn't wait to get into her Jacuzzi so that she could soak away the stress. She was a nervous wreck! Her best friend had just dumped a load of problems in her lap that she just didn't need.

DJ and Brandon had their faults as everyone does. But when they made a commitment to a person or project, it was a very rare day when they didn't come through. Shon knew that it was a blessing for her and Tabitha to find such good male partners who were real men.

DJ is a go-getter, a survivor, a good provider, and a great husband. But there were lots of times when she felt that Tabitha had the better man in some aspects. He was the brains behind their financial success. And she was proud that he was married to her best friend. They were good for each other--she, with her fiery mouth and temper--he, with his laid back style, all smooth and suave. They complimented each other in every way.

So why was Tabitha ruining her marriage? Why would she risk ruining her life like this? She hit her steering wheel with her hand in frustration. "Damn you, Tabitha!"

●●●●●●

BC was sitting in the guest bedroom of his two-bedroom apartment. He had converted the guestroom into a small office, with a nice desk, computer, printer, fax machine, and a fire proof filing cabinet.

At 6'1 and 195 1bs. BC was a good looking dark skinned man. When he was lucky enough to land a job with E & J

Investments over a year and a half ago, he joined a local gym to help keep his 35 year old body in tip-top shape.

BC loved his life. He made $50k a year and drove a Lexus that all the ladies loved. He worked at his own pace and in the leisure of his home. He had it made! And if everything went according to plan, his life would get even better. He came from behind his desk and went to answer the knock at the door.

BC looked through the peephole and saw the woman of his dreams. She was golden brown and beautiful.

"Hold on, Tabitha."

BC ran into the kitchen and pulled a bottle of Viagra out of a drawer. He swallowed a whole 50-milligram. Not that he had erectional dysfunction or anything, he needed the extra staying power because it was all in the plan, and it was working like a charm. He had already fucked the shit out of her this morning. Now the rich bitch was coming back for more! She had an insatiable sexual appetite. If he could just make her love him and leave her husband, she'd walk away with at least two million, minimum. Then he'd marry her and control her money.

BC was already getting her in tune with his domineering attitude. He treated her like she was shit whenever he got the chance. Hell, it must be working he thought, because if she didn't like it, she wouldn't have kept coming back for almost six months!

He threw the pill bottle back in the drawer and slowly walked back to the door.

"Hello, Tabitha, Come on in. I didn't expect to see you again today."

"I wanted to drop off the paperwork for the three properties that we won at auction."

BC got in her space. "Is that all you came for?"

She turned away and walked toward his office carrying her briefcase. BC grabbed her arm and jerked her back to him.

"I asked you a question. Is that all you came for?" he growled.

"Please, let go of me, BC."

He glared at her for a few seconds longer before he relaxed his grip. "Drop off the papers then, and get the fuck out. I don't need this shit."

"Don't act like that. I came over didn't I?"

"Fuck that! I'm tired of this shit! I want to spend more time with you, Tabitha. I'm not going to keep putting up with this sneaky shit."

He walked past her and into his bedroom.

Tabitha hesitantly followed him into the bedroom. She looked at his cheap bedroom furniture until her eyes settled on the queen-sized bed. She slowly removed her clothes and walked toward the dark man sitting on the edge of the bed.

●●●●●●

Tabitha was pulling on her panties. She had to get home and take a bath before her husband got there. She could see BC out of the corner of her eye lying in the bed butt naked, watching her. They had fucked for two hours straight and the man's dick was still rock hard. He was simply incredible! Some days they'd fuck for several hours, but she couldn't allow him to continue today.

Brandon couldn't give her a definite time on when he'd be home. And she could never allow her husband to find out about her affair. She knew that this was wrong from the first time she'd had sex with BC. But he made her feel different, afraid, exciting! Hell! She couldn't explain how he made her feel. He talked to her bad sometimes, and treated her rough and gritty. But she would except that from him because deep down she knew that she deserved it for betraying her husband.

Tabitha was so engrossed with her thoughts that she hadn't noticed BC leave the bed to stand in front of her as she put on her shoes.

"Did you hear me, bitch?"

"What? No, I didn't hear you. What did you say?" she asked, flustered.

"I want you to stay longer." He grabbed his dick and put it in her face.

"My dick is still hard. What the fuck is wrong with you? I'm not satisfied."

"I have to get home, BC. I do have a husband you know." Tabitha stood up to leave.

"Bitch!" He screamed as he backhanded her across the face. Tabitha was slammed into the dresser, knocking over BC's cologne bottles, before falling to the floor.

"Go home then, bitch! I don't need you in my life!"

Tabitha sat on the floor holding her eye and sobbing. "I'm sorry, I'm sorry! I didn't mean for this to happen!"

"Well, get out then, bitch! Come on, I'll help you." BC grabbed a handful of her dyed hair and pulled her to her feet as he shoved her out the bedroom.

He followed her into the hall and removed the paperwork that she brought from her briefcase. When he closed it, he threw it at her. Tabitha screamed as she used her forearm to deflect the flying briefcase. She quickly retrieved it from the floor and ran out of the apartment.

Chapter Twenty-One

Brandon & Tabitha

As Brandon pulled into the garage, he noticed his wife's Lexus in its parking space within the three-car garage. He had been thinking about her all day.

They had their problems, just like everyone else, but over-all they were cool. He was happy with his life, and he hoped that DJ and his problems didn't disturb that happiness.

As Brandon entered the kitchen from the garage, the first thing that he felt was the quiet solitude of the big house. He opened the refrigerator and removed a fresh, cold peach before he walked through the living room to go upstairs.

When he reached the top of the stairs, he still didn't hear Tabitha moving around.

"Tabitha!" He called, as he entered their spacious bedroom.

"In the bathroom, Brandon!"

"Hey, baby!" he said, as he entered the bathroom.

His wife was soaking in the Jacuzzi styled bathtub with soap all over her face and body. "Hey yourself. How was your day?"

"It was cool, nothing spectacular." Brandon tossed the rest of his peach and started to remove his shirt. "Mom and dad said hello."

Tabitha didn't respond. When Brandon finished undressing, he stepped into the tub and situated himself behind her.

"Give me that soap, girl, and let me rub you the right way."

She handed him the soap and bath towel so that he could do his thing.

"Brandon."

"Yeah, baby?"

"I love you so much."

He wrapped her in his arms, pulling her against his chest. "I love you too. Why don't you wash that soap off your face so that I can get me some suga?"

Tabitha gave a weak smile and rinsed her face. Then she slowly turned and let him see her bruised and swollen eye.

"What the fuck happened to your face?" he yelled, as he took her face into his hands. "Who did this to you, Tabitha? How did this happen?"

"Calm down, baby! Please calm down! I'm going to be alright, just calm down," she begged, as she started to cry.

Brandon pulled her close. "Shh, baby. I'll be alright, okay? Just tell me what happened. I'm calm. See?" he said softly, before gently kissing her cheek.

"I was... mugged, Brandon!" she stammered in between racking sobs.

"Shh, Shh, it's going to be alright, baby. Just tell me what happened."

"After Shon and I left the Convention Center today, we were walking to our cars when I realized that I had to pee too bad to make it all the way home. So I said goodbye to Shon and went back inside to use a toilet. That's when I called and talked to you." She broke down again.

Brandon let her cry. He wanted her to cry herself out so that he could get the whole story.

When she got control of herself she said, "When I finished, I left the Convention Center to head for my car. I guess that I was thinking about your trip to Houston." She shook her head. "I don't know what I was thinking! All of a sudden, someone came out from the side of a car that I had just passed and said, 'Give me your money.' When I turned to see who it was, they hit me in the face! When I fell, I dropped my purse. I vaguely remember hearing someone rummaging through it while I lay there. I guess I was knocked out or something."

"Did you call the police?"

"No. I just got the hell out of there before he came back!"

"Come on, baby." Brandon dried her off from head to toe. Then he wrapped the towel around her and led her toward their bedroom. "Get in the bed, baby. I want you to relax." Brandon pulled the covers down on the bed. After she lay down, he bent over and kissed her cheek.

"I love you baby. I don't ever want to loose you. Especially behind a senseless act of violence. Will you be alright for a little while?"

She opened her eyes and pulled him down on top of her. "Don't leave me, Brandon! Please, baby, don't leave me!" she begged.

Brandon held her tight and whispered in her ear, "It's alright baby, you're home now where it's safe. I just have to run to the drug store and pick up something for your eye. I'll be right back, okay?" He kissed her on the lips and she gave him her tongue. Brandon pulled softly and slowly.

"Promise me that you'll never leave me, Brandon! I want us to grow old together, baby. I just love you so much," she said.

"What we have is forever, Honey Love." She smiled as he used her pet name.

"Hurry back, baby!"

"I will. I'll pick us up a pizza on the way home too." Brandon pulled on a pair of shorts and left the room.

Tabitha waited until she heard the garage door open before she reached for the telephone.

"You bastard! I have a black eye!"

"Poor baby. Why don't you come over and let me kiss it and make it better for you."

"I'm not ever coming back over there. I had to lie to my husband because you can't control your temper, BC. And if you ever pull that shit again, I'll kill your ass!" She slammed the phone down and closed her eyes.

Three minutes later the phone rang.

"Hello!"

"Is Mrs. Elliott in?"

"Why are you playing on my phone, BC? Don't ever call here unless it's about business."

"It is business related. I have a few payment contracts that need your punk ass husband's signature."

"Watch your mouth, BC! He's my husband and your employer. Don't ever forget that!"

"What you think, I can't get another job?"

"I didn't say that."

"Whatever, Tabitha."

An uncomfortable silence passed between them for a number of seconds.

"Why don't you come and pick up the papers tomorrow. That'll give you an excuse to come back again on Sunday."

"You're real sure of yourself."

"Are you coming or what? I don't have time for games."

"Maybe, maybe not. I don't know yet. Brandon is supposed to go out of town tomorrow, so I may not need to come all the way out there to get those papers. He won't be around to sign them anyway."

"When will he be back?"

"Probably in a few days, maybe more. I don't know for sure."

"Maybe I'll just deliver the paperwork myself. If I do, I'll be sure to bring along a change of clothes." BC hung up the phone before she could respond.

Tabitha gently set the receiver into the cradle with a sigh.

Chapter Twenty-Two

Brandon, DJ & Fat Chris

DJ arrived in his gray Mercedes Benz CL600 at exactly 8:00a.m. The big powerful car would make the three and a half hour trip seem effortless. Brandon didn't want to leave Tabitha alone. But she assured him that she was alright by packing his suitcase and fixing him breakfast, which was a rarity in their household.

Once they were on Highway 45 going South, Brandon reclined the soft leather passenger seat and told DJ about Tabitha's mugging the day before.

"Is she alright?" DJ asked, with a grim look on his face. He didn't like it when his loved ones were harmed by elements within everyday street life.

"She'll be alright. Just a little shaken up is all."

"That's good. Shon was acting strange last night. I kept asking her what was wrong. I wonder why she didn't tell me about it."

"Tabitha said Shon had left before it happened so she wouldn't have known unless Tabitha called her," he said as he slid in a Tyrese CD.

"Wake me up when we get to the hotel."
●●●●●●

Fat Chris was misunderstood. First of all, he wasn't really fat, he was just big-boned. Americans feared what they didn't under-stand. They assumed that all Colombians were crazy, gun- happy drug dealers. He was neither crazy nor gun-happy, but he was a drug dealer. So the public perception was correct one-third of the time, he supposed.

Fat Chris was thinking this as he looked through the tinted windows of his limousine. He was accompanied by his two gargantuan bodyguards. Big Tree stood an imposing 6'8 and 270 lbs. Big Tree loved the drug dealer lifestyle. As a matter of fact, he thought as he looked over at his friend/bodyguard, he was loving it at this very moment. There was a naked little *senorita* in between his legs, noisily giving him head as they rode around town.

Fat Chris tore his eyes away from the lady's wiggling ass only to notice Big Jimmy. He too was watching the girl as he seemed to be salivating at the mouth while squeezing his piece through his pants in anticipation of getting his turn.

Fat Chris turned his attention to the passing scenery. It was time for him to get out of this business. Luckily, he was wise enough to have invested some of his money over the years, but nothing on the scale that he really wanted.

Fat Chris was a subscriber to *Black Enterprise Magazine*. As he thumbed through last month's issue while sitting on the toilet the other day, he was shocked to see a picture of his old friend DJ, from Dallas. The article described how DeJuan Jackson and Brandon Elliott became millionaires from buying land or houses at auctions. Fat Chris wasn't quite sure which, he just knew that he wanted a piece of the action.

Chapter Twenty-Three

Brandon, DJ & Shon

As DJ entered Houston he picked up his cellular telephone and got the number to the Hilton from information. Then he made reservations for a large two bedroom penthouse suite for two days. "Tank! Tank! Wake up man, we're here. Tank!"

"Yeah, yeah, I hear you, now shut up! You know that I hate it when people wake me up with a lot of noise."

"You told me to wake you up when we got here," DJ said defensively.

Brandon looked around at the passing cars. "I said wake me up when we got to the hotel. Shit!" He wiped the sleep out of his eyes. "Where are we staying anyway? Did you make reservation or what?"

"Stop asking so many damn questions and go back to sleep, why don't you!"

"Shit, I'm up now! I might as well keep you company. Where are we going?"

"To a soulfood restaurant in 5th Ward that I know."

"Man, it's a beautiful and sunny spring day. Why are we wasting it by spending time in Houston?"

DJ looked over at him. Guys from Dallas didn't like Houston too much. *If it ain't Dallas, then it ain't cool!*

He used to feel the same way. But once he started traveling to Houston regularly, the city had grown on him.

"Don't trip, homie, it ain't all bad. We'll find something to get into."

"Man, I want to get a room with some room service and chill. I don't need to do no sight seeing. In between looking at houses and checking on my eight stores, I get exhausted."

"Are you serious?" DJ asked. "You can't be serious. This is the largest city in Texas."

"And they don't have nothing on Dallas but the Gulf of Mexico. But I'm not hating on Houston, I'm just kind of tired, dog. I really have a lot of shit on my mind. Tabitha just got mugged and I would rather be at home barbecuing with her right now. And must I remind you that this isn't a vacation? You need to be trying to find me some heat, just in case I have to get off in Fat Chris' ass!"

"Will you please be cool? I have a man down here that'll get me whatever I need. Did you bring the Glock?"

"Yeah, it's in my suitcase. But that's my personal--I don't use it for jobs."

If you want to, we can go holla at my friend tonight."

"I thought that you said Fat Chris didn't believe in violence on Sunday."

DJ shook his head. "He doesn't, but you never know what's on a person's mind."

"Where's the meeting?"

"I told him to meet us at the Hilton downtown."

"The Glock will do for now. But if we decide to take him out, we'll have to get something else."

•••••••

Shon was on her way to Tabitha's house. After DJ left for Houston, she cleaned her house and got dressed to go shopping. It had taken everything that she had to keep her mouth shut about Tabitha's affair last night. DJ kept asking her what was bothering her. And every time he asked, she would bite her tongue to keep from blabbing.

Shopping was therapeutic for her. After she left the mall she decided to go and shake some sense into Tabitha's ass. As she turned onto her friend's street, Shon noticed a car sitting out front. Tabitha and Brandon lived in the middle of the block, so she didn't recognize the car as being the green Lexus loaned to BC until she got up on it. Damn, no she didn't!

Shon pushed the gas pedal and sped by Tabitha's house. Once she got to the end of the block she pulled over and called Tabitha with her cell phone.

"Hello!" Tabitha answered slightly out of breath.

"Girl, what you doin'? Whatever it is it can wait. Let's go shopping."

"I have a headache, Shon. I think that I have to pass, girlfriend. I'm going to take a nap."

Yeah right! Shon thought "Girl, take some Advil or something. I'll be there in five minutes."

"No!"

"What?"

"I mean... you don't have to come over, girl. My house is a mess anyway, and you know how I am about allowing people to see my house nasty. Let's get together tomorrow, Shon, alright?"

"Hell no it's not alright! Are you out of your fuckin' mind? I see BC's car outside your fuckin' house! I am so ashamed of you Tabitha, and you should be ashamed of yourself!"

"Who the fuck do you think you're talking too? Let me tell you somethin' Shon. Mind your own fuckin' business and stay the hell out of mine! I'm a grown ass woman and I can do whatever I want to! Now if you want to come over tomorrow and talk, then that's cool. But right now, I'm busy!"

Shon winced as she removed the phone from her ear. "The bitch hung up on me! I don't believe this shit!"

She put down the phone and pulled away from the curb. If Tabitha didn't want her help, then she would just take her nosy ass home.

"Ain't that a bitch!" she mumbled.

Chapter Twenty-Four

Brandon, DJ & Fat Chris

Brandon entered the living room area of the huge penthouse suite with a worried look on his face.

"You still didn't get an answer?" DJ asked.

"Nope, and I don't understand why. She's usually pretty good about answering her cell phone when she's not home. Maybe I should have taken her to the doctor. She could've had a concussion or something."

It wasn't like his wife to be unavailable. He had been trying to reach her ever since they'd checked in yesterday evening. DJ had called Shon to see if they were together, but Shon was home reading a book. Shon said that she'd talked to Tabitha earlier and that she was taking a nap and didn't want to be disturbed. But they planned to do some shopping on Sunday.

While Brandon was thinking about his wife, there was a knock at the door. DJ went to answer it, while Brandon reached around and touched the 9mm at the small of his back hidden by his suit jacket. DJ stopped at the door to look back at his friend. Brandon gave him a nod of assurance.

"Fat Chris! Welcome, my friend! Come on in." DJ stepped back and allowed Fat Chris and his gargantuan goons to enter the suite.

"It's good to see you, DJ. I've missed you, my friend." Fat Chris shook DJ's hand and gave him a good whack on the shoulder. He looked around the suite in admiration.

"Nice suite, DJ. I like to see that you're still living well and enjoying all that life has to offer." Fat Chris looked at the man standing in the middle of the room.

"And you must be Mr. Elliott," he said, approaching Brandon and offering his hand.

"My friends call me Tank," Brandon said, as he gave the man a firm handshake. "I hope that we are friends," he added.

"My friends call me Fat Chris. And if we aren't enemies, then what else could we be but friends?"

"Would you like a drink, Fat Chris?" DJ asked.

"No, thank you, DJ I'm trying to quit the alcohol." He patted his solid stomach. "I have to watch what I consume as I get older I'm almost forty."

"Please, gentlemen, let's sit down and get comfortable before we discuss business," DJ said.

Brandon noticed that the two goons remained standing on either side of the door. DJ and Brandon sat in the two sitting chairs facing each other. They were separated by the coffee table. Fat Chris occupied the big sofa facing the door.

"I'm going to be frank here gentlemen and lay all of my cards on the table. Is that alright?" Fat Chris asked, with a slight accent.

"Please do."

"Sure, go ahead, Fat Chris."

"DJ, when you retired without giving me time to find an adequate replacement for the Dallas area, I was highly pissed. A million dollars a month is nothing to sneeze at. And since you left, I've had nothing but problems fooling around with people who aren't honorable. You had balls, DJ, and your word was good."

He shook his head sadly before he continued. "I came to this country when I was two years old, and I've made my money. I'm tired of this dope business. I have some investments in real estate, ten rental houses and two apartment complexes, but I need something with a little more substance. I bring in about $8,000 a month with my rental houses and I gross around $72,000 a month from the two apartment complexes. I had my lawyer look into your company, E & J Investment Group. I also had him sit down and explain everything to me that your company did in detail just last night. He explained to me that there are several investment groups who take on investors and use their capital to secure tax lien notes."

He looked from DJ to Brandon. "I would like to invest ten million dollars into your company. But I don't want to be a mere investor. I want to be a full partner!"

With Fat Chris' revelation, Brandon and DJ made eye contact. This wasn't what they were expecting to hear on their drive to Houston. Surprisingly, he wasn't finished.

"Gentlemen, I too am a businessman. I understand that I have to bring something to the table. So with that in mind, I also will add my ten rental houses and my two apartment complexes. I have 275 apartment units within those complexes here in Houston. Once I finalize a few things, I'm leaving the dope game. And upon my retirement I'll need something to occupy my time. So I propose an office branch be established here in Houston. I'd like to be responsible for procuring tax-lien notes in South Texas."

Fat Chris noticed that the two men were speechless. "I understand that you gentlemen will want to discuss my proposal in private." He rose from the soft couch. "So I'll take my leave now."

Both Brandon and DJ stood to shake his hand.

"You caught us off guard with such a generous offer, Fat Chris. But yes, you're correct in your assessment. We do need some time to evaluate your offer. Especially the appropriation of a new branch here in Houston," Brandon said.

"I understand." Fat Chris turned and walked to the door.

"We'll let you know something within a couple of weeks or so," DJ said.

"Please do that, DJ. Have a safe trip home, gentlemen."

Chapter Twenty-Five

The Gang

Shon was on her way to Tabitha's house. No matter what Tabitha said or did, she wasn't going to just sit back and allow her to get caught with a man in the house. They had been through too much together to allow a few harsh words to come between their friendship. So she'd lied to her husband when he asked about Tabitha yesterday.

DJ and Brandon were on Highway 45 at this very moment, on their way back home. DJ had called her on his cell phone and told her to break out the champagne. They were all going out to celebrate tonight. Hell, she didn't feel like celebrating, she felt like crying. Instead she ran to her car to make the five-mile drive to Tabitha's house.

As she pulled up, she was relieved that BC's Lexus was nowhere in sight. As Shon approached the front door, she could tell that it hadn't been closed all the way. She pushed it open and walked in, but she quickly stopped in her tracks. There were bloody footprints in the front foyer leading to the door. They came from the living room. Shon slowly followed the footprints. The place was a mess. Vases were broken, lamps were knocked over, glass was on the floor, and the stereo system was pulled from the entertainment unit against the wall.

Shon thought that someone had broken into the house. She immediately started looking around warily, just in case the intruder was still there.

"Tabitha?" she called. Shon heard something in the kitchen and froze with terror. She noticed the bloody footprints were a darker red as they left the kitchen. She was so mesmerized by the bloody footprints that she jumped when she heard a voice begging, "*Help me! Help me!*"

Shon recognized the voice and flew into the kitchen. As she rounded the counter she slipped in a puddle of blood and went down hard.

●●●●●●

DJ was napping in the passenger seat when his cellular rang.

"DJ... DJ! Wake up and answer your phone!"

"Yeah, yeah, I got it." He turned down the car stereo and pulled the Nokia out of his pocket. "Hello!"

"Baby, I'm at Baylor Hospital."

DJ sat up straight in his seat. "What's wrong? You alright?"

"I'm fine, I'm fine. It's Tabitha, baby." Shon started crying.

DJ looked at his best friend and asked, "What's wrong with Tabitha, Shon?"

"Someone beat her and stabbed her, DJ. Oh, DJ, he left her for dead, and it's all my fault!" she cried.

"What room is she in, baby?"

"Room 301."

"Okay. We'll be there as soon as we can. Just take care of our girl. I love you."

"Alright, DJ... DJ?"

"Yeah baby, I'm here."

"Tell Brandon that I'm sorry, okay?"

DJ was silent for a few seconds. *Sorry for what*, he wondered. "Alright, baby. You just sit tight. Room 301, right?"

"Yeah."

"Bye, Shon." DJ slowly put the phone back into his pocket. Brandon had grown impatient. "So, are you going to tell me what's wrong with my wife?" he growled.

"We need to get to Baylor Hospital, dog. Shon said that Tabitha was beaten up pretty bad... and... and..."

"And what!" he screamed.

"Stabbed, dog! Tabitha got stabbed!"

"Stabbed where? Is she going to be alright? I didn't hear you ask that! Who stabbed her, DJ?"

"I don't know, dog!"

They were forty-five minutes outside of Dallas, passing through a little town called Innis. Brandon floored the big V-12 and reached Dallas County in twenty minutes.

●●●●●●

As DJ and Brandon came off the elevator and started up the hallway, Shon came out of a room up ahead. When she saw them, she ran into Brandon's arms.

"I'm so sorry, Brandon. Please forgive me. I didn't know that she was going to get hurt," she cried.

"Shhh, shhh." Brandon pat her on the back. "How is she, Shon?"

Shon pulled away and began wiping her tears. "She's going to be alright. She's asleep now." Shon saw Tabitha's doctor approaching and waved him over.

Brandon turned to see a young red headed man in a white lab coat.

"Doctor, this is Mr. Elliott," Shon said.

The young doctor offered Brandon his hand. "Mr. Elliott, I'm Dr. Hughes. I treated your wife when she was brought in today."

"How's my wife, Dr. Hughes?"

"Well, as I told Mrs. Jackson here, she'll heal up pretty good. She suffered a contusion on the left side of her head that required six stitches. Then there's the abrasions to her lips and eyes, caused by someone's fist, I suppose. She took a beating, Mr. Elliott. But my main concern was the stab wound to her left bicep. The knife went clean through. But there may or may not be nerve damage in that arm. Some surgery may be required to repair some muscle tissue. But it's really too early to tell. She's a young healthy woman and the body will heal itself.

"Can I see her?"

"I gave her a pretty strong sedative, so she'll be asleep for awhile. I should also warn you..." Dr. Hughes was hesitant.

"Warn me of what?" Brandon prompted.

"It seems that your wife may have been raped."

"Raped! By who?" Brandon grabbed the doctor by his collar but DJ was quick to restrain him.

"Who raped my wife?" he yelled.

Calm down, Mr. Elliott! This is a private hospital." the doctor admonished.

Brandon quickly got a hold of himself. "I'm sorry; this is very shocking to me. Please continue, Dr. Hughes."

"Your wife had sexual intercourse within the last 24 hours. There was some anal and vaginal tearing. We've taken samples and the results will be turned over to the authorities once they return from the lab. The police will want to speak to her soon. I'm sorry, Mr. Elliott."

"Thank you, Doctor." Brandon turned and walked into Tabitha's room as DJ and Shon followed.

Tabitha was resting on her back. She was hooked up to an I.V. and there were bandages around her head and arm. But the dark purple bruises around her eyes and mouth were a gruesome contrast to her beautiful honey colored skin.

Brandon fell heavily to his knees next to the bed and gently lifted her hand into his. "Who did this to my baby?" he whispered. "My beautiful baby."

Brandon looked at Shon. "Tell me what happened, Shon."

Shon only told him what she had to. She recounted how she found the door cracked and the trail of blood that led to her finding Tabitha in the kitchen. She also told him about the damage to the house.

"DJ, take Shon and go by the house and pick up some clothes and cosmetics for her. Check out the house from top to bottom, DJ. I need to know how this son of a bitch got into my house!"

"Alright, dog. I'll be back in a couple of hours. Come on, baby."

"DJ, here." Brandon reached into his pocket. "Take my house key. The alarm code is 26436. Set it when you leave."

"Alright." DJ took Shon by the arm and left him alone with Tabitha.

Brandon pulled a chair up next to the bed and continued to hold his wife's hand. "Baby, I swear, whoever did this to you will pay for it with their life!" he growled. He put his head down and said a prayer giving thanks that his wife's injuries weren't worse.

When he finished there was a knock at the door. A big bald headed man in a cheap suit walked into the room. "Excuse me. Are you, Mr. Elliott?"

"Yes, I am."

"My name is Reggie Leroy. I'm a detective with the Dallas Police Department. Can I have a word with you please?"

"Sure." Brandon rose and led the man into the hall.

"I just have a few questions." The detective removed a pen and note pad from his pocket. "Where were you around midnight to 12 noon today, Mr. Elliott?"

"I was on a business trip in Houston. I left Saturday morning and I returned about an hour ago."

"Where did you stay in Houston?"

"Look man, what is this about? Why are you asking me these stupid ass questions?"

"Well, Mr. Elliott, it's like this. Unless your wife knew the assailant, and I believe that she did, the husband or lover is always the first person that we look at as a possible suspect in a case such as this. 'OJ and Nicole'. You see where I'm going here?"

"Wait a minute! Why do you believe that she knew this person? Someone broke in and trashed my house!"

"Someone trashed the house alright. But most, if not all of it was done in a struggle. And there wasn't any forced entry. Whoever attacked your wife either had a key and knew the alarm code, or they were allowed entrance by her."

Brandon started to pace back and forth with a look of confusion etched across his face. "This shit doesn't make sense!"

"Well, Mr. Elliott, now I guess you can understand why I have to ask these questions. I have to clear you as a suspect before I can pursue other leads."

Brandon stopped pacing and asked, "What kind of leads?"

The detective looked uncomfortable with Brandon's question. "Are you sure that you want to know that, Mr. Elliott?"

"What other leads, Detective?" Brandon growled.

"Well...uh... there was a pair of men's briefs next to the bed in the master bedroom. When I looked through your dresser, all that I found were boxer shorts."

"I don't own any briefs!" Brandon didn't like where this was going.

"The sheets had been disturbed as well. It was obvious that someone had engaged in sexual intercourse recently. That may be

151

where the sexual assault took place. We've confiscated the sheets and our laboratory will run the result against anything that the hospital may have found."

"What else do you need to know? I need to get back to my wife." Brandon was both confused and frustrated.

"Where did you stay in Houston?"

"We stayed at the Hilton downtown."

The detective looked up from his pad. "We, sir?"

"Yeah, we. Me and my business partner, DeJuan Jackson. We stayed in a penthouse suite. The room was charged to our credit card in the name of E & J Investment Group."

"And where is your partner now?"

"He's at my house with Shon--that's his wife. She was the lady who found Tabitha."

"Yes, I spoke with her briefly. She was a little distraught at the time." He closed his note pad. "Alright, Mr. Elliott, I'm sorry for any inconvenience. I know that you want the perpetrator caught as soon as possible."

Brandon offered his hand. "Yes, thank you, Detective Leroy. I'm a little shook up right now."

"Here's my card. Please call me if you find out anything that'll help in the investigation. I'll also need to speak with Mrs. Elliott as soon as possible."

"Sure, yeah," Brandon said, absentmindedly.

Brandon resumed his vigil over his wife. "What the hell is going on, baby?" he whispered.

Tabitha's eyes opened heavily with sleep, swollen and bloodshot red. But she managed to find her husband next to her bed with his head down.

"Brandon," she croaked.

"I'm here, baby." Brandon gently kissed her lips. "Everything is going to be alright, okay?"

"Oh, Brandon, I messed up, baby. I messed up real bad this time. You're going to hate me! You're going to leave me, I just know it!" She whispered, as tears ran down her face.

"Whatever it is Tabitha, we'll work it out baby. Don't worry about anything. I'm here for you. Just get some rest and we'll talk when you feel better." He kissed her on the forehead as she closed her eyes and went back to sleep.

Brandon sat back down. His mind was racing. Could Tabitha have been having an affair? He didn't want to believe that she was even capable of doing that to him. And there had to be another explanation for the underwear being found in his house.

●●●●●●

A few hours later, DJ slowly opened the door and entered the room. When his eyes settled on Tabitha they were full of hate and disgust. Shon had confessed everything to him about Tabitha's affair. His first thought was how could she do this? Then he asked himself, what could she possible see in BC over the man sitting next to her bed? Brandon's eyes were always full of respect, love, pride and devotion for this woman. And it pissed him off that he was about to see all of those beautiful emotions dissolve, only to be replaced by pain and betrayal.

Brandon looked up and was shocked at the expression on DJ's face as he stared at Tabitha. "DJ!"

DJ tore his eyes away from Tabitha. "We need to talk, dog." DJ walked out of the room as Brandon got up to follow.

"What's up?" Brandon asked, as he fell in step with DJ down the hallway.

"The house was a mess, Tank. Shon is there cleaning it up now." DJ gave him Tabitha's overnight bag. "Shon packed this for her."

DJ looked down at the floor for a few seconds before continuing. "I have to tell you something homeboy. And it's really breaking my heart, man." DJ looked his friend in the eyes. "This is going to be hard for you to take, homie. But Tabitha has been sleeping with BC for five or six months."

Brandon's knees buckled. He had to grab DJ's arm to keep from falling down.

DJ made sure that he was okay before he asked, "What do you want me to do?"

"Get me his personnel file. Tabitha and Shon hired him, we just approved it."

"Is that all? You don't need a gun?"

Brandon shook his head. "Not on this job."

"I got you. When will she be able to go home?"

Brandon heard the malice in DJ's voice. "Let me tell you something, DJ. For better or for worse, that's my wife in there.

And you'll respect that fact and you'll treat her the same way that you treat me. The same as I treat you and your wife. With respect!

"DJ, don't get me wrong, dog. I'm hurt. I'm hurting like a motherfucker! But she's still my wife and I still love her. This is our problem. We'll deal with it. I'm not a punk or some trick, I'm a man, DJ, and I'll handle this my way, without any interference from you or Shon. Do you understand?"

"I got you, dog. I'm just a little upset right now. I'll e-mail that information or something. Hit me on the cell if you need me." DJ walked away.

Brandon knew that he'd hurt him. But Tabitha's infidelity was his problem. She was half of the family that he started and he would deal with the situation. He wasn't sure how but he had to find a way. He said a silent prayer before returning to Tabitha's bedside.

Chapter Twenty-Six

Tabitha

Shon arrived at the hospital early the next morning and found Brandon sitting next to the bed asleep.

"Brandon!"

"Good morning, Shon," Brandon said, as he rubbed the sleep from his eyes.

"Go home and get some rest, baby. I'll stay with her for a while. She'll be alright, she's a strong woman."

"I know she is, that's what I love about her. Can I ask you a question?" He rose from his seat.

"Sure, Brandon," she said softly.

"Why? What did I fail to do as a husband? Where did I fail her as a man, Shon? What area was I weak in? I've been asking myself these questions all night!"

Shon walked up next to the bed and gave him a big hug. "Baby, sometimes a woman gets hurt so much and so often that she grows hard inside. You're what we ladies like to call, 'A Do Right Man', and sometimes women can't believe their good fortune to find such a man. A lot of times they don't believe that their 'do right man' will forever do right. We constantly hear stories about dog ass men. So, the woman that has a good man starts second guessing him. She thinks that it's just a matter of time before he hurts her, just like everyone else did. I'm not saying that Tabitha felt that way." Shon looked at her girlfriend as she slept

"Tabitha's different, I think. Sometimes I've felt that she liked drama. Her life had gotten too comfortable."

"Are you saying I treated her too good?"

"No. I'm saying that some people are self destructive. I'm saying that maybe Tabitha isn't aware of her own self worth--not only to herself, but to you as well."

Brandon shook his head. "That's not good enough, Shon."

"Brandon, what could that man offer her that you couldn't give her ten times over? I know that it wasn't the sex, because we girls talk. And I know for a fact that you satisfied her in the bedroom. So don't devalue your worth, you're priceless, baby. And I want you and my girl to work this out. You hear me?"

Brandon kissed Shon and gave her a hug. "I'll try, Shon. It'll be hard, but I'll try." Brandon walked to the door. "Take care of her, Shon. I'll call you in a few hours. I have some business to take care of."

She waved him off. "Boy, go on, I got this."

Brandon watched Tabitha a few moments longer before he walked out the room.

"Thank you," Tabitha said, after Brandon had gone.

Shon was happy to see that her friend was awake. But she was still pissed off that Tabitha allowed her affair to come to this, so she told her so.

"Don't thank me for shit, Tabitha! I'm so mad at you that I don't know what to do. How could you be so stupid? How could you allow this to happen? You had to know that man was capable of hurting you, Tabitha!"

Tabitha started crying. "I'm so sorry, Shon. I was so ugly to you the other day. I'm such a selfish bitch sometimes!" She beat her fist against the sheet in frustration. "But this happened to me because I deserved it, Shon!"

Shon leaned over the bed. "You did not deserve to get beaten and stuck with a knife, Tabitha! Don't you ever think that. That man is a coward. Your husband is a real man. And you of all people should know the difference. I hate him for doing this to you and I don't feel sorry for what's going to happen to his ass!"

"What's going to happen to him, Shon?"

Shon turned her back to Tabitha and walked to the window. She shouldn't have said that and she knew it, dammit! DJ had made her swear a long time ago never to reveal that Brandon had been a professional killer. And as far as she knew, only her and DJ knew Brandon's secret. Tabitha had never given her any indication that she was aware of the origins of her husband's wealth, and she wasn't going to be the one to enlighten her.

"The police think that he raped you and they're going to arrest him." That was a lie, but she had to think fast as she gazed out the window. Shon hadn't told the police about BC, but Tabitha didn't know that.

"I had to tell them what happened, Tabitha." Shon returned to the bed. "That animal left you there to bleed to death!"

"I tried to end it, Shon. I allowed him to spend the night on Saturday. But all night I felt terrible because I'd allowed another man to sleep with me in my husband's bed. When we woke up Sunday, we had sex for the last time. Afterwards I tried to tell him that it was over, but he just flew into a rage. He started hitting me and saying that I was cheating him out of his millions! I still don't know what that was about. I ran into the kitchen and grabbed a knife to defend myself, but he was too strong and I ended up getting stabbed. While I was lying on the floor bleeding, all that I could think about was Brandon. I knew that I could never explain what had happened with a lie. So I just laid there, Shon and waited to bleed to death. I would rather have died on that floor than face living the rest of my life without Brandon."

Shon remained silent as tears rolled down their faces.

"I wouldn't blame Brandon for leaving me, Shon. Because if he brought a woman home and slept with her in our bed... I wouldn't forgive him!"

"Well baby, you're lucky to have the man you've married because he's different than most, and you know it. You're going to have to fight to keep your man, girl. It won't be easy, but nothing worth having ever is."

"When do I get out of here, Shon?"

"I'll go find the doctor and see if we can take you home."

Chapter Twenty-Seven

Brandon

Brandon was in a daze as he drove DJ's car. He didn't have a pre-planned destination, but somehow he ended up in front of a new style brick home that was just one of many duplicates in the Mesquite suburban subdivision. He had purchased the house a year ago as a 25th Anniversary present for his parents.

As Brandon sat in the car trying to get his thoughts together, he was realizing that he couldn't inform his parents of Tabitha's whereabouts without revealing the affair. Knowledge of her betrayal would only cause resentment and force his parents to choose sides. And Brandon had no doubt in his mind whose side they would choose. Eventually time would heal everyone's wounds, even his own. He was blessed to have a wife that was well liked by everyone in his family, and it was important to him that she remained so.

"Brandon, what's wrong, son?" His dad stepped back to look at the Benz. "Who's car is this?"

"Nothing's wrong, and the car belongs to DJ."

"Why are you just sitting out here? Come in the house. Did Leuwenia call you from work and tell you to come and check on me?"

Brandon laughed as he got out of the car. "I haven't talked to Momma since Friday. I just got back from a business trip in Houston. And why do I need to check on you? The post office stressing you out or what?"

"Shit, I've been there for thirty years now! It's 'bout time one of us gave up the fight. I'm thinking about retiring in a few more years and they can have it! But for now, I have to settle for a vacation," he said, as they walked into the house.

Seeing the old furniture that his parents refused to part with brought back memories of better times. Brandon sat in his dad's La-Z-Boy in front of the big screen. His father grumbled because he had to take the sofa.

"So, what do I owe for this unexpected visit? Your face is as long as your feet. What's bothering you, son?"

"We received an offer to expand our company and purchase tax liens in Houston, and it's a very generous offer. But other than that, I'm cool."

"Well, you look kind of depressed to me. You don't look like a man that received a generous offer to make more money."

The old coot was very observant, he thought. Always had been. Brandon decided to leave before his dad weaseled a confession out of him about Tabitha's misfortune. But before he could wiggle out of the La-Z-Boy his cell phone rang.

"Excuse me, Pop, but I have to get this. Hello!"

"Hey, Brandon."

"What's up, Shon?"

"Tabitha's doctor is releasing her. I'm going to take her home and help her get settled in."

"Thank you, Shon. Is everything alright?"

"She's stiff and sore. You'll have to change a few bandages from time to time, but my girl is tough. She'll live."

"Yeah, I know, Shon. I'll be home soon." Brandon hung up the phone. "I'll have to go, Pop. I'll tell Momma that I came by and that you were fine."

"I knew that woman had you checking up on me! Just because a man wants to take a few days off from work, something has to be wrong with 'em!"

"Well Dad, you never take days off. So I can see why Mom is concerned."

"I'm alright, I tell ya. I'm only fifty years old. What could be wrong?"

"Alright, alright, but if something is bothering you, I want you to let me know. I'll stop by later this week." Brandon walked to the door. "Bye, Pops!"

"Bye, son!"

●●●●●●

After Brandon left his parents' house, he still wasn't ready to go home. He wanted to put off the confrontation between him and his wife for a little while longer, so he stopped at K-Mart. There he purchased a pair of black Dickey cotton pants and a matching long sleeved shirt, a pair of black steel toe boots and a stocking mask that would cover his head and neck. In the Outdoor Sportsman section of the store, Brandon admired the various knives in the display case for awhile, but all that the salesman could get him to purchase was a spool of fishing line. After he left K-Mart he drove to Rexall Drug store and bought a box of latex gloves, a pen light, lighter fluid, and a pair of leather driving gloves that fit tight, yet comfortable on his hands.

DJ was standing at his curbside mailbox looking over the day's mail when Brandon drove into his circular driveway. "What's up, man?" DJ said, as he walked to the car.

"Nothin' good. What's up with you?"

"Just checking the mail."

"You feel like giving me a ride to the crib or what? I mean, I can keep your car if you're trippin'!" Brandon knew that he was upset with him for defending Tabitha last night, but Brandon was old school. Marriage was a lifetime commitment no matter what.

"I'm not trippin', dog. I just don't understand your forgiving ass attitude, that's all. If Shon ever tried to pull that shit on me, she's out of here!" he said, angrily as Brandon got out of the car.

"She fucked off on me, dog. And I'm afraid to go home because I might loose it and kick her ass my damn self! But I've never hit a woman and I don't want to start now. We all fuck up DJ, I understand that, man. She betrayed me and I'm hurting like I've never hurt before. But I love my wife, dog. And I want us to at least try and work this shit out."

"You're a better man than I am. Let me run this mail in and I'll take you home so that you can face your demons."

"Very funny, smart ass!" Brandon yelled, as DJ ran to the house laughing. He walked around the car and sat in the passenger seat.

As DJ got into the car, he passed Brandon a manila envelope.

"Is this his personnel file?" Brandon asked.

"Yeah, everything that we have on him anyway."

"Good."

DJ pulled into the street. "Shon called a little while ago and said that Tabitha was giving her statement to a detective." He glanced at Brandon as he drove. "You need to get to him before the cops do, dog.

"Yeah, I know. Don't trip."

"If the law gets to him first, we can bail him out and get him then," DJ said.

"The Dallas Police Department will have to coordinate with the Fort Worth Police Department, who'll have to coordinate with the Arlington Police Department. Ft. Worth Police will need to see a warrant before they can make an arrest on a complaint that was filed in Duncanville and turned over to Dallas. The bureaucratic process will give me all the time I'll need."

"Just be careful, man," DJ said as he came to a stop in front of his friend's house. "If you can handle things with Tabitha, tell my wife to bring her ass home."

"Alright." Brandon reached into the back seat of the Benz to remove his packages.

"What's that shit?"

"Tools of the trade, homie, and it's all perishable. I'll holla at you sometime tomorrow or the next day."

"Be careful, dog." DJ warned again.

"Always."

Chapter Twenty-Eight

Brandon & Tabitha

As Brandon entered the house, his nose and stomach conspired against him. His stomach rumbled in response to the delicious smelling aroma of southern fried chicken, cabbage, and greens that were floating through the house. He dropped his bags by the stairs on the way to the kitchen. Brandon hadn't eaten anything since he and DJ were in Houston.

"Your husband said to bring your ass home, girl." Brandon kissed Shon on the cheek and grabbed a drumstick off a platter full of chicken on the stove.

"I'm goin'. I just wanted to hook up a little somethin' for you and my girl before I left." Shon peeked at the cornbread in the oven before going to the sink to load the dishwasher.

"Where's Tabitha?"

"She's asleep upstairs. I stopped off at the drug store on the way home and filled her prescriptions. That stuff must be strong because she's out like a light."

"Good, because I almost didn't come home. I've been dreading the thought ever since I left the hospital."

Shon put down her dishrag and slowly turned to look at Brandon. She heard the sound of disgust in his voice. "Don't be like that, Brandon. Don't even entertain the thought of hating your wife. She made a big mistake, I grant you that. But she's still the same woman that you would have given your life for before your trip to Houston on Saturday! She loves you no matter what you might think. You still love her too, Brandon."

Brandon was getting uncomfortable, so he changed the subject. "What did she tell the police?"

"Everything. They plan to have him in custody sometime late tomorrow, if he hasn't fled by then. BC is originally from Louisiana and he may have gone back down there."

Brandon plucked a chicken wing off the platter.

"Get out of there! If you eat it all now, there won't be any left for dinner."

Brandon took a bite as he left the kitchen. "Go home, Shon."

"I'm goin', I'm goin'!"

Brandon picked up his bags and ran up the stairs. He stored the bags in the guest bedroom and went to take a shower. When he got out of the shower he put on a bathrobe and walked into their bedroom. Tabitha was on her half of the bed sleeping on her back. He sat down on his side of the bed and used a big towel to dry his feet.

"I thought I heard the shower."

"And I thought that you were asleep." When Brandon turned to look at her, he was instantly reminded of the hate that he felt towards the man that caused his wife to be swollen and bruised.

"I was, but I've been trying to fight it. I didn't want to miss you when you got home."

"You didn't want to miss me? What did you think that I was coming home to do, pack my clothes and move out?"

She ignored his question. "We need to talk, baby."

"Don't baby me! Don't even fix your mouth to use words of endearment, Tabitha!" Brandon went to the dresser and started to get dressed. "We'll talk when you feel better. I don't want your mind clouded with medication when I say what I have to say."

"Brandon, I'm sorry! I never meant to hurt you ba..."

He glared at her with a mixture of pain and hate in his eyes. "I have some work to do in the garage. I'll come up and check on you later," he said gruffly.

He stormed out the room and went to the guestroom across the hall to retrieve the 9mm Glock that he had placed inside one of his bags. He put the spool of fishing line in his pocket and went downstairs to his office. Brandon reached deep under his desk and pressed a button. The book case against the wood grained wall slid to the side by remote control to reveal three shelves full of weapons. He had the secret compartment installed when they first bought the house. At the time, he reasoned they would have children someday, and he would need a safe place to store the vast collection of handguns that he was collecting. But those plans had been placed on hold--possibly forever.

Brandon removed the clip from the plastic 9mm Glock and set it down on the shelf. He chose the heavy .44 Smith & Wesson. As he was returning to his desk, the telephone rang, and he snatched it up before Tabitha could answer.

"Hello...! Hello!" Whoever it was didn't say anything. He gently placed the phone back into the console on his desk. Someone had been playing on their phone for the past three or four months. He remembered asking Tabitha if she had received any strange calls, she said that she hadn't. Now he had a pretty good idea why. Their caller I.D. always read "unavailable" after he receive one of these strange calls.

Brandon pressed the button and left the office. As he passed through the kitchen on his way to the garage, he noticed that Shon had gone. He pulled a chair up to his work bench and set the gun down on the table along with the fishing line. Brandon pulled 12" of line off the spool and cut it with a pair of wire cutters. After removing two four inch bolts from the tool box, he used a hand clamp to close metal fasteners around the bolt and fishing line. He set the hand clamp to the side and held up his homemade garrote line with a bolt in each hand.

"Perfect!"

Brandon set the garrote line to the side and turned his attention to the heavy gun. Using an oiled rag, he wiped down the gun and all six shells. He didn't plan on using his gun, but you could never plan for the unexpected. Yet at the same time, you had to be prepared in case the unexpected occurred. When he was satisfied that the weapon was working properly, he put everything away and went back upstairs to the guest room to take a nap. He had a long night ahead of him.

Later, as Brandon removed the watch from his wrist, he noticed that it was fifteen 'til midnight. His nap had left him refreshed as he removed the matching diamond studs from his ear lobes before pulling on the black Dickey uniform. After he finished dressing he went into the master bedroom and retrieved a black backpack and a big black duffel bag from his closet. Then he grabbed a blue sweat suit along with a pair of blue sneakers and stuffed them into his duffel bag. It wasn't until he was leaving the room before he noticed that Tabitha wasn't under the pile of bedding asleep.

When he got downstairs and entered the living room, he saw that Tabitha had come downstairs to eat. She was sitting on the sofa with an empty plate next to her on the couch.

For the first time, Brandon took notice of the damage to their living room. The frame to the glass table was there, but the glass was missing. The vase that was supposed to be on the fireplace mantle was missing. The lamp that usually sat next to the couch on the end table was gone too. As he looked around, he got angrier and angrier, and since Tabitha was the primary cause of his anger, he decided to take it out on her.

While he was looking around their living room, Tabitha had remained silent. When he finally looked at her, he could see the discomfort that she was feeling in her eyes, but he didn't care about her feelings very much at the moment.

"Have you noticed that our living room looks like shit?" Brandon didn't wait for her to reply. "How in the fuck could you bring another man into our house?"

"I'm sorry, I'm so sorry, Brandon! I know that I messed up." She started to cry. "Hell, I can't even tell you why I did what I did!" she whined.

"If you don't know why you fucked off on me, then what's keeping you from doing the shit again?" Brandon dropped his bags and advanced on her. "When we met, I promised to never hurt you this way. Hell, you were afraid to commit to me because of shit other cats had done to you. You fuckin' hypocrite! You didn't have no problem kickin' your motherfuckin' legs up! And in our fuckin' bed no less! If you were a man I'd kick your punk ass right now!" he screamed.

Tabitha fell to his feet in racking sobs, clutching his pants leg. "I'm sooo sorry! Please don't leave me! I love you so much, baby!" she sobbed. Brandon was her world and her heart almost stopped when he came downstairs with a bag in his hand. He was leaving her, and that she couldn't bear. "Please don't leave me! I love you!" she screamed.

"You don't fucking love me, you love yourself! If you loved me, then you wouldn't have disrespected our marriage."

Tabitha looked up at him. "It wasn't like that, Brandon! I fucked up! But I don't care about him!

Brandon pushed her off him and stepped away. She tried to grasp his leg as he walked away. "Don't fuckin' touch me!" he screamed. "You fucked another man, I can live to accept that. What hurts the most is that you fucked him in our bed! In our house! That bed was supposed to be special! You insisted that we get a bed that hadn't been shared by anyone but you and me. I will never forget what you've done or how you've made me feel!"

Using the arm of the couch Tabitha climbed to her feet. "Brandon, I know that you won't forget. But please try to forgive me. I messed up, baby. What do you want me to do? I'll do anything for you, baby, just don't give up on me please!" she begged, as she walked up to him. "Just don't give up on us!"

"I don't feel lovey-dovey, so don't you even think about touching me, Tabitha," he warned. "I don't even like you right now. And that's fucked up, because you're my wife and I know that I still have love for you somewhere deep inside me. I just can't find it right now," he said, sadly.

"What can I do? Just tell me how to make you feel better. I can't go on feeling like this, Brandon. I have to do something to make it right again," she cried.

"The first thing that you can do is get tested for A.I.D.S! If the hospital tested you, then I want it in writing. Then you can get our house put back together. I also want a new bed and linen. Throw all the old shit in the trash. In the meantime, I'll be sleeping in one of the guestrooms." Brandon retrieved his bags and walked toward the kitchen.

"Where are you going at this time of night?"

"Don't question me! Don't even fix your mouth to ask me a question like that. You're the one in this marriage that can't be trusted!" Brandon went into the garage and slammed the door.

He placed the garrote rope and the pistol in his backpack. Then he went to his tool box and removed an automatic lock pick. It looked like a pistol with a long skinny barrel. Once the tool is placed in front of a lock, the user can squeeze the trigger and little steel teeth will rake over the tumblers inside the lock until the right combination is found thereby releasing the lock. He placed the tool inside the backpack. Brandon removed the license plate from the Lexus and installed a paper dealer's tag in its place. *It's better to be safe than sorry*, he thought.

Chapter Twenty-Nine

Brandon & BC

DJ had provided a detailed map with the exact location of the apartment complex where BC lived. Brandon parked his car in the back of an adjacent apartment complex between a Cadillac and a mini van. He put on his full face ski mask, but he didn't roll it down. Then he left the car and went for a walk. Brandon needed to find BC's exact location and check out the lighting in the area.

BC lived in an upscale apartment complex. There were several BMW's, Cadillac's and Lexus' in the parking lot. Brandon's senses were on alert. It was important that he not be seen--or worse--remembered. He was keeping a sharp lookout for any type of security patrol. Every now and then, the headlights of a late night straggler would warn him of danger. When this happened, Brandon ducked inside a breezeway.

It had taken him about ten minutes to find the apartment building that he was looking for. There were three floors with four apartment units on each floor, and one light fixture next to each door. But there weren't any apartment unit windows in the direct view to BC's door. On his way back to the car, he noticed the green Lexus sitting in front of the building. When Brandon got back to his car, he let his seat back and went into a light sleep.

At 3:10am, Brandon was squatting down in front of BC's apartment door with the lock pick softly humming as it did its job. Once all the tumblers fell, the lock snapped back. Brandon winced at the loud pop of the lock in the hollow breezeway. He quickly stored the lock pick in his backpack and removed the big pistol from the small of his back, and slowly turned the doorknob and silently entered the apartment.

The light over the oven cast an eerie glow over the dark apartment. Brandon closed the door and stood still to allow his eyes to adjust to the dim lighting and the lay of the place. The pistol led the way as he advanced through the apartment looking for his target. He could hear a television playing in the far bedroom to his right, but he checked the first door to his left before advancing. The bedroom had been converted into an office, but BC wasn't there. He crept to the second door in the hallway, and peeped around the corner. The television illuminated the back part of the bedroom. Brandon saw that the bed was empty. Damn! Brandon's first thought was that BC had abandoned his apartment and fled. That's when he heard the toilet flush inside the room.

BC barely had his eyes open as he left the bathroom. He was trying to navigate back to his bed when Brandon blocked his path and used the big .44 magnum to viciously backhand him across the face. BC crashed into the wall and fell to the floor in a daze. Brandon put the gun in the pack over his back and advanced on him. BC spit four bloody teeth out of his mouth and tried to sit up.

Brandon went to one knee and grabbed BC by the throat with his right hand and used the other to methodically beat the man in the face, breaking his nose and ripping the eye lid off his right eye. BC made grunting sounds at every punch from Brandon's fist. Every time he tried to scream, Brandon hit him in the mouth. BC was drowning in his own blood.

With a sudden burst of strength, BC used his hips to flip Brandon over his head. Brandon crashed into a wall but he quickly recovered and jumped to his feet. BC was so punch drunk that he couldn't take advantage of the unexpected somersault that he used on his attacker. When he got to his feet, he was so disoriented that he didn't realize that Brandon was behind him. Brandon put his shoulder into BC's back and rammed him into the wall, knocking the wind out of him. He slung BC to the floor on his stomach and put his knee in the center of the man's back. Brandon dug into his pocket and removed the homemade garrote. He wrapped the fishing line around BC's neck and pulled on the steel bolts using a sawing motion. BC was thrashing around trying to reach back and stop the choking, but Brandon was using his knee as leverage riding BC, constantly sawing on his neck. The thin fishing line sliced through skin and muscle like butter. Brandon didn't stop sawing until the garrote line touched the man's spinal cord. It took a few long seconds before BC's body realized its head was gone. Throughout the violent encounter Brandon hadn't said a word. He quickly removed the line from BC's neck and ran into the bathroom and flushed the garrote line down the toilet. He flushed it once more for good measure before going to the sink to rinse BC's blood from his gloved hands.

Brandon left the apartment with the ski mask pulled down over his face as a precaution. If he ran into anyone they'd never be able to sit in court and point him out. He walked at a fast pace, in case someone heard the noise and alerted the police. Brandon reached the car and removed his boots and put on the sneakers. He didn't want to transfer any blood or carpet fibers from BC's floor to his car. Once he placed the boots in the duffel bag, he got in the car and drove back to Dallas.

Brandon pulled into a quiet but basic looking apartment complex and found a parking space. He removed the Dickey outfit and put on the sweat suit. He stuffed the outfit into the duffel bag. He removed the pistol and the lock pick from the backpack and stuffed the backpack inside the duffel bag along with his leather gloves. He grabbed the lighter fluid and a book of matches and threw the duffel bag over his shoulder. Before he left the safety of the car, he looked around and made sure no one was around. He found what he was looking for on the other side of the apartment complex. Brandon poured lighter fluid all over the duffel bag and its contents before tossing it into the big trash dumpster. Striking a match in cupped hands, he lit the whole book and was gone before the small ball of fire turned night into day.

••••••

As Brandon entered the house and walked through the kitchen he noticed Tabitha lying on the sofa watching him.

"What?" he asked.

"I didn't say anything."

He walked into the living room. "Why aren't you in bed?"

"I wanted to wait for you." She looked at his outfit. "Why do you have on different clothes?"

"I told you about those damn questions!"

Brandon never came home at 5:20 in the morning. She had been harboring fears that he might try to find another woman to get back at her, and to see him stroll in wearing a different outfit just confirmed her fears.

She got off the couch and faced him. "Let me tell you one damn thang! Yes, I fucked up. But I want us to work it out. And I want you to forgive me. But I'm not going to sit here night after night waiting up for you and wondering if you're spending time with some bitch just to spite me!"

"Tabitha, go to bed. I don't feel like talking to you right now, let alone argue."

"That's bullshit! You come home at five in the morning and you won't tell me where you've been? Fuck that, Brandon! Who is she?"

"Who's, who?" Brandon was amused that she was feeling insecure after the shit she pulled. He decided to let Tabitha wallow in her discomfort and continue to think that he'd spent the night with some woman.

"Don't you dare play dumb with me, Brandon Elliott. I'm not stupid! Where are you going? I'm not through talking to you!" she said while following him up the stairs.

Brandon ignored her badgering and walked into the guest bathroom. He locked the door before taking a shower. When he came out of the bathroom with a towel wrapped around his waist. Tabitha was standing next to the door in her bathrobe. "Will you please take your ass to bed? I don't have anything to say to you, alright?" He went into the guestroom and slammed the door. He never saw the tears roll down her face.

Chapter Thirty

Detective Reggie Leroy

Detective Leroy was wondering what the hell was going on. He was on his way to the Elliott residence to inform the couple that their employee, Bill Cole, was dead.

Leroy received a courtesy call from a female detective with the FT. Worth Police Department, named Menyon Canada. He didn't particularly cotton to female detectives, but he was forced to coordinate with her because of jurisdictional red tape, especially in light of recent developments. Detective Canada was supposed to issue an arrest warrant for Bill Cole this morning. But instead of calling to confirm an arrest for aggravated assault, she gave him a preliminary report on a murder victim.

Bill Cole had been brutally beaten and decapitated. That had been her preliminary cause of death. They wouldn't know for sure until an autopsy was performed, but one thing was for sure, Detective Canada would have her hands full with a murder investigation. And to top it off, the Feds were snooping around and asking for copies of their reports on the case. Neither he nor Canada knew what that was all about.

"Mrs. Elliott, how are you feeling today?"

"I'm sore, but better than I was, thank you. What can I do for you, Detective?"

"I need to speak with you and your husband, if I may." Leroy noticed that she hadn't invited him into the house. Man, he hoped that this nice couple didn't have anything to do with this murder.

"Well, Detective, my husband is still asleep if..."

Tabitha was interrupted by Brandon as he jogged down the stairs dressed in a woven leather Sean John sweater and blue jeans.

"I'm up baby, let him in."

"Please come in, Detective. He's awake."

Leroy met Mr. Elliott at the bottom of the stairs and offered his hand. He was wondering why an obviously successful business man would be asleep at 2:00pm on a Tuesday afternoon. Leroy knew the coroner on the scene used a rectal thermometer to estimate the time of Mr. Cole's death. Detective Canada told him that the window was between 2:45am to 4:30am as the coroner's best guess.

"Would you like a cup of coffee or a soft drink, Detective?" Mrs. Elliott asked as they walked into the living room.

"No, thank you. I just wanted to let you know that Bill Cole was found dead this morning in his apartment." Leroy watched their reactions to the news closely. He could tell by her eyes that Mrs. Elliott was genuinely surprised, but Mr. Elliott didn't bat an eye. *Interesting!*

"How did he die? What happened?"

Detective Leroy answered Mrs. Elliott's questions, but he made eye contact with Mr. Elliott as he spoke. "It seems that he was viciously beaten and then decapitated. Mr. Bill Cole obviously pissed someone off--the wrong someone, I figure." He broke eye contact to examine the bruises on Mrs. Elliott's face. *Shit!* he thought. If someone beat his wife like that, he probably would have done the same thing. He sympathized with these people, but he still had a job to do.

"Mr. Elliott, where were you this morning around 2:45 and 4:30?"

"I was up late last night talking to my wife, Detective. I'm sure that you'll agree that we have plenty to discuss in light of what my wife has been through. But for the record, I won't shed a tear because he's dead."

Leroy nodded his head in understanding before turning his attention to Mrs. Elliott. "Would you know if your husband was at home around 2:45 to 4:30, Mrs. Elliott?"

She interlocked her arm with her husbands before answering the question. "My husband was here taking care of me, Detective Leroy. Why wouldn't he be home? He's always home well before 2:30am ever since I've known him. And if you're trying to imply that my husband may have had something to do with BC's death, then I'm going to have to ask you to leave! And in the future, if there's any reason for you to discuss this topic again with either of us, please give us timely notice so that our lawyers can be present to protect our rights. They have the death penalty in this state, you know. We wouldn't want to be railroaded into the chamber!" she said sarcastically.

Leroy was amused at the fire the little lady displayed in protecting her man. "Mrs. Elliott, I don't think that your husband will ever need a paid criminal attorney, you'll do just fine. But I do have one more question and I'll leave you two good people."

He looked at Mr. Elliott. "As I said, Bill Cole was viciously beaten. And if there was a struggle and there obviously was, Bill may have scratched his attacker. If so, the perpetrator's skin may be under Bill's nails, and that'll supply us with DNA evidence. Furthermore, the perp may have bruised and swollen knuckles. May I see your hands, Mr. Elliott?"

"No, you may not! You've over stayed your welcome Detective and I want you out of my house. Now, dammit!" Mrs. Elliott screamed.

"Calm down baby, it's alright. I want the Detective to get it out of his mind that I had anything to do with this vicious crime. That way he can devote his energy to pursuing the real criminals." Brandon turned to Detective Leroy. "And if Bill does have skin under his nails, I'll submit to a DNA test at any time, Detective." Brandon held out his well-manicured hands.

Detective Leroy couldn't see any discernable bruises or busted knuckles. "Thank you, Mr. Elliott. I'll be talking to the Detective in charge of the case. I'll report the outcome of this interview with her; she may wish to speak with you as well."

"Bill was in possession of company property. When can we expect those things to be released?"

"Well, Mr. Elliott that will probably be up to Detective Canada of the Ft. Worth Police Department. As I said, she'll be in touch. You people have a nice evening. And I apologize, Mrs. Elliott, for any inconvenience."

Interesting. Very interesting, Leroy thought as he walked to his car. Was Mrs. Elliott being overly protective? Or did she and her husband have somethin' to hide? One thing was for sure, unless the perpetrator left behind fingerprints or DNA evidence, this case would be nearly impossible to solve without an outright confession from the killer. And Leroy didn't believe in fairy tales.

Chapter Thirty-One

The Meeting

Brandon called an emergency meeting after Detective Leroy left his home. He had the floor as DJ, Shon and Tabitha listened to him from the sofa.

"As I said over the phone, BC was found dead late this morning. I really don't give a damn about that as you probably know. My concerns are business related. BC had some very important paperwork in his possession that needs immediate attention. Deadlines are coming up and agreements need to be made with delinquent property owners. We also need to find an adequate replacement to fill the open position as soon as possible."

Brandon switched topics. "The last order of business that we need to discuss is an offer from a businessman in Houston who wishes to become a full partner in our firm. He's offered to pay us ten million dollars as well as provide some very profitable rental properties that will become assets of E & J Investment Group." Brandon gave the ladies some time to absorb this new development. So much had happened since their meeting in Houston, that they hadn't had a chance to discuss Fat Chris' proposal.

"The proposal that we've been offered provides that we establish an affiliate in Houston. Which means, we'll have to develop a subsidiary division down south and train the appropriate personnel to help our new partner secure delinquent tax lien notes." Brandon held up his hand to hold off their questions. "But that's not all.

This new office will also pursue procurements of real estate in all of the South Texas area. As it stands, DJ and I each own 40

181

percent of E & J Investments. Shon and Tabitha each own 10percent. If we accept this proposal the breakdown will be 25percent for me, DJ, and our new partner. The remaining 25 percent will be divided between Shon and Tabitha--that's 12.5percent a piece, ladies." Brandon smiled and started to pace.

"We're not only business partners, we're family. We've been fortunate enough to have made some good money in the last two and a half years and it helps that we haven't had much overhead. We're not hurting for money in any way. If we accept the offer from Houston, me and DJ stand to make four million a piece, Shon and Tabitha will take one million a piece. But it's going to take capital to start a new division and it's going to take capital to develop a real estate division." Brandon faced the trio and made eye contact with each of them.

"I want to re-invest the ten million, guys. There's over five million people in the Dallas-Ft. Worth Metroplex area. We're fortunate enough to live in one of the fastest growing cities in the country. I want to take advantage of that by developing a solid real estate company here in the Metroplex.

Listen to what I said now. I don't propose that we start a Northern Division of E & J Investments, because if we do that and become successful at it, we'll have to share our profits with our new partner." Brandon shook his head. "I propose that we start a new company entirely."

"Shon?" Brandon took a seat on the love seat as Shon took the floor, looking very much the businesswoman in her Chanel business suit.

"I won't miss BC. I know that sounds cruel, but I slipped and busted my ass in Tabitha's blood. Nuff said."

Shon let her eyes roam around the room for a second and her gaze settled on Brandon. She knew that he had killed BC, but it hadn't made her feel any different about him. On the contrary, she kinda felt protected. She knew that this wasn't a normal feeling if you considered she had a husband to do that. But Brandon made her feel secure in a big brotherly kind of way that she liked.

Shon self-consciously ran her hands through her shoulder length hair. "We need to have someone pick up the Lexus. I'll handle that as well as deal with regaining the paperwork that we need from his apartment. As far as the business opportunity in Houston, I'll leave that up to you guys. You've made some very profitable decisions for this company in the past and I see no reason why we should deviate from that now. But for the record, I'm in favor of accepting the proposal. Tabitha?" Shon said, as she gave up the floor.

Tabitha had discarded her robe for a J-Lo designer pink sweat suit for the meeting. She dreaded facing her friends and business partners after her embarrassing affair. Not to mention the bruises to her face that she couldn't hide with a pound of make-up. But this was her job, and these people were her family.

"First of all, guys, I want to thank all of you for your concern and attention." She was finding it hard to maintain eye contact with anyone. "I've been an ass. And the bottom line is, I fucked up! I'm not going to make excuses for what I allowed to happen. I embarrassed my husband and myself."

DJ gave her his handkerchief for the tears on her face.

"Thank you, DJ." She cleared her throat before resuming. Some how she found the courage to look at her husband. "I'm aware that I've lost your trust. But please give me a chance. I promise to rebuild it and cherish it forever. BC is dead, and I just want to forget that entire negative situation. I talked with Shon earlier and we both agreed that it would be best if she handled all business concerning that man and the obtainment of our property."

"As far as the Houston proposal goes, I'm sure that there's still a lot that needs to be discussed and considered concerning the start up of a subsidiary before a final decision is made one way or the other. Basically, as far as I can see, we need to research the Houston market thoroughly for profitable real estate and tax lien opportunities. I'm aware that it's going to be hard to find a negative reason to turn down the ten million dollars. And I'm also aware that such a large infusion of capital will allow us to pursue a larger property base at auctions or to start a brand new company."

As usual, Brandon was impressed with her mind for business. She could always look deep into a business opportunity and foresee the positive as well as the negative to make a clear and calculated assessment of the deal. He just wished that she was as astute in her personal life. Forever the businesswoman, he listened as she continued.

"On its face, it looks like a wonderful opportunity for us. But I suggest that this new partner be dedicated to the procurement of quality properties to ensure company growth. And is he willing to put E & J Investment Group as top priority over any other business interests that he may have? If the answer is yes, then I'm willing to go along with whatever you guys decide. DJ?"

DJ stood up and brushed the wrinkles from his khaki slacks as he took the floor. "I also agree that Shon should handle the BC situation. This has been a sad uncomfortable time for everyone."

DJ focused on Tabitha. "Tabitha not only hurt Tank, but she hurt us as well. But Tabitha is a part of our family, and in time we'll all get past this."

Turning to Brandon he said, "I'll find a replacement as soon as possible to start working towards obtaining settlements for our existing tax liens, that shouldn't be a problem.

As far as our partnership offer is concerned, we still have a lot to consider towards accepting the deal. This will be a great opportunity for not only company growth but personal growth as well. And as soon as Tabitha is feeling better, I think she would be the best person to assess all the intangibles of the deal that she touched on earlier. Tank?"

"If there isn't any more business, I move to adjourn until future business related issues call for reconvening.'"

"I second."

"I third."

"I fourth."

"Ladies, please excuse us, but I need to have a word with DJ." Brandon made a head gesture for DJ to follow him. "Let's go bust some balls, dog."

Brandon led DJ past the foyer and through the dining room to a large game room. A huge brown felt topped pool table dominated the middle of the room. Ms. Pac-Man, Galactic, and an old school pen ball machine lined the wall. But no game room is complete with out a big screen television with the PlayStation hook-up. Brandon had placed the 72-inch plasma screen in the back of the room and surrounded it with three calfskin leather La-Z-Boy recliners. The television was rarely used until football season. He and DJ liked to watch the Dallas Cowboys on Sunday.

"You rack em'," DJ said, as he chose his favorite stick from the set against the wall. "So how did everything go last night?"

"Break em'," Brandon said as he backed away from the table and turned to select a stick. "Everything was straight. But just in case that cop comes back around, I need you to take my pistol and door pick with you when you leave. Stash it at your mother's house or something." Brandon lined up the cue ball to take his shot.

"Why didn't you trash the pistol last night after you used it? You know better than to keep a dirty gun. That alone will get your ass a life sentence!" DJ was looking at him like he was crazy.

"Chill out, fool! I didn't use the gun. Well, not in the way you're thinking." Brandon knocked down three shots before missing to relinquish the table to DJ.

"Boy, you've been practicing!" DJ lined up for a shot. "So if you didn't use it, why you wanna get rid of it?"

"Because I smacked him with it and knocked out his teeth. There might be blood or sweat on it that I can't see or wipe away. You'd be surprised at the shit those police forensic labs come up with. I have a motive to want him dead, so I'll be their number one suspect. But hopefully they won't find anything." Brandon tried a bank shot.

"How did you do it then?"

"Damn!" Brandon missed his shot. "You don't disturb Tiger when he's making a game winning putt on the 18th hole, do you? He asked sarcastically as he gave up the table to DJ.

"That's why I don't play or watch golf." DJ lined up his shot. "So, how did you do it?" DJ asked again.

"I choked him with a piece of fishing line until his fuckin' head came off!" Brandon threw down his stick and went to sit in the La-Z-Boy.

DJ hung up their sticks before he joined his friend.

"You know what, DJ? If your game is tight enough to talk my woman into giving you some pussy, I can accept that. I can accept it because any woman can be had if you catch her at the right time. She might be having problems with her man. She might be single. She might be drunk. She might be horny. Hell, she might just like your damn car! I've been offered so much ass when I'm in my Corvette, that it ain't even funny. But to know me personally and still come into my house and fuck my wife, in my bed! And before you leave, you beat the shit out of my wife and leave her for dead! That's totally fuckin' disrespectful to me, DJ! That's why I had to kill his ass that way. I don't give a fuck what my wife did. It's my job to protect her. And if her ass needs kickin', I'll do the kickin', dog!"

DJ could feel his pain. He understood the level of embarrassment that he felt. Tank needed a friend, someone who wouldn't laugh at his pain or ridicule and judge him. So he chose to remain silent and let Tank get it off his chest.

"When I came home from college and educated myself on the art of committing the perfect murder, I read and watched documentaries about people that are either on death row, or serving life sentences. A lot of people get caught because they don't give their actions any thought." Brandon pulled back the handle of the La-Z-Boy and propped up his feet. "I promised myself that I would never kill for emotional reasons. All the hits were about business, never personal. But when I made that promise I failed to take into account that someone could actually offend my sense of honor and pride." He slapped the armrest in frustration. "Not to the point where I'd feel the need to take another life." Brandon shook his head back and forth. "I don't know, DJ. Maybe I'm getting soft. I hear money does that to you."

"Bullshit! I would have knocked his ass off too!" DJ sat in contemplation for a few seconds. "Or, I would have paid you to do it."

They both burst out in a fit of laughter.

●●●●●●

While their men horsed around in the game room, the ladies made a retreat to the master bedroom. Tabitha sat on the bed and watched Shon as she tried on different pairs of shoes. Shon had just finished changing the bandage on Tabitha's arm.

"Girl, I don't know what I would've done if you hadn't come over." Tabitha propped a pillow behind her back. "I wanted to ask Brandon to change it, but I was afraid that he was going to curse my ass out."

Shon was busy trying on a pair of green Dolce & Gabana pumps. "Girl please! You know that man loves your ass! He's supposed to be pissed off. Give it a little time and he'll start getting horny. Give him some, and you're on your way to getting over this mess."

"How do you know it'll work?" Tabitha asked hopefully.

"Trust me, I just know. There's power in between those legs girl! Don't you know anything?"

Shon tried on another pair of shoes out of Tabitha's vast collection. "Girl, where did you get these? Whenever I'm in your closet I feel like a kid in a candy store."

Tabitha ignored her and said, "I have to get tested before he'll even come near me. I even have to get rid of this bed." Tabitha pouted. "I love this bed."

188

"That's the problem, heffa. You loved too much in that damn bed! It's full of BC juice!"

"Fuck you bitch!"

Shon laughed, "Whatever, ho'! You opened the door for that one."

"Shon, I'm worried about something."

Shon could easily discern when her friend was serious, so she gave Tabitha her undivided attention. "What are you worried about?"

"That damn detective! He was asking some very serious questions that scared the hell out of me."

"Now I'm worried. What kind of questions?"

"He said that BC was killed around 2:30 to 4:00 in the morning or something like that. Then he asked Brandon where he was in between that time frame." Tabitha was staring off into space as she spoke. She was doing everything that she could to justify Brandon's absence from their house last night. "Brandon said that he was here talking to me all night."

"I still don't see your problem."

"Shon, he didn't come home until 5:05 this morning! And when he came in, he had on a totally different outfit all the way down to the shoes on his feet! Me and my paranoid ass, I accused him of being with another woman." Tabitha shook her head negatively. "Brandon has never stepped out on me. I don't know how I know, maybe it's female intuition. I keep telling myself that all of this is just a bad ass dream. But I know that I'm not that lucky, Shon."

"What else did the police say?"

"Detective."

"Whatever!" Shon snapped.

"He said that BC had been decapitated, so I got to thinking."

"Uh oh, we're in trouble now!"

"Will you stop joking? This shit is serious!" Tabitha snapped.

"I'm sorry. You're right."

Tabitha gazed at her for a second longer before she continued. "Like I said, I got to thinking. If BC's head was cut off, maybe Brandon was drenched in blood and had to change before he came home." She looked at Shon in hopes that she could add or subtract an opinion to her conjecture. But Shon just sat in her chair biting her bottom lip with a fixated stare and at the carpet. "Say something please! I'm a nervous wreck here!" Tabitha climbed off the bed and paced around the room.

Shon knew that Brandon killed BC as soon as her husband got off the phone with him. When DJ told her about it, they shared an awkward moment of silence. Once again, she found herself torn between her allegiance to her husband and her best friend. Tabitha had made her promise not to reveal her affair to DJ. And DJ had sworn her to secrecy about Brandon's other life as an assassin. She was so sick of all these damn secrets.

"Shit!" Shon rubbed her temple worriedly. "Tabitha, I think that we need to talk about your hus..." She was interrupted by DJ as he abruptly entered the room. *Thank goodness!* she thought.

"Shon, let's go baby. We have to stop by my momma's house." DJ approached Tabitha and gave her a hug and kiss. "How do you feel, babygirl?"

"I'm better, DJ, thanks for asking. And thank you for supporting me today. I never should have gotten myself into this mess. I just don't want to loose my husband, DJ." Tabitha decided to pick his brain. "Is he going to leave me? Has he told you his plans?"

DJ smiled, "Nice try, babygirl. You know it's not cool to try and play us against one another. That shit ends friendships," he said seriously. "We all make mistakes Tabitha, Brandon is aware of that. The important thing is to learn from your mistakes and grow a little wiser because of it. That way, an argument can be made that the hardship was worth the pain. You have family in us, and we're your support system. Don't forget that, babygirl."

"That's sweet, DJ. Thank you, baby." She kissed his cheek and gave him a hug.

"Bitch, get your hands off my husband!"

"Screw you, hussy!" They all laughed as they left the room.

Chapter Thirty-Two

Almost Back To Normal

After the death of BC, Brandon and DJ decided to delay making a decision one way or the other on their expansion offer. Brandon wanted to be sure the authorities didn't have enough evidence to arrest him for the murder. It had taken DJ over three and a half weeks of greasing the right hands with cold hard cash before Brandon was able to rest comfortably at night. The cops didn't have a shred of physical evidence against him.

Before Brandon attacked BC that night, he made sure not to allow any of his flesh to be exposed. A single scratch would have been the equivalent of falling down to his knees in front of Detective Reggie Leroy and confessing every detail of the crime. DNA evidence was sometimes called genetic fingerprinting. That scratch would justify the Texas court system handing down a sentence of death by lethal injection. Throughout Texas highways, citizens of the state and tourists alike are constantly warned by signs that read "DON'T MESS WITH TEXAS!" And those signs mean what they say. Texas leads the nation in putting more people to death yearly than any other state in the union.

Brandon felt confident when he offered to submit to a DNA test for Detective Leroy. The night before, he'd examined every inch of his body in search of scratched skin.

Detective Menyon Canada refused all of Shon's requests to release the property of E & J Investments until Brandon made himself available by coming to Ft. Worth Police Department Headquarters and submitting to an interview. But Detective Canada didn't ask him too much more than Detective Leroy did. Still, it had taken an additional month of constant badgering before

Shon was able to gain a victory with the release of the company's property.

By August, Tabitha had replaced all the damaged furniture in their living room. She also purchased the new bed that her husband requested for their bedroom.

Brandon had come home one evening to find Tabitha's negative results from her HIV test lying on his bed in the guestroom. She'd done all that he'd asked of her. She occupied her time by researching the Houston market on her PC. So far, all of her reports were favorable.

Brandon also noticed that her bruises had faded. She was looking as beautiful as ever. He was finding it harder and harder to ignore her. Every day she would prance around the house in see-through teddy's or sexy nightgowns. But he was determined not to allow his flesh to break his will.

Brandon and DJ both agreed that it would be best to hire a woman, so DJ took his task to heart and found a gorgeous young woman, named Toni Alexis, to replace BC. Shon and Tabitha were acting catty towards the young lady, but Brandon was happy to have her. Toni was light brown with shoulder length hair and voluptuous curves, and being born and raised in Dallas was a plus. She had a business degree from Prairie View A&M, which enabled her to quickly grasp the duties of her job. Toni couldn't believe her good fortune the day Brandon handed her the keys to a green Lexus.

Two months after BC's death, everything was getting back to normal. Brandon and DJ decided that it was time to sit down with Fat Chris and work out a few details. But instead of them traveling to Houston, Fat Chris insisted on coming to Dallas. He chartered a plane and flew onto a small private airstrip in Oak Cliff. Brandon and DJ went to pick him up and take him to dinner.

Chapter Thirty-Three

Brandon, DJ & Fat Chris

Fat Chris was sporting an Armani suit and carrying a suitcase as he exited the small airport and walked towards DJ's Mercedes. He was cursing someone out over the cell when he slid into the backseat.

"Check this out B. You better have all my fuckin' money o all my product!" Fat Chris waived at DJ to go ahead and drive "What money? Mutherfucka, those suit cases that you sent wa short $225,000! This is the third or fourth time that you've shor changed me, but one thing is for sure, it'll be the last. I want m money within the next two hours or you're a dead man, amigo And after you bring me my money our business together will be finished. What? I know that you can't get to Houston in two hour unless you fly." He held the phone away from his ear. "Where wil we be in the next two hours?"

"Chili's Restaurant on Camp Wisdom Road in Oak Cliff. Brandon said.

Fat Chris repeated the information into the phone. "Yeah, I'n in Dallas. Now get your dumb ass over here with my money!"

DJ pulled into the restaurant parking lot as Fat Chris hung up the phone.

"I'm sorry guys, I didn't wish for you to hear that conversa tion. But I'm sick and tired of dealing with this guy."

"Don't trip. Sometimes you have to chew a little ass, Fa Chris. That's the cost of being the boss," DJ said, as he got out th car. "Hand me that suit case and I'll put it in the trunk."

"Man, I'm starving!" Brandon said, as they walked into the restaurant.

DJ laughed. "You're always starving, let you tell it."

The Tex-Mex restaurant was three-quarters full. The scent of grilled beef and chicken permeated the air, only to enhance everyone's appetite as they entered the eatery. There were cowboy hats and sombreros hanging on the wall and cactus plants at every table. Brandon requested a booth in the non-smoking section to the left of the entrance. He hated cigarette smoke and he wanted to enjoy his meal in peace.

The three men observed proper business etiquette and refrained from discussing the expansion throughout their meal. Fat Chris sat in the middle of the booth with his back to the front window of the restaurant as DJ and Brandon sandwiched him in. When the waiter removed their empty plates they all ordered a glass of Hennessy and got down, to business.

"Fat Chris, I need you to understand something before we agree to accept your offer," Brandon said. "As a partner of E & J Investment Group, by no means are you allowed to engage in any dope transactions. As a matter of fact, I insist that we all sign a business contract that binds us as partners. There will also be a morality clause inside this contract that forbids any illegal activity."

Fat Chris smiled. "I have no objections to your demands, my friend. I'm more than ready to get out of this business. People aren't as solid as they used to be."

The waiter approached their table with a tray of drinks. After he walked away, Fat Chris continued.

195

"I don't want you to worry that I'm dealing dope down in Houston. I've given all that up. Byron is the only loose end that I have. He thinks that Fat Chris is a fool. But I have a little surprise for him." He looked at DJ. "But I need your help to spring my little surprise."

"What's up? If I can help, you know I will," DJ said.

Fat Chris sipped his drink. "As I said, Byron is a loose end, and as you know, I hate loose ends. They give out so much time nowadays that people are forced to spend decades behind bars. But the state and federal government will also reduce those decades for cooperation and testimony. It's a no-win situation for people in the business. Shit, a person's word alone can get you life imprisonment! Who wants to do decades in prison, DJ? Most people would rather loose street credibility nowadays, as opposed to spending a third of their life in a jail cell."

DJ nodded his head in understanding and said, "Brandon here helped convince me of just that. It's very rare that a successful player in the game avoids prison or death long enough to see retirement."

"We've been lucky, my friend. But Byron has tried to fuck me too many times to allow him to live. If he gets cornered he'll talk and I know it. I remember you telling me about a professional a few years ago that always came through. I also recall that he was expensive."

DJ was getting uncomfortable with the direction this conversation was taking. He drained his glass of Hennessy before risking a peek at Tank as Fat Chris continued.

"I need such a professional now, my friend. I don't care about cost. Do this for me and I'll be able to sign any contract that you put in front of me, in good faith. That suitcase in your car has eleven million dollars in it. I promised you gentlemen ten million in cash to become your partner. The extra million is what I'm willing to pay to be able to walk away from this business worry free. However, if you accept the briefcase, you're not only accepting me as a partner, you're also accepting responsibility for eliminating my problem."

When DJ and Brandon made eye contact, Brandon gave an almost imperceptible nod that Fat Chris didn't see.

"We accept responsibility, my friend, and welcome you into our family at E & J Investment Group," DJ said, offering Fat Chris his hand.

Brandon also shook his hand and welcomed him into the fold of what he and DJ started.

DJ called the waiter over and ordered a bottle of champagne to celebrate. DJ was bragging to Fat Chris about their city's night life. But Brandon's mind was on the hit that he secretly accepted. A hit didn't usually cost anywhere near a million dollars! But according to the law, if a person was caught trying to solicit a murder for hire, they'd be looking at some hard time. If the murder was successful and you were later fingered as the moneyman, you could expect to receive a sentence somewhere around 25 to life, and that was just at state level. If the federal government decided to prosecute, they wouldn't bat an eye at handing down a sentence of life without parole. The sentence would be enhanced to death by lethal injection for a drug lord who ordered the death of a man. Fat Chris was a smart man. He knew DJ would keep his mouth shut if he was caught trying to solicit a murder for hire. In essence, Fat Chris was paying DJ such an enormous fee so that he could wash his hands of all responsibility by placing it into DJ's hands and inadvertently, Brandon's as well.

Brandon would later tell the police that he was so consumed with his personal thoughts, that he just naturally assumed the shadow suddenly cast over the table was made by their waiter returning with DJ's order of champagne. Suddenly at point blank range, three very loud gunshots were fired in quick succession directly over his head, causing him instinctively to dive for cover.

Brandon and DJ were finally allowed to leave Police Headquarters at three in the morning. The police asked back-to-back questions in an effort to piece together the events that led to the assassination of their new business partner.

DJ and Brandon didn't get off the floor of the restaurant until they were sure the shooting was over. The restaurant was in a state of pandemonium as families and couples fled after getting a look at the bloody corpse of Fat Chris.

DJ recognized Byron when he approached the table. He was wearing a baseball cap pulled down low over his face with a pair of shades. But he didn't see the pistol in his hand until he aimed it at Fat Chris' head. DJ could have very easily given this information to the police and walked away with a cool million. But he had too much street in him to ever become Joe Blow the good citizen. He didn't tell Brandon about the shooter until he pulled up to his friend's house.

"Are you sure?" Brandon asked, as he looked at DJ in disbelief.

"It was him alright. Think about it, dog. Who else knew where he was besides us and Byron? I use to see the cat in traffic from time to time. He had a little paper, but nothing like he made from fuckin' with Fat Chris."

"Why would he do it himself?"

"Hell if I know. I guess Fat Chris really pissed him off. But you heard their conversation while we were in the car. Fat Chris threatened to kill him. You never tell a man what you're going to do to him." DJ slammed his hand against the steering wheel. "Fat Chris underestimated his opponent and it cost him his life."

Brandon nodded his head. "That it did, dog. That it did."

"We have eleven million dollars in the trunk. What do you suggest that we do with it?"

"If we keep it, we'll have to wash it."

"What do you mean if we keep it? What else would we do with it?" DJ asked sarcastically.

"Maybe he told someone about our deal. If he did, they may knock on our door someday and ask for Fat Chris' money."

"Shiiit! What money?"

They both laughed.

"We're going to have to deposit it into our Cayman account just like we did when we started the company. But we'll each keep a million in cash and use it for bills and spending money."

DJ liked that idea. "That means we'll have to go on another cruise to deliver it."

"Yeah, but in the meantime, place it in that big ass safe that's stashed in your closet. We have to make a decision about Byron's ass before we do anything else." Brandon had a grave look on his face.

"We did get paid for it, didn't we? What do you need?" DJ asked.

"You can start off by getting me some information on the cat." Brandon looked down at his favorite Sean John suit. "That clown ruined my suit, fool!"

"Shit, mines too, dog. I got brain and hair in my mouth after he fired that first shot. Scared the shit out of me!"

"I'll holla," Brandon said, as he got out the car.

"One!"

Chapter Thirty-Four

Tank & Tabitha

After Brandon washed traces of Fat Chris out of his hair, he went into the guestroom and climbed into the queen-sized bed and was asleep in a matter of seconds.

Tabitha heard Brandon go into the bathroom and close the door. It had been over two months since they'd made love, and making love to him was all she thought about lately. She had tried enticing him to come to her, but she seemed invisible to him. Around other people they shared an unspoken agreement to act as though everything was okay between them. But as soon as they were alone he would shut her out and go into his shell. It pissed her off to be ignored by her man. But she bit her tongue and endured his rejecting her because she'd brought it upon herself. Tabitha came to a decision. It was time for them to get over this. Either he still wanted her or he didn't. She knew she couldn't go on like this for much longer.

●●●●●●

Brandon moaned in his sleep. He was dreaming, but he'd never had a dream that felt so damn good. As he slept on his back, he reached down to squeeze his dick. His hand was quickly engulfed in hair. He woke up with a start and threw back the covers.

"Tabitha what are you doing? Ooh shit!" he moaned, giving into the good feeling that she was giving.

Tabitha removed him from her soft and warm mouth to stroke his balls with her tongue.

"Oooh, Tabitha, I missed this. Come up here girl. Shit that feels good!"

Tabitha ignored him as she put his dick back into her mouth and bobbed up and down.

He held her head and ground his hips in a circular motion. Brandon loved it when she gave him head, but he wanted to be inside her body. "Stop! Come up here...! Oh...! Now!"

She popped him out of her mouth long enough to say, "No," before going back to torturing him with pleasure. Tabitha sucked and licked on him for ten minutes longer. When she came up for air, she quickly crawled up his body and straddled his groin while reaching down to guide him into her pussy. She had never been so hot in her life! All she could think about was getting him into her before he remembered that he was angry. Tabitha sat on top of him looking into his eyes while squeezing his member with her inner muscles. Slowly she started grinding against his pelvis faster and faster.

Brandon held Tabitha's ass in his hands and helped her find a familiar rhythm.

"Ooooh, Brando...! Oh shi...! Fuck me baby...! I missed you sooo much! Fuck me, yeahhh!" she whispered. Tabitha leaned forward and put a swollen nipple in his mouth. "Yes...! Bite it. Ooooh!" she moaned, as she stuck her tongue in his ear.

Brandon rolled her over onto her back and threw her legs on his shoulders. He long stroked her like a man just paroled. "Yeah, I missed this pussy, girl!" He was breathing hard as he slammed into her. The smell of their lovemaking permeated the air.

"Fuck meee! Ooooh, yes! Don't stop...! Don't stop...! I'm gonna' cum! Cum with me!" she panted breathlessly. Tabitha grabbed his ass and rode with him. "I'm cummmin', Brandon!"

"Me too...! Oooh...! Oh shiiit!"

"Ooh, Yees...! It's so damn good!" she screamed as she clung to him in pure ecstasy.

When they caught their breaths, they held each other in a tight embrace, sharing gentle kisses and words of endearment.

"I love you, Brandon," she said, softly as she lay on top of her man and nibbled his ear.

"I love you too, Tabitha."

"Can we start over, baby? Please come back to me. I want another chance."

"You could have ruined our future together, Tabitha."

"I know," she whispered.

"Before we were married I knew that there was always a possibility that one or both of us would have an affair. I don't know, Tabitha. Maybe I should have talked to you about it. But I assumed that you were aware of where home is. In other words, I can fuck a thousand different women, but no woman comes before you, girl! And I'll never allow another woman to take me away from you. He rubbed his hand back and forth across her ass.

"Yes I'm hurt and I feel betrayed. I've given you everything that you could ever want out of life. I finally just stopped asking myself why? Knowing the answer wouldn't change the circumstances. I don't have many hang-ups and I'm confident of who I am. I'm also aware that sometimes people do some dumb shit!"

Tabitha winced, but she kept her mouth shut and let him finish.

"I was pissed off more because you let that cat put his shit in you without protection. That was some stupid ass shit, Tabitha. You not only put your ass at risk, but mines as well. You're an educated woman and I expected better from you. I understand that a woman is weaker than a man, so I can see how you could be persuaded to engage in an affair. But don't ever do what you did the way that you did it ever again!"

Tabitha raised up and straddled him before saying angrily, "You sound like you're telling me that it's okay to fuck around!"

"I didn't say that it was okay! I just know that I can never be a gullible motherfucker and assume that my dick is the only dick that you're fucking. Just respect me enough to make the bastard wear a rubber."

"There won't ever be a next time. I told you that I was sorry, Brandon!"

"In a perfect world I might be able to believe that, Tabitha. But this isn't a perfect world. Your actions don't show me that I can trust you at all right now. And yeah, sure you're sorry at the moment. When truthfully, you're more sorry you got caught."

Tabitha climbed out of the bed. "Fuck you, Brandon! You're talking to me like I'm a fuckin' slut! I don't just fuck every dick that I see or go to bed with every man that comes my way!"

"If you're not a slut you could have fooled me, because that's how you were acting a couple of months ago. And fuck you too!"

I don't have to take this shit!"

"No, you don't! You can get the fuck out if that's what you want to do, because I don't need the shit you've been putting me through. If I wanted a ho, I would've rented one. I damn sure didn't intend to make a ho into a housewife!"

Tabitha was in tears, but she was determined to have the last word. "I fucked up and I apologized for that more than once. And if you want a divorce you'll have to fight me tooth and nail to get it because I'm not leaving you and I refuse to let you give up on this marriage! And for your information, my momma didn't raise no whores!" Tabitha ran out the room before Brandon had a chance to make things worse that they were.

Chapter Thirty-Five

Byron

On a beautiful Saturday afternoon, everyone was playing their car stereo systems in freshly washed rides, all vying for attention. The slow moving traffic was bumper to bumper as teenagers and young adults cruised back and forth past Glendale Park.

Inside the popular weekend spot, Byron Williams was throwing a big barbecue for his family and friends. He had invited over a hundred people to come and enjoy themselves on his food and booze. Originally when Byron planned the barbecue a few weeks ago, he didn't have any particular reason for doing it other than to show some love and have a good time. But since then, a lot had changed with the death of his supplier, Fat Chris. Byron had made millions with Fat Chris. And now it was time for him to get out of the game and enjoy his money.

He was sitting on the hood of his Mercedes under a big shade tree watching everyone enjoying themselves at his expense. All dope dealers with money suffer some level of paranoia. Ever since he'd gathered all the cash he'd been wise enough to save over the last three years, he hadn't felt the same. He'd known that he had a significant amount of money put away. But at the end of his self-audit, Byron was amazed to realize that his self worth was over five million dollars.

The game wasn't nice. Byron had robbed, stolen, and cheated every chance he could to reach the level of financial security that he had achieved. He knew he'd hurt a lot of people during his climb, and he was aware that his past actions came with consequences. He believed what went around came back around. But he never dwelled on it, and his beliefs sure didn't stop him from blowing Fat Chris' brains out. The way Byron figured it, Fat Chris would have killed him eventually anyway. Byron just beat him to the draw, so to speak.

Fat Chris had threatened him several times. Usually, it was after Fat Chris had discovered that the suitcases Byron had sent to Houston didn't contain the entire agreed upon amount. It takes a very long time to count a half a mil' to a million in small bills, and Fat Chris rarely counted the money at all. Many times, Byron would purposely hold back $100,000 or more, and most of the time, Fat Chris never noticed the short.

It really wasn't a big deal when Fat Chris threatened him last weekend. But he mistakenly showed his hand when he said that their business dealings were over. Byron knew that Fat Chris intended to make good on his threats. By killing Fat Chris first, Byron effectively eliminated two other threats, because with Fat Chris no longer being able to send the large shipments of cocaine to him in Dallas, he now had a legitimate excuse to quit the game. And if he wasn't in the game, he wouldn't be a target of law enforcement or jackers.

Byron's distributors grumbled when he informed them that he was out. But he knew they secretly wished that they too could afford to walk away from hustling.

"Boy, quit daydreaming and take this plate."

Byron was brought back to the present by the soft voice of his latest conquest. He hurriedly jumped off the car to grab one of the two heaping plates of steaming barbecue before she dropped them. "Good lookin', Boo. I'm starvin!" Byron sat down on the car to eat his food.

"You're welcome," she said, as she waited for an invitation to join him. He had been acting real moody lately. Here he was throwing a big ass barbecue, yet he'd separated himself from everyone, to sit under a damn tree.

"What's wrong, Boo? Sit down and eat. I told you about that proper shit!" he said.

"What's wrong with you, Byron?" she asked in between bites of her pork ribs.

"Nothin'. Why you ask that?" Byron set his plate to the side so that he could work on a beef brisket sandwich.

"You've been acting funny lately, like there's something on your mind. I'm here for you if you need someone to talk to," she said sweetly.

Monica was a beautiful brown skinned woman with shoulder length hair and a body that men have been known to have gunfights over. Byron had met her at the Cliff Club about three months ago. She was sexy as hell that night. But it was the sway of her ass that got his attention. Monica had a walk out of this world. He stepped to her and they'd been kickin' it ever since.

Byron would look at her sometimes and see a hint of regalness. Today she wore a simple white Polo shirt with matching shorts. There was nothin' hoochie about Monica and that's what he liked most about her. She was definitely high maintenance. But hell, so was he.

"I'm cool! Preciate it though."

"Byron, I can tell something is bothering you. Talk to me," she pleaded.

"Monica, I'll never let my left hand know what my right hand is doin' and you know that. So don't go trying to stick your nose in my business, hear?"

"I'm not trying to get in your business! I'm trying to be your friend, as well as your woman." She sat down her plate. "And if you have a problem with that, then let me know, because I don't like the way you've been acting and I'm letting you know." She rolled her eyes.

Byron jumped off the car to stand in between her legs. "I have shit on my mind, Boo. But it doesn't concern you and it's nothin' that you can help me with. I have to work out something by myself." He took a hold of her hands. "I'm from the streets, Monica and there's certain rules that I have to live by. We're leaving for the Bahamas tonight baby, and after we leave I'll feel better, okay?" He needed to get her off his back.

Monica decided to leave it alone for now. She was tired of feeling neglected. Whatever he had on his mind was getting on her damn nerves. But he was good to her in other ways that she liked. Byron had money and he wasn't stingy with it. Plus, the sex was simply delicious.

She checked him out from head to toe. He had on a white tank top with brown Rocawear shorts and matching Nike leather sandals. A wave cap covered the fresh cornrows she'd laced up last night. But he was a little small for her taste at 5'8 and 195 lbs. Byron wasn't the most attractive man she'd ever had. Monica liked him though and he'd certainly do for now.

"If you promise me that you won't be a party pooper in the Bahamas," she pouted. "Then, I guess I can look over the way you've been acting."

Byron smiled displaying his diamond encrusted grill. "Yeah baby, I promise. Now let me taste some of that barbecue sauce."

Monica moaned as he sucked her tongue. When they broke the kiss, there was a smoky look in her brown eyes. "You better not start something that you can't finish!" she warned.

Byron looked around. The main crowd was about 50 yards away. As far as he could tell, no one was paying them any attention. They were too busy eating, drinking and jamming to the Biggie Smalls "Life After Death" CD which was bumping out of someone's trunk. He turned to Monica and asked, "What you tryin to do?"

"Whatever you're trying to do!" She was up for a challenge. Byron helped her off the car and led her to the passenger seat of his Benz. "Get in and get naked!" he said excitedly.

They got off on having sex in the car. There was a thrill in knowing that there was a possibility they might get caught doing the nasty. Monica had slipped out of her shorts and popped the seat back to a reclining position by the time Byron slid into the driver's seat.

He quickly started the car to get the air conditioner running.

"Damn baby, you ain't playing!" he said, as he pulled down his shorts and boxers in one stroke.

Monica showed him she wasn't playing by wrapping her hand around his dick and pulling him across the console and in between her legs. "Hurry up, B! I'm so wet baby. Put it in!" She moaned and wrapped her legs around his waist as he slid into her. "Yess...! You fit me soo right, baby," she whispered.

"Damn, Monica! It's warm and tight, just like I like it. Shit!"

"It's all yours big daddy! Fuck meee!" she moaned, as she rotated her hips. "Oooohh yes! You do it sooo good. Fuck me baby, don't stop please, don't stop!" Monica squeezed his rotating ass and tried to pull more of him into her. "Yeees, don't stop! This some good dick, boy!"

"Yeah, and I'ma' tear this pussy up!" he yelled, as he stroked in and out of her.

"Fuck me! Fuck me! Shove that big dick in me baby! Yeah, like that!" she moaned. "Oh I love it when you do it like that! Squeeze my titties baby. Ohhh yeah! I'm close Byron! Cum in me baby! Yes...Yes...Yes!"

Byron pumped harder and faster as he neared climax. "I'm gonna cum baby! I'm fixin' to cum!"

"Me too! Ohh shit!" she screamed.

"I'm cummiinnggg! Ugghh!" Byron tensed as he released his seed into her warm body.

"Damn, that shit was good." Monica sighed as she felt him growing soft inside of her. He gradually slowed down and collapsed in exhaustion. "I hope that we get a chance to make love on the beach during our trip, baby," she mused.

"We will, baby. Even if we have to go in the middle of the night."

"Byron turn the air conditioner up, I'm sweaty!"

As Byron turned to flip the switch, he looked right into the eyes of his drunk ass Uncle Allen. He had been watching them fuck through the driver's side window with a big ass grin on his face.

"Uncle Allen, what the hell you doin'?" Byron quickly jumped into the passenger seat to let Monica get dressed. He snatched on his shorts and hopped out the car, nearly knocking his uncle down in his haste. "Man, what you doin' peepin' in windows and shit?"

"Shit, I saw the car rocking from way over there." His uncle pointed toward the crowd. He tried to get another peek at Monica. "You got one of them hoodrats in there, nephew?"

Byron blocked his view and pushed him back. "This my woman, man! I don't fool around with hoochies and hoodrats no more. I got a jazzy woman now," Byron said, proudly.

"Yeah? Well that's good for you, nephew. But I sure know one thing." He wobbled from side to side a little bit before steadying himself. "She sho'll got a nice set of lungs, the way she was screamin' and carrin' on."

Byron laughed at his favorite uncle. He was a good man and a good provider to his family. Uncle Allen just drank too much sometimes, especially at barbecues and other family gatherings.

Byron gave him all of his discarded clothes. He recognized the Sean John T-shirt and jeans that his uncle wore now. The old man thought he was clean as a clap doctor.

Byron needed to get rid of his uncle. He figured that Monica would be too embarrassed to leave the car and face his family if his uncle went back and blabbed about what he'd caught them doing. He pulled a big wad of cash out of his pocket.

"Is Uncle Joe drunk too?" Byron asked, as his uncle leered greedily at the hand full of cash.

"Yeah he's drunk. His big ass been drinking all day. Why? You want me to give him that money?"

Byron ignored the question and asked his own. "What about Aunt Ilean?"

"You know she don't partake in alcohol, nephew. My sister is a Christian woman," he slurred, proudly.

"I need you to go across the bridge and pick up a few more cases of beer. But I don't want you driving. Get Aunt Ilean to take you." Byron gave him three hundred dollars. He knew it was too much, but hey, it was his favorite uncle. "Keep the change, man."

His eyes lit up. "Thank you, nephew! And tell your girlfriend that I said thank you, too. She got a nice set of lu..."

"I know, I know! Byron said, irritable as he guided his uncle towards the party. "Go find Aunt Ilean."

"Okay, nephew."

Byron got back in the car and said, "Sorry about that, baby. My uncle is a little drunk."

Monica had overheard their exchange. Byron had called her jazzy. Maybe they had a future after all. She'd made reservations as Mr. and Mrs. Byron Williams for their trip to the Bahamas. Monica was going to find out what he was really made of. Byron talked a good game, telling his uncle that he didn't mess with hoochies any more. Time would tell.

"Baby, I'm ready to go. I still have some packing to do before we leave tonight," she said.

Byron was ready to go too. He turned to see how the barbecue was going, wondering if he would be missed. "How would it look if we left early?"

Monica folded her arms and crossed her legs to look at him like he was crazy. "Are you serious? All they care about is free food and booze. Once they got a few drinks in 'em, they wouldn' care if you hadn't bothered to show up at all!"

Byron knew that she was right. As he turned to look at the crowd again he noticed two of his associates walking towards his car. They were the most vocal in displaying their displeasure with Byron's decision to quit the game. He decided to get rid of Monica for a minute.

"You're probably right, baby. Why don't you fix us a coupla plates to eat on the plane."

Monica looked horrified. "What? That is so ghetto! We'll be flying first-class. If you get hungry they'll provide the food. Not you, Byron!"

"Alright, baby, calm down. Damn. You know that I need you to teach me shit like that. But fix me a plate anyway. I need to talk some business for a minute."

She rolled her eyes as they got out the car.

"What's up, Big D, Terry?" Byron shook hands with the big men. They both were about 6'2 and 220 1bs. and they always dressed in hip-hop gear. Big D was the darker toned of the two and he usually served as the spokesman. He wore an Allen Iverson jersey with matching shorts, while his brother rocked a throw back Dr. J hook-up.

Big D got right to the point. "We need to talk, B."

Byron leaned against the car and crossed his arms. "What's on your mind, playboy?"

"Our money is what!'

"Are you still on that? Listen dog. I'm out. Find you another supplier."

"We can find another hook-up. But there's all types of things that you have to take into consideration when you do that." Big D counted them off with his fingers. "Trust. Can we trust the guy not to set us up and jack us someday? Is he working for the po-po's? Is he an undercover cop himself? How many times have he stepped on the product? Will our customers like the product? Etcetera, etcetera. You know how it is, Byron!" he shouted, throwing his hands up in frustration.

Byron got off the car and glared at him. "What you sayin'? You sayin' I can't quit?" Byron was getting pissed. He had a pistol under the seat and he wouldn't hesitate to bust a cap in their asses. "What do you expect me to do, sell dope for the rest of my life?"

"No, we don't. We're just tryin' to get where you're at, homeboy, and we can't do that if you quit on us now."

Byron sighed. "What do you want from me, man?"

Big D looked at his brother for a second before turning back to Byron. "We want you to plug us in with your connection down in Houston."

So that was it. These clowns wanted to be king ding-a-ling. Byron shook his head and said, "Can't do it."

Big D exploded. "Why not? You can't help us out? You hatin' on us or what?"

"Fuck you, Big D! I'm not a hater! I don't give a flyin' fuck who takes my place. I didn't say that I wouldn't plug you in, I said that I couldn't!"

"Why?" Big D asked.

"That's what you should've asked me in the first place. Instead, you called me a hater!" he seethed.

"My bad, dog. I didn't mean to offend you. I'm just frustrated a little bit that's all," Big D said, backing off.

Byron could relate to feeling frustrated because that was just how he felt when Fat Chris threatened to cut him off. He looked up at Big D and said, "I can't hook you up because my connection is dead. If he was alive, I wouldn't have a problem with helping you."

"What do you mean, he's dead? You just got a shipment in two weeks ago!"

Byron nodded his head. "Yeah, I did and it was my last shipment too. Dude got killed last week."

"Damn!" Big D turned to his brother and said, "We can't win for loosing, Terry." He turned back to Byron who was leaning up against the car again and asked, "Where did they get him?"

"What do you mean?"

"Where did he get shot?" Big D asked.

"Who said he got shot?" Byron asked, suspiciously.

"You did."

"No I didn't. I said he got killed."

"Well, how else do you kill somebody in this business?" Big D was trying to recover from his slip.

Byron gave him a piercing stare for a few seconds longer before speaking again. "I guess you're right. You never hear about people getting stabbed and shit. Fat Chris got shot in the head, or so I heard."

"For what? Who did he fuck over to get smoked?"

"Why are you asking so many questions?" Byron was thinking more and more about getting his pistol.

"Why are you trippin'? You've been acting paranoid as a mutherfucka! I just wanna know so I don't make the same mistake. This is a dangerous business, man. I don't only live and learn, I also learn from other peoples fuck-ups!"

Byron knew that he should just shut up, but he couldn't help himself. "He came up here and got fucked off in some restaurant. End of story, you dig?"

Big D shook his head from side to side. "That's fucked up! Do you think there's going to be repercussions from his homeboys in Houston?"

"Hell if I know. They don't know who did it anyway." Byron noticed Monica on her way back with their plates. "I'm fixin' to bounce, y'all."

"Alright, B." Big D offered his hand. "We'll see you in the club or somethin'."

"And you know this man," Byron said, before the two men turned and walked away.

Big D got behind the wheel of a customized yellow Saleen Mustang while Terry fastened his seat belt on the passenger side. As Big D maneuvered through the congested parking lot, he turned to Terry. "What do you think?"

"I think he's a piece of shit!"

"Yeah, me too. But I mean about Fat Chris."

"I think he knows more than he's telling us. He did it himself or he paid someone to do it," Terry said, as he watched a woman in a pair of tight shorts walking along side the car. "Damn she's fine!" he yelled, grabbing his crotch.

Big D ignored him. "If Byron's really out of the game, he's no good to us walking the street. He might drop salt on us and fuck up our plans." Big D blew his horn at a guy in a Honda Accord that was blocking him in. "This place is packed."

It's like this every weekend," Terry said, as he checked out a group of women in a Lexus, before adding, "But you're right, we'l have to take him out of the game permanently."

"When should we do it?" Big D asked, finally getting out of the crowded parking lot and onto Ledbetter Road, the main thoroughfare to the big park.

Terry turned to Big D and said in a deadly tone, "As soon as possible. Definitely within the next few days."

Chapter Thirty-Six

Tabitha & Shon

Once a month, Tabitha and Brandon's mother, Leuwenia set aside a Saturday morning to cruise Mesquite's suburban neighborhoods hunting for garage sales. After Tabitha dropped her mother-in-law at home, she went to Town East Mall to spend the rest of the day with Shon. They had agreed to meet in the women's shoe department inside of Foleys. But since Shon called to say that she was running late, Tabitha decided to try on a few pair of shoes while she waited for her girlfriend.

Tabitha chose two different sets of pumps and turned to the female salesperson that was hovering nearby. "Let me see these in size eight please."

"That's a nice choice. I can see that you have good taste. Just have a seat here and I'll be right back." The salesperson hurried off to the back.

Tabitha kicked off her loafers to rub her feet. Leuwenia must have taken her to every damn garage sale in Mesquite. She smiled as she thought of her mother-in-law. Tabitha felt blessed to have her in her life. When she and Brandon first married, Leuwenia helped her out a lot by giving her marriage advice. She told her which meals he liked best and made damn sure that she knew how to prepare them.

Leuwenia could tell that something was bothering her, but Tabitha just couldn't bring herself to confide in the woman about her affair. She wouldn't ever be able to face Brandon's mother again if she found out her secret.

Tabitha's train of thought was interrupted as Shon asked "How long have you been waiting?"

"Not long, not long at all. I'm just waiting to try on some shoes in my size." Tabitha checked out Shon's outfit. "Did you come straight from the gym?"

"Yeah. Why?" Shon asked, as she looked down at her sweat suit. When she looked up Tabitha was fanning her face and holding her nose.

"You stink!"

"I do not!" she shouted. "I took a shower before I left the gym, heifer. And this is not the same sweat suit that I worked out in, thank you very much!" she said, snapping her fingers.

Tabitha was still laughing when the salesperson returned with her shoes.

"Here you go. We had both of your selections in stock." She set the boxes down and removed the lids. Tabitha slipped into the black pumps first.

"How do they look on my feet, Shon?" She asked, as she pranced back and forth.

"They look cute. But you already have a pair just like them in your closet."

"No I don't. Girl, I swear you don't recognize quality when you see it. The pumps in my closet cost $250." She pointed to her feet. "These just cost $85." Tabitha threw her hands in the air. "See the difference?"

Shon eyed her up and down. "Yeah, I see the difference. Next you'll be justifying why you chose to wear that skirt and blouse by Lane Bryant today.

"Fuck you, bitch!"

"You too, heffa!"

The salesperson was looking from one to the other getting nervous.

"Are you trying to say that I'm fat?" Tabitha shrieked.

Shon cupped her hands around her mouth. "Moo! Moo!"

Tabitha stomped her foot. "I am not fat! I'm just a little bloated," she whispered. "I'm still fine!"

"Whatever rocks your boat, girlfriend. Just hurry up with these cheap ass shoes. I'm starving!"

The salesperson thought she was about to loose a sale so she jumped in to do her job. "Well, actually these are quality pumps. You can't always judge quality by price."

Tabitha and Shon looked at each other and burst out laughing,

"I'll take the black, sweetheart. I really don't care for the red ones." Tabitha slipped off the shoes and removed her credit card from her Fendi bag. "Ring that up, honey."

"Right away, ma'am."

They decided to have lunch at Salads R Us. It was situated in between Taco Bell and Hot Dog Heaven inside the Food Court of the mall. The ladies selected a table on the second level where they could eat and watch the shoppers. Everyone seemed to have shopping to do this weekend. The mall was packed with a diverse group of people from all cultures. Shon and Tabitha had a good view of all the stores they planned to hit.

Shon took a few bites of her Caesar salad before she noticed her friend hadn't touched her food. "What's on your mind, Tabitha?"

"It didn't work, Shon," she whispered.

What didn't work?" Shon asked, with a puzzled expression.

Tabitha played around in her seafood salad before she reluctantly replied, "I tried to seduce Brandon and it didn't work!"

"What do you mean that it didn't work?" Shon sat down her fork. "That was two weeks ago. I remember, because you called me early the next morning. And as I recall, you were pissed off at him," she accused.

"You would've been pissed off too if your man called you a whore. He actually asked me to make my next lover wear a condom! I can't live like this Shon, it's killing me inside. Can you understand that?"

Shon sighed. "Baby, you broke the man's heart. And maybe he's been betrayed by another woman before. Did you ever think about that?" she asked softly. "Maybe lashing out at you by calling you a whore was a defense mechanism. I don't know. But you do need to sit him down and talk to him about how you feel. You have to get him to open up. This isn't a game. We're talking about your marriage, Tabitha." Shon pointed her finger at her friend. "You fucked up. And you can't give up until the problem is resolved."

"Don't you think I know that?" she cried "Every time I try and talk to him about our marriage, he turns somber. But it's all gravy when the topic's about business. I think he's given up on our marriage, yet embraces me as a business partner."

"So I guess I shouldn't assume he's moved back into your bedroom."

"Please, don't waste your breath."

"Well, have you asked him why the hell not? You did have sex, so he's not against touching you. You're about to fuck off a good man," Shon said, raising her voice.

"What are you getting mad at me for?" Tabitha asked incredulously.

"Because you're not happy. Yet you tell me that you know you're responsible for the problem that led to your unhappiness. But I can't see shit you've done to solve the problem except fuck him."

"Fuck you, Shon!"

Shon pointed her finger at Tabitha's chest and said, "No! Fuck you, Tabitha! It was your fucking that started this mess in the first place, remember? Everyone was happy and everything was going along smooth, until you decided to fuck everything up by dropping your drawers! Your little affair is even causing problems between me and my husband. Not to mention you got BC killed!"

"What? I got BC killed?" Tabitha didn't understand.

Shon was shaking her head as she stood up to leave. "Nothing, Tabitha. Please forget I said that. I didn't mean it like that."

"No!" Tabitha cried, as she stood up to face Shon. "I won'
forget it. What are you not telling me?"

Shon noticed they were causing a scene. Everyone around the
food court was looking at them. "I have to go home, Tabitha."
Shon said as she walked away.

Tabitha grabbed her bags and went after her. She had to run
to catch up after coming off the escalator. "Shon, will you wait up
please!"

Shon was walking fast through the crowded mall. "Go home
Tabitha. Just leave me alone, please!"

Tabitha grabbed Shon's arm to stop her from running away
Shon turned and slapped Tabitha hard across the face. Tabitha
dropped her bags in shock.

"Don't fucking touch me!" Shon screamed.

Tabitha was rubbing her cheek. She'd forgotten all about BC
"No you didn't, bitch!"

"Just leave me alone, Tabitha." Shon turned to walk away
but as she took a step, she was violently yanked down by her hair
After she crashed to the floor, Tabitha straddled her body and tried
to pummel her across the face. Shon was kicking and screaming as
shoppers crowded around them to watch the cat fight. Tabitha
zeroed in on Shon's eye as she balled up her fist and cocked back
her arm. But before she could deliver the vicious blow, she was
snatched off Shon's body by a pair of strong arms.

"Put me down! I'm gonna kill you, bitch! Don't ever put your
hands on me again!" Tabitha screamed.

Shon got to her feet, and ignoring Tabitha's tirade, she ran through the crowd of rubberneckers.

"Put me down, motherfucker! I don't know you!" Tabitha screamed, as she tried to wiggle free.

The big man holding her yelled, "Someone call the police!"

"Motherfucker, if you don't put me down, I'm going to press charges against your ass for sexual assault. I can feel you grinding against my ass!"

The big man quickly lowered her to her feet. "I wasn't sexually assaulting you, ma'am! I was just tryin' to be a Good Samaritan!" the farmer in overalls bellowed.

Tabitha ignored him. She retrieved her bags and pushed through the crowd with tears in her eyes. Once she was safely locked inside her car, she lowered her head to the steering wheel in wracking sobs.

Tabitha realized what she'd known all along. It was just too coincidental. She hadn't wanted to believe her husband was capable of taking another human's life. Now she knew for sure she was the cause of BC's death. Tabitha tried to hate BC for what he'd done to her but her nature was to forgive. That's what her parents taught her to do. God, what was she going to do now? BC didn't deserve to die. Tabitha found a handkerchief and cleaned her face. What else is Shon not telling her? She's supposed to be her best friend, dammit! Right or wrong, they're supposed to be there for each other. She started her car. Shon was right about one thing; she needed to be more assertive. Brandon was going to talk to her today. She couldn't love a murderer.

Chapter Thirty-Seven

Brandon & Tabitha

Her husband was in the living room talking on the phone when she entered the house from the garage.

"Do you have any idea when he'll be back?" Brandon needed to tie up loose ends, but Byron was proving to be elusive.

"I couldn't find out. But no one takes three week vacations do they?" DJ asked.

"I've never heard of it myself. I'll be ready when the time comes, so don't trip. But the sooner the better. We need to take a little vacation ourselves. I get sick to my stomach when I think of all the interest payments we're loosing by not having that money in the bank."

"Tank, hold the phone for a minute. I need to holla at Shon. She's been waiting for me to get off the phone for a minute."

"Handle your business, I'll wait."

Tabitha had sat down on the love seat to wait for Brandon to finish his phone call. But she was getting impatient.

"What happened to your face?" Brandon asked.

She was startled from her thoughts with his question. "Huh. What did you say?"

"I said, what happened to your face? It's red."

"I'll wait for you to get off the phone. I need to talk to you about that and some other things that's been on my mind."

Brandon held the phone away from his face. "DJ has me on hold. What's up?"

She switched over to sit next to him on the couch. "Me and Shon just had a big fight in the mall." She looked away nervously.

"Don't worry about it, Tabitha. Y'all always get into it over one thing or another. That's what friends do sometimes. Is that why your cheek is red? Shon slapped you?" He had a big ass grin on his face.

"Yeah, as a matter of fact she did. I kicked her ass too!"

"What? How could you allow an argument to come to blows? What were you arguing about anyway?"

"While we talked over lunch, I was trying to explain why I was feeling bad about the state of our marriage." She turned to look into his eyes. "You know, about your unwillingness to meet me half way towards repairing our relationship. She asked me why I haven't asked you to move back into our bedroom. When I said that I didn't know, she went off on me by saying that it's my fault all these things happened." As tears rolled down her face, Tabitha crossed her arms and rocked back and forth.

Brandon was a little surprised to see her cry. Usually she was angry and later she'd turn sad after she'd gotten into it with Shon. But he'd never known her to cry over it. Then too, their arguments had never escalated to blows. He hung the phone up and put his arms around her.

"It'll be alright. We'll work out our problems in time," he said softly.

"No!" Tabitha broke free from his embrace to look him in the eye. "I'm not finished yet." She had to know for sure if her husband had killed a man because of her affair.

"Shon said that my mistakes are causing problems between her and DJ. Brandon I love Shon and DJ. I don't know if I could live with the thought of destroying our marriage and theirs. I can see how you might not ever forgive me, because I can't forgive myself for ruining what we've had." She was pouring her heart out to him. But she was afraid of what she'd see in his eyes after she made her next statement.

"Brandon, Shon also said..." Tabitha was cut off by the ringing of the telephone.

"Wait a minute, hold that thought."

"Hello!

Tabitha got up and started to pace. She was full of nervous energy.

"How did that happen?" she heard him ask into the receiver.

"Alright, I'll holla at you later." Brandon hung up the phone.

"Tabitha, come here for a minute, come sit in my lap. I need to talk to you, baby." He held out his hand to her.

Tabitha was so shocked at his request that she actually started to deny it. But she was craving his touch so damn bad that her resistance was weak, and she'd never been one to turn down affection. She settled into his lap and put her arms around his neck.

"I know that I haven't been responsive lately. But I've had some things on my mind that I've needed to work out on my own."

He gently kissed her lips. "And contrary to what you may believe, I can and will forgive you. It'll take time, but eventually the pain will fade. You are the love of my life, baby, and it'll be that way forever. The past is history and we need to learn from it, so that we don't repeat past mistakes. But let me be clear here, Tabitha. Don't ever fuck off on me again. Ever!"

"Oh, Brandon, I love you so much, baby. I'll do anything you ask of me for as long as we live. I just want to make you happy."

He smiled. "You know what we need to do?"

"What?" she asked.

"We need to break in that new bed, don't we?" Brandon started kissing her on the neck.

"But it's the middle of the day."

"Well, if you don't want me to make love to you, I understand."

"Shit!" She jumped off his lap and grabbed his hand. "Come on, boy. The only thing I'm turning down is my collar!"

Brandon laughed as she pulled him to his feet and led him to the stairs. He realized once again how much he loved this woman. Brandon meant everything he said to her--he just hadn't planned on saying it today. She had been feeling miserable and uncomfortable for the last two months, and that's just how he wanted her to feel, as punishment for what she'd done. Hopefully she learned quick flings weren't worth loosing the person she loved most.

DJ's last phone call had tipped him off and sped up his plans. He didn't know how much information DJ had revealed to Shon, but he would make it a point to find out. He knew it was only a matter of time before Tabitha brought up the subject again of his whereabouts the night BC was killed. And when she did, he wasn't going to disappoint her.

They were wet with sweat as Tabitha collapsed on top of her husband. She was trying to catch her breath after riding her stud to a very much needed climatic orgasm. Brandon was palming her soft ass with his big hands while running his fingers through her damp hair with the other.

"You know what?" he asked, softly.

"What?"

"I worked up an appetite."

Tabitha laughed, "How? I did most of the work," she said as she gently kissed his lips. "Brandon?"

"Yeah, baby?"

"I love you so much. I want to make you proud to have me as your wife."

"I'm already proud of you, Tabitha."

"No. Seriously."

"I am serious, I'm proud of you now."

Still straddling him, she sat up with a suspicious expression on her face to see if he was kidding. "Why would you be proud of me, Brandon?"

"Well, let's see. When we're in public at family functions and stuff, you cater to me as well as compliment me as my other half.

You're smart and beautiful. Your business sense is as sharp as anyone I've ever met. And you're an overall good person, baby. I can't think of a better woman to share my life with."

Tears of joy rolled down her face. "You're making me cry!" she said happily as she kissed him all over his face.

"Baby?"

"What?" She mumbled.

"I'm hungry."

Tabitha rolled off of him and out the bed. "You're always hungry after you get some!"

He laughed as he crawled out of bed. "You shouldn't work a brotha' so hard."

"Well be prepared to put in a little overtime tonight,"

Brandon followed her into the bathroom and admired the view as she bent over to run water into the large bathtub. Once they had settled comfortably in the water, Brandon decided to broach the subject of BC's death. They needed to clear the air on this topic and lay it to rest. He preferred to be on the offensive rather than the defensive. She was his alibi for that night and it was important she never waiver from being so. He didn't believe he'd ever be convicted for the crime. But murder doesn't have a statue of limitations and he did have a motive to want the man dead. As long as the authorities continued to believe he didn't have an opportunity to kill BC, he was cool.

Tabitha was sitting in between his legs. "Give me the soap and I'll wash your back," he said.

Tabitha relaxed. She enjoyed being pampered by her man.

"I want you to do something for me," he said.

She looked over her shoulder at him and asked, "What, baby?"

"I need you to make an attempt to resolve your differences with Shon. I shouldn't have to tell you how important it is we all go the extra mile to keep our relationship intact." Brandon set down the bath towel and hugged her tight. "To have a friend who only has your best interests in mind is a priceless commodity in this day and age. Not to mention the fact you two have to work together. So for the betterment of our company and your continuing friendship, fix it, Tabitha."

"Alright baby, but..."

"No buts! Just do it!" he said sternly. "There's something else that you need to do for me."

"What?" she pouted.

"BC is dead... and I wanted him that way. After tonight, I don't want his name mentioned ever again in this house. I wasn't home the night he was killed. So you've probably been wondering if I had something to do with his death."

Tabitha tried to turn around to face him but Brandon squeezed her and wouldn't allow her to.

"Let me finish," he growled. "You need to learn a little something about the world we live in. Before I went to college, I hustled in the streets. And in the streets there are rules of survival every hustler lives by. If you see something that's none of your business, then you didn't see it. If you did something that could get you the death penalty or a long stretch in prison if you leave witnesses, then you don't leave any." He turned her around to face him.

"Just because I use proper English and live in a big crib and drive fancy cars doesn't mean I'm soft. So don't ever get it twisted. You've already showed me that I have to keep you on a short leash because you can't be trusted. So why would I be foolish enough to provide you with information that could possibly get me the death penalty some day? I'm not perfect, nor do I claim to be. There may come a day that I hurt your heart in some way. But I'll never allow you to place me in a situation I can't walk away from. 'Hell has no fury like a woman scorned'!"

Brandon softened his voice. "This issue is dead. I don't ever want it discussed again--not even with Shon, Tabitha. You asked me never to leave you. One of the reasons why I married you is because you make me happy, and I wanted to spend the rest of my life with you. But have no illusions. A judge can break our asses up by sending me to prison."

She hugged him tight as tears ran down her face. Tabitha realized that he had given her a confession just as much as a denial, but she would do as he asked and drop the subject forever. If Brandon was willing to go the extra mile for her, she would make damn sure she did it for him. She took a deep breath and slowly exhaled. Oddly, she felt at peace and secure again. It had been months since she'd felt like this, and the feeling was alien to her in a way.

"Baby?" he asked, tentatively.

"Hmmm?"

"Can we *please* go eat now?"

233

Tabitha laughed as she kissed him and reached for his member in the water. When she broke the kiss he was hard as a rock.

"We have to feed this big boy first, Brandon," she said, seductively as she straddled her husband.

Chapter Thirty-Eight

Brandon & DJ

Sunday morning, Brandon waited until Tabitha went to church before he called DJ and asked him to come over. When the doorbell rang announcing DJ's arrival, Brandon answered the door seething with anger.

"Come in." Brandon let DJ close the door as he went to the game room and sat in the La-Z-Boy. He was afraid that if he remained standing he might hit his best friend in his big ass mouth.

"What's up, dog?" DJ set his briefcase down before he took a seat in the adjacent La-Z-Boy.

"I'm just curious as to why you felt compelled to tell Shon that I killed BC. And while you explain yourself, please be free to let me know anything else that you might have told her," he said, sarcastically.

"She's my wife, Tank, my other half."

"Fuck that!" Brandon leaned over and looked into his eyes. "I shouldn't have to tell you this shit, DJ. A woman is weak! Do you think she'll stand up and keep her mouth shut when the pressure is applied?"

"Yeah, I believe she will." DJ said, in defense of his wife. "I never would have told her if I didn't believe that. I don't just talk to her about our business. I talk to her about shit that I've done in the past too. We don't keep secrets from each other."

"Oh yeah? So what you sayin'? You knew all along Tabitha was fucking around with BC?"

"You know I didn't know about that shit!"

"Well, why didn't you? You and Shon don't keep secrets remember?'

"That was different and you know it. She was trying to keep Tabitha's secret."

"Well, why in the fuck couldn't you keep mines, DJ? As a matter of fact, as I see it, she's shown her loyalty to Tabitha twice and her disloyalty to you twice." Brandon said.

DJ looked confused. "What are you talking about?"

Brandon sighed. "Shon didn't tell you about Tabitha's affair because she didn't trust you not to tell me. Second, she betrayed your trust by telling Tabitha about a murder she shouldn't have known anything about."

DJ blew out a breath and ran his hand across his face in frustration. "What do you want me to do about it, Tank?"

"Check your wife, DJ," he growled. "And check her good. Because I'm telling you to your face, I'm going to always look out for me."

"What's that supposed to mean?" DJ asked.

"It means that I'll pay for you and your wife's funerals before I allow either one of you to send me to prison. Is that clear enough for you?"

"Man, you are really trippin'!" DJ said, incredulously.

"I'm just keeping it real, homeboy. Do you think this is a game? I love you and Shon, DJ." Brandon had tears in his eyes

"Fix the problem before I have to. That's all I'm saying about the situation. Just fix it, DJ!"

The two men were quiet for several uncomfortable minutes as the Dallas Cowboys pre-game show played on the big screen television. DJ set his briefcase on his lap and removed a manila envelope.

"I had a little trouble obtaining significant background information on Byron."

"Why is that?" Brandon asked.

"Because he's never been in enough trouble to warrant a criminal record." DJ scanned the contents of the folder. "City records list him as the owner of three different residences. It took some time, but I was finally able to find out which of the three is his primary residence. He lives in an affluent part of Lancaster. That suburb is about six miles from here, give or take."

"I'm not real familiar with the Lancaster area, but I'll find the house. All I need is the address."

"According to the Department of Motor Vehicles, he's got three cars registered in his name. A 2004 Corvette, a 2004 Cadillac Escalade, and a 2005 Mercedes Benz," DJ quoted.

"Sounds like he's got all the bases covered. Sports car, utility truck, and a luxury car. Nice."

"I have something else for you, too." DJ removed a brown paper bag from his briefcase and passed it to Brandon.

Brandon pulled out a shiny blue steel .22 semi-automatic from the paper bag. "It looks brand new."

"It is. I got a good price on it too. The cat threw in the silencer for free," DJ said proudly.

"It'll get the job done." Brandon put the gun back into the paper bag and set it aside.

"What should we do about getting Tabitha and Shon to kiss and make up?"

DJ shrugged. "Hell if I know. I got on her ass about that shit too! She was sulking around the house all night."

"We'll give it a few more days. As soon as Byron's out the way we can get the girls to kiss and make up on the cruise. I haven't even mentioned it to Tabitha yet."

"Yeah, it'll be a surprise to Shon, too."

"Hey, turn to FOX. It's about time for kickoff. You get the sandwiches and I'll get the beer out the trunk," DJ said. They'd forgotten all about their disagreement, or so Brandon thought.

●●●●●●

Later that night, as Tabitha slept, Brandon crept from the house dressed in all black to do a little recon. As a safety precaution, he had switched the license plates for paper dealer's tags on his Lexus Coupe earlier in the day. That hadn't taken very long, but it took over an hour to find Byron's house within a maze of unfamiliar streets. He did two passes familiarizing himself with the neighborhood and making a mental note of the exact location of Byron's house. Three streets over he killed the lights and engine allowing the Lexus to quietly coast to a stop in front of someone's home. He stealthily slipped from the car and jogged to the side street alley that would lead him to the back of Byron's residence.

All the houses inside the community had eight-foot wooden privacy fences surrounding the backyards. As he walked along,

Brandon counted off each fence on the left side of the alley. When he arrived at the tenth house, he crept up to the dark garage and used a penlight to take a look. Parked side by side were Byron's Corvette and Escalade--the Mercedes Benz was missing. As he pocketed the penlight and left the way he came, he was wondering if Byron usually parked his Benz in the back driveway or the circular one out front. Brandon decided that the best course of action would be to drive by the front of the house during the day and make forays up the alley at night. As Brandon drove away he made a mental note to stop by his parents' house in the morning.

Chapter Thirty-Nine

Big D. & Brandon

Like Brandon, Big D and Terry had also done reconnaissance on Byron's crib. But they'd taken it a step further and ordered a youngster to sit in a nondescript sedan with dark tinted windows up the street. Brandon had just missed Byron by thirty minutes. Big D hadn't been informed Byron had returned from his trip until 7:45 in the morning. But it had taken him a little longer than usual to get out of bed. He and his wife were trying to make a baby so he had to perform on call whenever his wife claimed she was most fertile. Shit! She was just horny this morning and he was too damn weak to resist her.

"What's so funny?" Terry asked, from the passenger seat.

Big D wiped the smile off his face. "Nothing. Nothing at all," he said, as he gripped the steering wheel with both hands. They wanted to take Byron out as soon as possible so they were coordinating and organizing to do just that. "I think 10:00 am would be the perfect time to hit his ass. The neighborhood should be virtually empty during that time."

"That's too soon," Terry said, as he looked at his watch. "It's 9:05 now. We'll have a better chance if we take our time and do it right. He ain't goin' nowhere."

Big D turned down the radio. He was anxious to see the expression on Byron' face. "What time, then?" he asked.

"I think we can have it all planned and laid out by noon."

"We may need four or five more guys. Five would give us ten and as you know there's strength in numbers. Byron's not afraid to pop them pistols!" Terry warned.

"He won't have a chance because he doesn't suspect what's comin' his way," Big D replied confidently.

●●●●●●

Brandon didn't go to his parents' house until he was sure they'd left for work. He used his own door key to get in. When he climbed into the attic, it had taken him awhile to go through all the boxes stored away up there before he was finally able to find what he was looking for. After he'd transferred the contents of the box into his duffel bag he decided to go by Byron's house to see the neighborhood in the daylight hours.

As he turned onto the designated street his heart started beating rapidly. There was a big beige colored Mercedes Benz sitting in front of Byron's house in the circular driveway. He maintained a speed of twenty miles per hour as he surveyed the block. The same cream colored sedan he'd seen last night was still the only car parked along the curb. *The beautiful neighborhood seemed just as peaceful and quiet in the daylight hours as it did at night,* Brandon thought. After going around the block and making a second pass of Byron's house, he drove to a Motel 6 to get a room. Always mindful and being cautious, he used an assumed name and paid in cash. Removing the duffel bag from the car he went to his room to make preparations.

When Brandon arrived back to Byron's neighborhood, he parked the Lexus two streets over and called DJ from the car.

"Hello!"

"It's me."

"What's up, dog?" DJ asked.

"It's time for you to make those travel arrangements we discussed."

DJ was slow to respond. He was contemplating the meaning of Brandon's statement. "Is it a wrap?"

"Not yet, but it will be real soon," Brandon said.

"How soon do you want to leave?"

"Shit! It's Monday now. See if you can get us out of here this week. Friday would be lovely."

"Cool. I'm on it. One! "

Brandon looked around before leaving the car. *It was a beautiful morning*, he thought as he walked down the sidewalk. He had borrowed his father's old postal uniform along with a worn leather mailbag and baseball cap. The pants were a little tight in the thigh area, but other than that, the uniform fit perfectly on his frame.

Brandon had promised himself this would be his last job. To his horror, he had come to realize he was actually starting to look forward to his next opportunity to take a human life. All he needed was a justifiable reason.

He also realized he didn't have to kill Byron. After all, Fat Chris was dead. But he got off on the precise planning and preparation of a job more than performing the actual hit. There was a perverse feeling of exhilaration and triumph that rode roughshod over his conscience. Never the less, he would make it a point to quit this shit and maybe take up deer hunting, he thought as he turned the corner and walked up Byron's street.

He carefully but discreetly scanned the street with his keen eyesight hidden behind a pair of dark shades. There wasn't any human activity he could discern. The only thing out of place was the sedan parked along the curb. Everyone else either parked their automobile in the circular driveway or the garage. He dismissed the oddity as a threat as he walked passed the Mercedes in Byron's yard.

The base around the front door was tarnished oak, but the majority consisted of tinted glass, which allowed him to see clearly through the big house. Brandon pressed the doorbell and held it down for a good ten minutes before he saw movement from inside.

Byron was slowly maneuvering down the stairs in a bathrobe. He snatched open the door and asked Brandon why he was ringing his damn doorbell.

Brandon reached into the mailbag over his shoulder and wrapped his hand around the butt of his pistol and said. "I have a special delivery that can only be delivered to you, sir."

"What? A package?" he asked curiously.

"No, a bullet!" He replied, as he withdrew the pistol and shot Byron in the center of his forehead.

The man was dead before he hit the floor. Brandon quickly located the spent shell and swallowed it. He removed a handker-chief from his pocket and used it to close the door and wipe off the doorbell. After he had placed everything back into his mailbag, he casually strolled back up the street the same way he had come.

● ● ● ● ● ●

Three hours later, Big D, Terry, and their associates quietly crept up to Byron's house and had it covered on all sides. They didn't want Byron to have any opportunities for escape.

Big D and Terry used the Mercedes as cover. Terry was first to reach the front door. He occupied the left side while Big D was on the right. Big D peeped inside through the glass door. One, two, three quick times. It was the third quick peep that he noticed the body lying to the left side of the door in the foyer.

"Shit!" he said, to no one in particular.

"What?" Terry whispered.

"There's a body on the floor."

Terry peeped inside and he too saw the body. He motioned to his comrades for assistance before storming the house. Big D slowly turned the knob and pushed the door open.

"Go, go, go!" he screamed, as the men charged through the door with pistols drawn in search of a target. Two men ran upstairs while Terry and four others searched downstairs.

Big D dropped to his knees and rolled the body over, only to look into Byron's dead eyes. A Trickle of dried blood had run down his nose. As he rose to his feet he heard his comrades yell "clear" after they'd searched a room and found it free of danger. He remained at the door so they wouldn't receive any unexpected guests from the rear. After the men cleared the house, they returned to the front foyer to gawk at Byron's body.

"Is there a pulse?"

Big D looked at him like he was crazy, but he answered the man's question. "No. He's dead. Get these guys out of here and get me that rookie."

They all walked out into the sunshine to wait for the coroner.

Big D watched the rookie approach in a wrinkled suit obviously bought off the rack. "I thought you said he didn't have any visitors?'

"He didn't, sir."

Big D rolled his eyes and sighed. "Let's try this again. I have a dead man in there. I've been around the block a time or two, son. So I recognize a recent kill when I see one. Do you understand that, Agent Aaron?"

The nervous rookie was sweating profusely. This was his first assignment and he didn't want to blow it, so he'd taken No-Doze to help him stay awake. He was sure there weren't any visitors to the house he was assigned to watch.

"I understand, sir," he answered.

"I want you to think clearly. Take your time. It could be anyone. A fireman, policeman, cable repairman, neighbor...?"

The young agent cut him off. "How about a mailman?" he asked excitedly and eager to please the more experienced agent.

"The mailman?" Big D looked around and noticed the mailboxes were stationed along the curb. "What did the mailman do, Agent Aaron?"

"Well, I couldn't see him after he knocked on the door." He turned to point towards his car. "That big tree blocked my view," he lied. He couldn't tell the special agent he was busy writing his girlfriend a letter.

"Why didn't you park closer to the house?"

"Because in training we were instructed to park at least four houses away whenever possible."

Big D was seething. "I guess common sense was never factored into your training, Agent Aaron. Because common sense would have dictated you find an unobstructed view of the fuckin front door!" he screamed, as spittle flew into the frightened agent' face.

He quickly regained control of himself long enough to get a description of the assassin before turning the crime scene over to Terry. The undercover special agent had to fax an emergency report to his superiors in Washington, D.C. This situation was about to get real interesting.

Chapter Forty

Big D

He watched Brandon do a series of stretching exercises in preparation for his morning run. He had watched Brandon off and on for a few years now. And every time he caught a view of him he was always dressed nice. That was impressive to him because it showed character. Today he wore a gray Jordan sweat suit with matching sneakers as he left the house jogging at a smooth gait.

He knew the route Brandon would take. After he had faxed his report to Washington, D.C. a few days ago, he was immediately ordered to increase surveillance on the subject. Last night he received a top-secret communiqué instructing him to make contact with Mr. Elliott for possible recruitment. He started his car and drove past the early morning jogger.

Brandon loved to jog through the park at this hour because it was usually deserted. But as he ran along he noticed a tall well built man standing off to the side of the track path next to a tree, as if he were waiting for someone. Brandon looked around in alarm to see if there were others lying in wait. That's when he noticed the yellow Mustang that passed him earlier. When he was twenty yards away he started walking, never taking his eyes off the good-looking man. When Brandon was five yards away, the big man spoke.

"Mr. Elliott, can I have a word with you, please?" he asked as he met Brandon on the path.

Brandon eyed him suspiciously. "It's not everyday that I have meetings in a park at 5:30 in the morning. Especially with men in Armani suits. But what can I do for you?"

The big man reached inside his jacket and Brandon tensed.

"I work for the government, Mr. Elliott," he said as he withdrew a leather bound I.D. badge. "I'm Special Agent Willie Cobb of the Federal Bureau of Investigations."

Brandon smiled. "So what does the FBI need to talk to me about, Agent Cobb?"

"Let's walk and talk if you don't mind." They fell into a casual walk along the path. "I'm going to get right to the point if you don't mind."

"Of course, please do," Brandon replied.

"I really don't expect to hear an admission of guilt from you Mr. Elliott. That's not what the government is after."

Brandon stopped and turned to the agent. "An admission of guilt to what?"

Agent Cobb looked into Brandon's brown eyes with his own for a few seconds before answering the question.

"I'm not looking for an admission to your being paid to do wet work."

"Wet work? I'm not familiar with that term," he lied.

"It's slang for what professional hit men do."

"The government is obviously barking up the wrong tree. I'm a businessman, not a killer."

The agent resumed their stroll through the park and ignored Brandon's statement.

"You see, Mr. Elliott, a few years ago your business partner, along with several other individuals that I can't name, were under investigation by the Drug Enforcement Agency or the D.E.A., if you will. They worked in conjunction with the FBI. We were called in because the D.E.A. suspected that someone was carrying out contract killings. Several people were getting killed and there was never much physical evidence left behind. It's always been known that drug dealers often place contracts on rivals or people they deem are a threat to their survival. There were rumors DeJuan Jackson had direct access to a professional. It was further rumored he helped organize and set into motion several hits for his associates, using this professional. So ultimately a second covert investigation was launched."

Brandon stopped and asked, "So what does all this have to do with me?"

The big agent laughed. "Please, be patient with me, Mr. Elliott. I'm long winded sometimes." They resumed their walk.

"Everyone that was remotely close to DeJuan Jackson was investigated thoroughly. At first you were cleared. We couldn't find any bank records to justify how you gained the capital to open your first car stereo store. So we just assumed the money was a loan from Mr. Jackson. And you've done well with that business endeavor, I must say. What do you have now, six stores?"

"Eight."

"Yeah, you've done good. But back to the subject. We red flagged your name. And when Bill Cole was killed and you became a suspect in his murder, our computers picked it up and you were brought back to my--I mean--our attention. I personally assigned a fresh batch of agents to go through your life history with a fine tooth comb." Agent Cobb stopped and gazed at Brandon with a look of admiration in his eyes.

"At first it didn't add up. I kept wondering how you could be such an effective assassin. You had no military training, no ROTC in high school, no prison record. You don't even have a juvenile record. And to top it off, you have a business degree. So once again I was starting to doubt my instincts and training. With your background I couldn't go by the age-old adage, 'If it looks like a fish and smells like a fish...it's a fish'.

About a month and a half after Bill Coles' death, I was ready to give up and pull the agents off your case. And as luck would have it, we caught a break. Actually it was two. But I'll tell you about the second one later."

"What was your first break, Agent Cobb?" Brandon asked curiously.

Agent Cobb had a mischievous grin on his face. "We found a record of your library card, Mr. Elliott."

Brandon was unnerved by this revelation, but he kept his composure and remained poker-faced. "And what could my library card possibly reveal to you, Agent Cobb?"

He smiled at Brandon. "It told me you were interested in novels and documentaries on true crime stories. It told me you were interested in weapons and their maintenance. It told me you were interested in hand-to-hand kill methods. Shall I go on?" he asked, sarcastically.

"Since when did it become a crime to read, Agent Cobb?" Brandon countered, just as sarcastically.

The agent didn't like Brandon's cocky attitude so he decided to take him down a notch.

"There isn't a crime against reading, Mr. Elliott. But murder is a crime. Let's not forget that, sir! And to a trained agent, you and I both know why you chose these particular subjects to study. So let's not play games here. As I said earlier, we're not particularly interested in pursuing you for prosecution."

"So what are you pursuing me for?"

The agent dismissed his question with a wave of his hand. "We'll get to that." They resumed walking. Agent Cobb took a few seconds to regain his composure.

"Our second break came when Fat Chris was killed. The investigation took a new turn," he said, as he ran his palm across his bald head.

"You and Mr. Jackson were at the scene and I'm still not sure why, because Mr. Jackson disassociated himself with Fat Chris almost three years ago. The description of Fat Chris' killer was inconclusive. But we strongly felt Byron Williams was involved. If we were successful in taking Byron into custody, we planned to approach you and Mr. Jackson to aid in his prosecution. We had enough to put him away for life on drug charges alone, but with your help we could get the death penalty. Unfortunately he was killed at his home a few days ago." He glanced at Brandon before he continued. "An emergency autopsy was performed the same day. A .22 caliber bullet was removed from his brain. In my report I emphasized the fact that within the last four years several people have been killed execution style by a .22 caliber pistol. Furthermore, all of these killings were related in one other special way..."

Brandon took the bait and asked, "And how's that?"

"They were all done by a professional!"

"I'll ask you again. What does this have to do with me?
Brandon was growing impatient.

"I'm sure you're aware of the new government branch called
The Department of Homeland Security. The department was
formed to operate within the border of the United States, while the
Central Intelligence Agency operates outside the borders. As of
now the people of America are under the impression that a terrorist
looks like a person of Middle Eastern descent. But the truth of the
matter is, a terrorist could look just like you and me, and every
other race of people in America. As a matter of fact, under the
Patriot Act passed after 9/11, any Blood, Crip, Ku Klux Klan
member, or Joe Blow citizen that commits an act of terror can be
labeled a terrorist. And the day is fast approaching when citizens of
this country will be labeled that way." The agent motioned to a
park bench. "Let's have a seat."

As the sun had risen, Brandon noticed more and more
activity throughout the neighborhood as people went to work and
children walked to school. He sat next to the agent and listened as
he continued.

"Covertly, the CIA has professional hit men on their payroll.
They're usually disguised as analysts, bankers, accountants,
businessmen, general laborers, engineers, the list goes on and on.
When they are called upon to do a job, there's certain parameters
that are looked at and analyzed thoroughly so as to choose the right
professional for the assignment. Every professional operates
differently in incorporating their kill shots. While others prefer
hand to hand kills, which enables the assassin to disguise the real
motive of the killing by making the local authorities believe it was
a mugging gone awry.

What I'm revealing to you is not something the government
advertises. The Department of Homeland Security is no different
from the Central Intelligence Agency. We are currently recruiting

professionals to operate within our borders, Mr. Elliott. Our primary source of recruits comes from our nation's military. But every now and then a specialist of your ability is brought to our attention, and if he can be controlled, we'll seek out his services."

Brandon laughed. "I can't believe this shit!"

"Believe it, Mr. Elliott. Because a representative of your country is here in the flesh. You'll be hired as an analyst and paid a yearly salary of $55,000 plus benefits and a bonus of $20,000 in additional income if you're ever called upon to perform a job. You won't have an office and you'll never be required to report to work inside one. Essentially you'll be what the CIA calls a 'sleeper agent'. You'll be assigned a handler and contacted by him alone. But in the meantime, you just continue to live your life. The government will require you to attend a four week covert special operations school in Virginia sometime within the next year or two."

"What if I say no? What if I say I don't know what the fuck you've been babbling about for the last hour?"

"Then I'm instructed to continue in my investigation until I have enough to take to a federal prosecutor. The government doesn't need any physical evidence to win a conviction under federal conspiracy laws. All I need to do is break down someone who knows your secrets."

Brandon thought about DJ and Shon. "I didn't know the government was into blackmail, Agent Cobb."

"That's good. Most of the sheep in this great country of ours are asleep as well." His voice grew hard. "Did you honestly believe it would always be peaches and cream?" he asked incredulously as he looked around at the surrounding prosperous neighborhood. "Look at where you live, what you drive, and how you dress.

You're living the American dream. So why not show your appreciation and serve your country by helping Uncle Sam get rid of a few terrorists?"

Brandon stood up to leave and turned back to the agent. "Like I said earlier, I don't know what you're talking about."

As Brandon turned to leave, Agent Cobb jumped off the park bench and yelled, "What about Tabitha, Shon, and DeJuan? You think they might know what I'm talking about?"

Brandon stopped in his tracks and slowly turned to face Cobb. "You stay the fuck away from my family. This is about you and me."

"I'm sorry, Mr. Elliott. But I have too much power to play fair. It's as simple as that. To me personally, you're no more than recycled garbage. But to your government, you're a diamond in the rough. So you can either go to work for the good guys or go to prison with the bad ones. It's your call, Mr. Elliott!"

Brandon sighed. He was in a no win situation. Byron was supposed to be his last kill. But it seemed the killing would never end. He had to stall for time.

"I'm going to need a little time to think about this."

"I need an answer now."

"Fuck you then! I won't allow you to rush me into making a decision as important as this." Brandon turned to walk away.

"Wait a minute." The agent caught up to Brandon. "How much time do you need?" he asked, calmly.

"A month."

"A month? That's to fu..." He caught himself. "Alright, Mr. Elliott, a month it is." He removed a business card from his wallet and passed it to Brandon. "If I don't hear from you in thirty days you'll hear from me."

Brandon slipped the card into his pocket and broke into a smooth-gaited jog.

Chapter Forty-One

The Gang

With a sigh, DJ placed the last bundle of hundred dollar bill on the smallest stack. For the last two hours he'd been in the dining room counting and stacking money in preparation for the first leg of their journey which they would embark on later in the day. The valuable experience gained from past trips to the tropical paradise afforded them security in knowing what they could get away with and what they couldn't.

Closing his eyes, DJ sat back to relax while he waited for Brandon and Tabitha to arrive with more luggage. The plan was for each one of them to carry a suitcase containing two million dollars, while the other suitcase would only contain clothing. Another million would be divided between the four of them and strapped around their waists on money belts.

DJ was going over their plans step by step in his mind when he heard the sound of the doorbell. Shon and Tabitha hadn't spoken since their little altercation last weekend. DJ didn't inform her of their little trip until he had all the travel arrangements set for Friday, as Tank requested. That was Tuesday. So his wife had three days to contemplate how she'd go about rectifying the rift between herself and her best friend. One thing was for sure; it was time for them to mend their fence so their trip wouldn't be so damn stressful. There's nothing more uncomfortable than being confined with two bickering women.

●●●●●●

"Shon!" DJ yelled. "Get the door!"

Sweaty from her morning run and still wearing a pair of bike shorts and sports bra, Shon ran downstairs barefoot and opened the front door. Ignoring Tabitha, she looked at Brandon and said, "DJ is in the dining room."

Brandon smiled. "Well good morning to you too, Shon." Carrying two suitcases, he stepped in the doorway and gave her a peck on the cheek.

With two large suitcases of her own, Tabitha brushed past Shon and followed her husband to the dining room.

"You ready to sit in the sun and dance the night away?" DJ asked, with a big grin on his face. "Sit those down right there next to ours."

"Hell yeah, I'm ready. Is everything set?" Brandon asked, as DJ came around the table to give Tabitha a kiss and hug.

"It's set. I chartered a small plane to fly us to the Gulf of Mexico. From there we'll get on a very nice luxury yacht that'll take us south of Cuba and on to the Cayman Islands."

"I thought you said we were going on a cruise, Brandon!" Tabitha asked, in disappointment.

Brandon put his arm around her and gave her a kiss. "We are going on a cruise. The ship will be a little smaller is all."

"With this kind of money it's too risky," DJ said.

"Damn right it is. I'd be sick if this kind of money was ever confiscated. There's no telling what type of new requirements customs implemented. This way we can float into a dock and leave the ship with our suitcases full of clothing to show customs agents. Once we're cleared and given their stamp of approval, we can come back and retrieve the luggage full of money. Great plan, DJ."

"Thanks. You ready to get to work? We have a lot of packing to do."

"Yeah, let's do it." Brandon turned to his wife. "Baby, why don't you go talk to Shon and let us knock this out."

"I'll stay and help. I don't mind."

Brandon gave her a stern look. "What did I ask you to do? Someone has to be big enough to apologize. So handle that Tabitha!" he growled.

"Alright, already! I'm going!"

●●●●●●

Shon dried off from her hot shower and slipped on a pair of panties and bathrobe. When she entered her bedroom what she saw stopped her in her tracks. Tabitha was propped up in her bed reading an Essence magazine and wiggling her toes like she didn't have a care in the world. Shon put her hands on her hips and loudly cleared her throat.

Tabitha lowered the magazine. "Girl, I have some throat lozenges in the car. Put some clothes on and go get you a few. I don't want you giving that to everyone on our trip." Tabitha went back to pretending to read the magazine. She knew they needed to break the ice some how.

Shon just shook her head and went to the dresser to find a bra. "You have your nerve, Tabitha. You jump on me in the mall and now you're taking over my bedroom." With her back turned she dug around in her lingerie drawer. "And just as a fair warning to ya, heffa, I'm not looking for underwear. I'm trying to find my pistol."

Tabitha laughed and lowered the magazine. "Shit! It wasn't that serious, girlfriend. We were both over emotional and we over

258

reacted that's all." Tabitha rubbed her cheek. "I had your finger prints on my face for three days. Had to use about a pound of make-up, wainch!"

Shon laughed as she turned to face Tabitha with her hands behind her back, trying to hook her bra clasp. "I'm sorry about that, girl. I know this might sound like a cliché or something, but I was on my period."

Tabitha stood up and tentatively approached her best friend with tears in her eyes. "I'm sorry too, Shon. Someone needed to set me straight. And what better person than my best friend!"

She held out her arms and the two women embraced and had a good cry. When they pulled apart, Tabitha went to the bathroom and returned with a roll of toilet paper to dry their eyes. They decided that there was a week's worth of gossip to catch up on, so they climbed into Shon's queen-sized bed and sat Indian style.

"Girl, did you see all that money down stairs?" Shon asked in disbelief.

Tabitha nodded her head. "That's a lot of money alright."

"That's only nine million. There's two more in the closet safe."

"Yeah, but do you know where it all came from?" Tabitha asked, as if she had a juicy secret.

"DJ got it from our new business partner."

Tabitha looked at her like she was crazy. "Business partner! When did he tell you that?"

Shon thought about it for a second. "I think it was the night he came home after three in the morning. Yeah, I remember because I was all cranked to chew a piece of his ass. But I shut up when he showed me all that money.

Tabitha smacked her lips. "Well, Brandon told me everything. And just so you know, we don't have a new business partner."

"What? Then where that money come from? What did Brandon say?"

Tabitha ignored her questions. "Girl, I'm thirsty. What you got to drink in this house?"

"Heffa, you better quit stallin' and tell me what's goin' on!"

Tabitha giggled like a little girl. "Alright, you talked me into it." She lowered her voice to a whisper as if she was afraid of being over heard. "They came in late that night because they were answering questions at the police station."

Shon's eyes got big. "Police station? What kind of questions? What they do?"

"They didn't do anything! Someone walked in and shot the man from Houston while they were having dinner."

"Shot him! For what?"

Tabitha's expression was grave. "Girl, I don't know! Brandon said it probably had something to do with drugs."

"Drugs? DJ isn't involved with no drug dealers! You know that."

Tabitha shook her head. "DJ didn't have anything to do with it. The man had a beef with someone and they shot him for it. That's all Brandon knew. And believe me when I tell you, I picked his brain good, girl. If he knew anything else, he would've told me."

"So where did the money come from if the guy is dead?"

"He brought the money with him to their meeting. But that's not the question you should be asking. Where did that extra million come from? That is the question."

Shon looked puzzled. She'd never thought about that. "You're right, Tabitha. The deal was for ten million. If Brandon and DJ were thinking of upping the ante, they would have said something."

"I know that. And I also know a person doesn't just accidentally pack an extra million dollars." Tabitha was also perplexed and it showed on her face.

"What did Brandon say about it?" Shon asked.

"He hasn't said anything about it to me. And I didn't ask him because I didn't know. You're the one who said there was nine million downstairs and two more in the safe."

"Yeah, I did didn't I!"

The two women sat in silence for a few seconds, consumed in their own thoughts.

"You're not thinking what I'm thinking are you?" Shon asked.

"What?"

"But that wouldn't make sense."

"What?"

"I was thinking they may have received a better offer than they first let on. But that doesn't make sense.

"You're right, it doesn't make sense. They're our husbands before they're our business partners. And we all profit, no matter how you split it. But I know what we should do."

"What?" Shon asked.

"Let's just ask them. Hurry and get on some clothes. I can't wait to hear this."

DJ and Brandon were sitting at opposite ends of the big table, wrapping large stacks of money in plastic and gray duct tape when their wives joined them. Each woman held a serious expression on her face.

DJ looked up resenting their intrusion. "We're not finished yet. We'll call you when we're ready."

It had been decided Tabitha would be the designated speaker.

"We need to ask you guys a question. I'm sure that it's nothing. But why is there an extra million dollars, when we all agreed on ten?"

Brandon and DJ were speechless as they looked at each other across the length of the table. They hadn't thought to devise an explanation to account for the extra million. But DJ hadn't got this far in life by being stupid. He was an opportunist and he saw a wonderful opportunity before him now.

When Brandon threatened to pay for his and Shon's funeral for having loose lips, he had wracked his brain to come up with an insurance policy. DJ figured if Brandon didn't so much as slap Tabitha for having another man in their bed, he was willing to bet his house Brandon would never harm Shon if there was a chance Tabitha would find out he'd killed her. But that would only insure Shon. He had to insure himself as well, and he knew just how to do it.

DJ looked from Brandon to Shon and finally to Tabitha.

"The extra million was for a job."

"What kind of job, DJ?" Shon asked.

"DJ!" Brandon yelled.

DJ ignored Brandon. "Fat Chris paid us an extra million to kill..."

Brandon stood up and cut him off. "What the fuck are you doing, DJ?" Brandon growled.

"You threatened to kill me and Shon the other day. Well, you might as well kill us now because Tabitha needs to know just how cold hearted your ass can be. She has the right to know the man she married!" DJ yelled.

"Why would Brandon threaten you and Shon, DJ?" Tabitha asked, calmly. "And why would Fat Chris pay you guys a million dollars to kill someone?"

"Tabitha, don't pay this fool any attention. He's trippin'." Brandon came around the corner of the table and grabbed her arm. "Let's go home."

Tabitha snatched her arm free. "I'm not ready to go home. And don't pull on me like that. I'm not leaving until I get some answers!"

"I'll answer your questions. Just come with me." Brandon tried to regain a hold on her arm but she twisted away and ran to the other side of the table.

Shon stood next to Brandon with a look of pain and disappointment in her eyes. "You threatened to kill me and DJ, Brandon? After all these years of loving you like a brother, you'd actually turn on me like a dog?" She turned to her husband. "DJ, please tell me he didn't do that!"

DJ nodded his head. "Hurt me too, baby. All I've ever done is love him," DJ said, sadly.

"But why?" Tabitha yelled. "What happened? What did you do to him? Brandon isn't like that at all!"

"DJ is right, Tabitha, you don't know this man. And I hope you can forgive me for keeping the truth about him away from you, girl." Shon looked at Brandon. "I'm so disappointed in you right now." She sat down as tears rolled down her face.

"Tabitha, we were paid to kill this guy because that's what Brandon does. Well, he doesn't any more. And I can't give him all the blame because I'm the one who got him the jobs."

Tabitha was still confused. "What jobs? What do you mean that's what he does? I don't understand!" she said, more confused and frustrated.

DJ sighed. "Tabitha, Brandon is a hit..."

"STOP!" Brandon yelled as he held up his hand. "That's enough, DJ. I see what you're trying to do and I'm not mad at you for doing it. Checkmate, dog," he said, calmly. "I'll explain everything from beginning to end. Please have a seat."

Brandon waited for DJ and Tabitha to get comfortable before speaking. "Tabitha, Shon, what I'm about to say is never to leave this room."

Brandon looked at his wife. "Baby, I'm not going to lie and say I've done these things for us. I did it for myself and I accept responsibility for my actions." He turned his attention to DJ and Shon. I owe you two an apology. You are not only my business partners, you are my brother and sister as well. DJ, you're right, Tabitha does have a right to know the truth. Because unfortunately, the game don't stop!"

Chapter Forty-Two

Tabitha

The man she loved was a cold-blooded murderer! That's all that went through her mind as Brandon told his story. How could she not see it? Was she naive? Did her knowledge of his crimes make her a murderess or an accessory to his madness?

Their business and their wealth was founded with drug and blood money. And Shon has known this all along? How could she not tell her she was married to a monster! What kind of friend keeps a sick ass secret like that?

Tabitha felt numb inside as she half listened to Brandon as he talked about a job with the government. Tears rolled down her face. She decided then she wouldn't be going on the trip with them. As a matter of fact, she didn't want to have anything to do with either one of them ever again.

They were all talking together as if what Brandon had just revealed to them was old news, which it obviously was to everyone but her. She scooted back her seat and slowly rose from the table.

Everyone stopped talking and looked at Tabitha expectantly. She knew they all were wondering how she would react to Brandon's revelation and she wasn't going to disappoint them.

Tabitha looked down at Shon across the table. "How could you?"

"How could I what?" Shon asked, innocently.

"You've known all this time I'm married to fuckin' Ted Bundy, and you haven't said shit to me about it!" Tabitha screamed. "BC? Yeah, I could accept that, and in a sick kinda way, I understood it!" She looked at Brandon and DJ. "But to take a human life for capital gain? Ya'll are sick!"

Brandon tried to come around the table to comfort her. "Tabitha, let me explain, baby!"

Tabitha ran in the opposite direction. "Don't come near me, Brandon! I don't want you ever touching me again!" she sobbed. "How could you do this to us? What makes you think I'd accept this?"

"Because I love you and because you love me, baby," he said calmly.

"I don't even know who you are! Our life isn't what it seems. You've been living a double life you son-of-a-bitch! And you dragged me into it with you!"

"I'm the same man I've always been, Tabitha. Just calm down baby, please!" he pleaded.

"I am calm." Tabitha ran her fingers through her hair and wiped her face. "I'm calm enough to know what's right and what's wrong." She took a deep breath. "This marriage is wrong." Tabitha looked at Shon and DJ. "This friendship is wrong."

"Tabitha don't say that! I'm sorry I..."

Tabitha cut Shon off. She didn't want to hear any apologies. "I'm going to the house and pack my things."

"No, Tabitha!" Brandon yelled before trying to come around the table.

"Leave me alone, Brandon!" Tabitha ran in the opposite direction.

"Baby, I love you. Don't run away from our problems. Let's work it out, please. That's what couples do, Tabitha," he pleaded.

"How can you work out your past, Brandon? Can you bring all those people back? And now the government wants your services. How can we work that out?"

"Fuck the government! I'm not going to work for them! I'm through with the killing. It's over, Tabitha. Yes, I did it for financial gain, baby. And yes, it was wrong. But let he whom is without sin cast the first stone, Tabitha."

"Fuck you, Brandon! An affair is nothing compared to what you've done! I deceived you for six months. You've been deceiving me since the day we met! And you would've gone on with the deception if it weren't for DJ. So fuck you! I don't want anything to do with either of you! You're all sick, and I was cursed the day met you!" Tabitha ran out the dining room and slammed the front door.

Brandon was stunned. Tabitha had never talked to him like that. Shon's shouting brought him out of his daze.

"Brandon! Brandon! Go after her. Get your wife back!"

When Brandon opened the door, Tabitha was backing the Mercedes out of the driveway. He had to get to her before she drove away so he broke into a run and dived onto the hood of the car.

"Tabitha! Stop the car!" he yelled as he held on to the windshield wipers.

In her fear to get away, Tabitha hit the gas pedal and swung out into the street.

Brandon's face smacked into the windshield with the unexpected acceleration, busting his nose.

Tabitha put the car in gear and slowly pressed the gas. She didn't want to hurt Brandon, she just wanted him to let her go. Trying to see around him, she drove slowly down the quiet neighborhood street as Brandon's nose bled on her windshield.

He held on for dear life while screaming at her to stop the car. After swerving all over the road for half a block, Tabitha came to her senses and pulled over to the curb and stopped the car.

"Put it in park and kill the engine!" Brandon yelled.

Tabitha did as he asked. She knew she would have to play him to get away from him, but get away she would. She meant everything she'd said in the house.

Brandon slid off the hood after she killed the engine. He had to make her understand. More importantly, he had to make her stay. Brandon used his shirt to wipe away the blood that flowed from his nose as he stood next to the driver's side door, silently looking at her.

"Well? What? Say something. Your ass wouldn't have jumped on my car like Batman if you didn't want something."

"We need to talk."

Tabitha sighed, and ran her hands across her stomach as tears filled her eyes. "What is there to talk about, Brandon? You chose your life and you brought me into it. But it's all been based around deception, lies, and death.

"No," Brandon said. "Our life has been based on love. Don't you ever doubt how I feel about you. What I do in the street has nothing to do with you."

"Yes it does. When you put your life in danger, you put my life in danger." She looked into his eyes. "We are one, Brandon. Don't you understand that, baby? If something happened to you, it would kill me inside."

"Nothing's going to happen to me, baby. That street shit is over. Once we take this money to the Islands, it's over. Please believe that," he pleaded.

Tabitha closed her eyes and leaned on the steering wheel. Brandon reached in and ran his hand through her hair.

"We'll talk when you get back."

"What do you mean, when I get back?"

Tabitha looked up at him. "I'm not going to the Islands. I need some time to think. I need some time alone. Can you understand that, Brandon?" She asked, sadly.

He looked up at the sky and took a deep breath before looking at her with tired and pain filled eyes. "I love you."

"I know you do. And I love you, too. I just need some time to myself. I'll be home when you get back, I promise." She started the car.

Brandon stepped away from the car and watched her pull away from the curb. As blood continued to drip off his chin, he stood in the middle of the street and watched his lifeline turn the corner at the end of the block, going the opposite direction from their house.

Epilogue

The strong baritone of Barry White's voice softly sifted through the speakers giving Toni's apartment a luxuriating romantic ambiance. It was well past noon and she was curled up underneath her soft silk comforter listening to Barry and contemplating what she'd do to help occupy her time for the next four weeks. But she wasn't too worried about it. Something or someone would pop up to help keep her mind off missing her man.

Ever since she'd gone to work for E & J Investment Group a year and a half ago, she'd been fortunate to meet some very interesting people. Toni didn't care much for Tabitha and Shon. But Brandon and DJ were sweethearts. Brandon was so damn sexy with those wide shoulders. Toni squeezed her legs together in an effort to stop her 'kitty kat' from tingling. She had a hungry appetite for sex. Maybe it had something to do with her two-year vow of celibacy. Thank God she wasn't doing that any more! Her man had worked her to four orgasms already today and she was still hungry for more.

She threw back the covers and ran to the bathroom. *Might as well get it while the gettin's good girl,* she told herself as she crept silently into the steamy bathroom and pulled back the shower curtain. Toni's mouth watered as she watched him lather up his muscular body.

"Can I do that?" she asked, with a mischievous grin on her face.

He turned to stare into her smoky brown eyes before allowing his own to slide down her voluptuous body. He stopped briefly at her swollen nipples and again at the neatly trimmed triangle between her legs before a smile of welcome was etched across his handsome face.

"Is that all you want to do is play with the soap?" he asked, as she got into the shower.

Toni took hold of his member and was pleased with the instant response to her touch. "I wanna play with this too. And I've got to have it one more time before you leave for the east coast," she purred, as she dropped to her knees.

●●●●●●

After Brandon got dressed and left for the airport, he swore at himself for not leaving sooner. He had forgotten about the evening traffic. It was stop and go as he entered the expressway. At this rate he'd be lucky to reach D-FW in an hour, although he wouldn't feel too bad if his flight to Virginia took off without him.

Brandon had tried to come to grips with his forced recruitment. They'd been waiting almost a year and a half now for the dreaded telephone call that would change their lives. After Brandon had been outwitted by DJ and forced to tell Tabitha all of his secrets, he thought he'd foreseen a way out from under the government's thumb. They all agreed the government prosecutors could never coerce them to testify to something they swore they knew nothing about.

So Brandon had felt cocky and confident exactly thirty-five days later when Special Agent Cobb once again interrupted his morning run through the park. But his confident attitude was short lived. Once again, he had underestimated his opponent. He remembered the conversation like it was yesterday.

●●●●●●

"Good morning, Mr. Elliott. I gave you a five day grace period after our agreed upon thirty days. Happy to see me, I hope." Wearing a jogging suit of his own, the big agent fell in step beside Brandon along the track path.

Brandon ignored his question and got right to the point. "I didn't call you because I have no intentions of ever helping you. The call would've been just as much a waste of my time as this trip out here is for you," Brandon said with a smirk.

"On the contrary, Mr. Elliott. You will go to work for the government, and you will do an exceptional job. The alternative dictates that you do so."

"How so? Are you going to threaten my friends to help you convict me for something they know nothing about? I don't think so."

Cobb turned to Brandon. "Do you love the individuals you speak of, Mr. Elliott? I mean, wouldn't you do everything in your power to help out a friend in need?"

"Get to the point. I have better things to do with my time, Agent Cobb."

Agent Cobb didn't like being patronized. His voice grew hard. "During our previous conversation I mentioned that DeJuan Jackson had been under investigation. I may have failed to mention the investigation was a successful one. You see, Mr. Elliott, DeJuan unknowingly sold over two kilograms of crack cocaine to federal agents.

I also may have failed to mention his girlfriend at the time, a one Shondalyn Edwards, was also implicated, and she will go down as a co-conspirator. The now Mrs. Jackson accompanied DeJuan in transporting drugs to some of the meeting points, where agents not only purchased drugs, they also have some very nice footage of DeJuan removing the drugs from the trunk of his car. Mrs. Jackson is so photogenic." Agent Cob couldn't resist pulling his chain. "Two kilo's of crack will get them well over a life sentence in federal prison."

Agent Cobb took a few seconds to nonchalantly admire his manicured nails and give Brandon time to come to grips with this new dilemma. "On the other hand, Mr. Elliott, I can make all of that dope go bye, bye. Your call, sir!"

Brandon knew he could never allow DJ and Shon to face drug charges. One or both would be sure to break at the thought of spending the rest of their natural lives behind bars. And he didn't want to see his friends in jail anyway. So in the end he submitted to the government's will. But not without demands of his own!

Brandon had been a highly recruited high school football player so he knew how the recruitment game was played. He'd gone off to college and left DJ behind and he wasn't going to let history repeat itself. Cobb did a lot of bitchin' and grand standing but in the end, he gave Brandon what he wanted. DJ would be his handler. And it would be just like old times except now they'd both be in the employ of Uncle Sam.

●●●●●●

Brandon pulled the Lexus into the airport parking lot and reached for his cell phone to call DJ.

"Hello!"

"Where you at?" Brandon asked loudly, as an airplane flew low overhead.

"I'm on the highway. I should reach the airport in about ten minutes."

"Did you have a chance to drop that paperwork that I gave you off to Toni?"

DJ laughed into the phone. "Yeah. That girl can't get enough of me... I mean work. She loves her job."

"That's good. I'm glad we hired her."

"Me too," DJ said.

"Hurry up and we'll have a drink before we catch our flight."

"One!"

"One!"

As Brandon sat at the bar inside the airport sipping his drink, he found himself thinking about Tabitha, which was something he couldn't seem to stop doing. When he returned from the Cayman Islands, his worst fears were realized. She'd packed her clothes and moved out. She'd even taken her prized shoe collection. Brandon was devastated. He'd begged, pleaded, and threatened her parents to reveal her whereabouts but it was all to no avail. They claimed they hadn't heard from her.

Eventually, he developed a daily routine to help ease the pain by occupying his time constructively. He threw himself into developing their new real estate firm. Every night he checked his answering service in hopes of hearing the voice that could make all the pain and loneliness go away. But it wasn't to be.

Brandon took a sip of his drink before reaching into his left breast pocket. He looked at the small figure in the picture swaddled in soft baby blankets and smiled. He kept the picture over his heart rather than in his wallet because that's where his son belonged. He turned the picture over and scrutinized Tabitha's handwriting for the thousandth time since he received the non-descript envelope with a New York postmark and no return address last week. But the words she'd written didn't tell him how they were or where they were.

"Mercel, nine months old." By his calculations, Tabitha had to have been two months pregnant when she left him.

She withdrew $200,000 from their shared savings account by way of cashier's check. There was over $250,000 in her own personal checking and saving accounts and she'd cleaned these out too so he wasn't worried about her and his child ever going hungry or having inadequate shelter. But providing for his wife and child was his responsibility and he was going to do everything in his power to find his family. He'd hired the most prestigious private investigative firm in Dallas to help get his family back.

They traced the cashier's checks to Seattle, Washington. And so far, that's all they had until the envelope arrived with his son's picture. Brandon didn't feel comfortable with taking advantage of the government's extensive resources to help find his wife but if it took too much longer, he would be forced to take that route. In the meantime, he had to continue to live his life one day at a time.

DJ slapped Brandon on the back and brought him out of his reverie. "Wake up, man." DJ looked at his watch.

"Finding a parking spot is a bitch ain't it?" As DJ climbed on the barstool next to him, he replaced the picture of his son over his heart in his shirt pocket.

"Yeah, it is." Brandon replied.

Before DJ could order a drink their flight was called over the airport public address system.

"Well, homeboy, you ready to go work for Uncle Sam?" DJ asked, as they climbed off their barstools.

"Yeah, I guess so."

"Don't sound so sad about it. Who knows, maybe this gig will lead to the White House someday."

"Shit! I have enough problems of my own. Running a country is the last thing I need on my agenda. Let's just stick to killing terrorists, will ya?"

"Whatever you say. I got your back."

"Bet, because I got yours too, homey. Let's go see what these government boys talkin' 'bout."

Street Knowledge!
"So Real You Think You've Lived It!"

Street Knowledge Publishing Order Form

Street Knowledge Publishing, P.O. Box 345, Wilmington, DE 198
Email: jj@streetknowledgepublishing.com
Website: www.streetknowledgepublishing.com

For Inmates Orders and Manuscript Submissions
P.O. Box 310367, Jamaica, NY 11431

Bloody Money
ISBN # 0-9746199-0-6 $15.00
Shipping/ Handling Via
U.S. Priority Mail $5.25
Total $20.25

Me & My Girls
ISBN # 0-9746199-1-4 $15.00
Shipping/ Handling Via
U.S. Priority Mail $5.25
Total $20.25

Bloody Money 2
ISBN # 0-9746199-2-2 $15.00
Shipping/ Handling Via
U.S. Priority Mail $5.25
Total $20.25

Dopesick
ISBN # 0-9746199-4-9 $15.00
Shipping/ Handling Via
U.S. Priority Mail $5.25
Total $20.25

Money-Grip
ISBN # 0-9746199-3-0 $15.00
Shipping/ Handling Via
U.S. Priority Mail $5.25
Total $20.25

The Queen of New York
ISBN # 0-9746199-7-3 $15.00
Shipping/ Handling Via
U.S. Priority Mail $5.25
Total $20.25

Don't Mix The Bitter With The Sweet
ISBN # 0-9746199-6-5 $15.00
Shipping/ Handling Via
U.S. Priority Mail $5.25
Total $20.25

reet Knowledge Publishing, P.O. Box 345, Wilmington, DE 19801
Email: jj@streetknowledgepublishing.com
Website: www.streetknowledgepublishing.com

The Hunger
ISBN # 0-9746199-5-7   **$15.00**
Shipping/ Handling Via
U.S. Priority Mail   **$5.25**
Total   **$20.25**

Sin 4 Life
ISBN # 0-9746199-8-1   **$15.00**
Shipping/ Handling Via
U.S. Priority Mail   **$5.25**
Total   **$20.25**

The Tommy Good Story
ISBN # 0-9799556-0-2   **$15.00**
Shipping/ Handling Via
U.S. Priority Mail   **$5.25**
Total   **$20.25**

The NorthSide Clit
ISBN # 0-9746199-9-X   **$15.00**
Shipping/ Handling Via
U.S. Priority Mail   **$5.25**
Total   **$20.25**

Bloody Money III
ISBN # 0-9799556-4-5   **$15.00**
Shipping/ Handling Via
U.S. Priority Mail   **$5.25**
Total   **$20.25**

Court in the Streets
ISBN # 0-9799556-2-9   **$15.00**
Shipping/ Handling Via
U.S. Priority Mail   **$5.25**
Total   **$20.25**

A Day After Forever
ISBN # 0-9799556-1-0   **$15.00**
Shipping/ Handling Via
U.S. Priority Mail   **$5.25**
Total   **$20.25**

Street Knowledge Publishing, P.O. Box 345, Wilmington, DE 198
Email: jj@streetknowledgepublishing.com
Website: www.streetknowledgepublishing.com

Dipped Up
ISBN # 0-9799556-5-3 $15.00
Shipping/ Handling Via
U.S. Priority Mail $5.25
Total $20.25

Playn' for Keeps
ISBN # 0-9799556-9-6 $15.00
Shipping/ Handling Via
U.S. Priority Mail $5.25
Total $20.25

Stackin' Paper
ISBN # 0-9755811-1-2 $15.00
Shipping/ Handling Via
U.S. Priority Mail $5.25
Total $20.25

Love Lust and Lies
ISBN: 0-9799556-7-X $15.00
Shipping/ Handling Via
U.S. Priority Mail $5.25
Total $20.25

No Love, No Pain
ISBN: 0-9799556-6-1 $15.00
Shipping/ Handling Via
U.S. Priority Mail $5.25
Total $20.25

Pain Freak
ISBN: 0-9799556-3-7 $15.00
Shipping/ Handling Via
U.S. Priority Mail $5.25
Total $20.25